FAMILY MAN

The Unreal Story of Charles Manson's
Right-hand Man

Chuck W. Chapman

BLACK BED
SHEET

Family Man
A Black Bed Sheet/Diverse Media Book
August 2020
Copyright © 2020 by Chuck W. Chapman
All rights reserved.

Cover art by Chuck W. Chapman with Nicholas Grabowsky
and copyright © 2020 Chuck W. Chapman and Black Bed Sheet
Books Author photo by Kathrine McCollough.

Library of Congress Control Number: 2020942896

ISBN-10: 1-946874-28-0
ISBN-13: 978-1-946874-28-3

Family Man

A Black Bed Sheet/Diverse Media Book
Antelope, CA

"Look down on me and you see a fool,
Look up at me and you see a god,
Look straight at me and you see yourself."

--Charles Manson

Preface

I first became interested in the Manson murders, i.e. the Tate-Labianca homicides, around the age of seven when I watched the made-for-TV movie *Helter Skelter*, based on author and prosecutor Vincent Bugliosi's book of the same name. Soon thereafter, I read the book and as Bugliosi promised on the cover, it scared the hell out of me. At the same time, it awoke in me a lifelong fascination for the case and all things Manson and Family related. Over the past 10 years, I have re-read every book I had on the subject and purchased many more. I have watched and re-watched every interview I could find with Charlie and the other Family members. I have researched news footage, listened to lectures and podcasts, and pored over photos and police reports. I have interviewed people who knew Manson personally, people who have devoted years of their lives studying the case and even spent many hours listening to private telephone conversations with Manson himself. I have explored every avenue I could find to get the best possible understanding of the murders and the events leading up to them, as well as the trials and aftermath.

Vincent Bugliosi's job as prosecutor was not to find the truth, but to secure a conviction. He did so masterfully. While the tale of a black-white race war inspired by The Beatles' "White Album" and hippie cults wanting to rule the world from a bottomless pit in the desert makes for a fascinating story, it makes little sense and seems highly unlikely as a motive for murder in the real world. The more research I did on the case, the more I came to doubt the official narrative told in court and popular literature. The story that you are about to read, in my opinion, gives a much more accurate accounting of what really happened that fateful summer of 1969 and the time leading up to it.

While this is a work of historical fiction, I do believe it paints a far more realistic portrayal of events than has been presented for mass public consumption thus far. The story itself is a work of fiction, but the people, places, and primary events depicted are all too real. Billy "Shep" Shepherd is a fictional character that has been placed into these real-life events to give us a first-hand narrative of how, and most importantly, *why* they happened.

Some fictional events have been added to give Shep a background and paint him into these pictures. In some instances, Shep has been added to the characters that were present. At other times, he has been substituted for people that were actually there. The timeline of some of the events in the building of the "Family" and their locales have been rearranged and some omitted to present a more enjoyable read. All the major events and their sequence are 100% true and told as accurately as my research has led me to conclude that they really happened. Many of the words attributed to Charles Manson are actual quotes from Charlie himself, taken from interviews, tapes, and non-fiction books, and inserted here if they fit the context. Others are simply my interpretation through reading and/or hearing Charlie's speech patterns, of how I think he would have carried his part of the conversation.

This book is in no way meant to glorify the killers or is it meant to denigrate the victims, but to portray both as being flawed human beings, possessing all the good and bad that each of us has within us.

Charles Manson was by no means innocent, nor should he be looked at as a hero, but neither should he be viewed as the personification of evil incarnate that he has so often been portrayed as. Charlie had unique musical and artistic talent and was a thought-provoking philosopher. He was intensely loyal to the people he cared about. He was also a drug peddler, a pimp, a petty criminal, and a master manipulator.

Many lives were forever altered, and some ended, because of the events portrayed herein. I feel that this book brings a new perspective to a case that has fascinated millions for more than 50 years. I also believe that the more we understand about the human condition in the most extreme cases, the more we understand ourselves.

CHAPTER I

I first met Charlie Manson in the summer of 1967. I was doing my best to sleep on a park bench with the sun's evening rays beating down on me in Berkeley, California when this crazy-looking little guy in jeans and a denim jacket just appeared at my head. It was as if he'd materialized out of nowhere. I sat up as quickly as I could and nervously spat out, "What do you want?"

"Want. Want. What do I want? Hmmmm."

He rubbed his stubbled chin and looked around the park, the world, the universe. He was staring straight at...no, *through* me with the most piercing brown eyes I had ever seen. A full head of dark hair was parted on the left, partially covering one of those eyes.

"Well. That's a hard question. Want. Maybe I want to rule the world. Maybe I want all your money. Maybe I want to get laid."

He must have seen the look of alarm on my face because then he broke into a half grin and said, "Maybe I just want to sit down."

He sat down beside me, and in an instant what had been panic on my part went straight to calm. "Cool as a cucumber," as my old man used to say. He put his hand on my shoulder, the touch surprisingly light and the nails surprisingly well-maintained. He looked at me sincerely, and declared, "There. That's good. Yeah, I think I just wanted to sit down. Now, why don't you tell me what *you* want."

1

His question took me back. It had been what? Two weeks? Wow. Only two weeks since I'd left my parents' home in rural South Carolina. It was the only life I had ever known and the only one I once thought I would need to know. I remembered telling my mom and dad that I wanted to take some time off between high school and college.

I was nineteen, had done one year at the local tech school and had planned to transfer to one of the big state colleges, but then everything fell apart. My best friend got drafted into the army. Two weeks after his basic training, he had stepped on a land mine in a town with a name that I couldn't pronounce in Vietnam. A week later my girlfriend dumped me for a senior journalism student at USC, and I just felt that I needed to take a break. A break from school, a break from responsibility, a break from hearing bad news, and a break from my parents.

Needless to say, they didn't take it well. I had "lucked out" and had been declared undraftable because of the broken arm I received in second grade when that dumbass, Norm Williamson, had shoved me off the swing at school during recess. My arm was broken so badly that the bone had poked through, and even though I felt little effects of it now, it had grown back a little crooked and was enough to disqualify me from military service. Little did I know then, but ol' Norm had done me a huge favor and may have saved my life. Norm himself eagerly enlisted as soon as he hit eighteen and got his ass shot off less than three months later. Karma truly is a bitch.

I don't think I would have done well in Vietnam. I was quiet, a bit shy, and not really into violence. I had shot target practice with my dad a few times, but I could never have even considered going hunting and killing a deer or anything and thankfully, my old man never asked. I supported my country and prayed and hoped for the safe return of my friends that were in Vietnam but honestly I, along with what seemed like more and more of the country every day, really didn't understand what we were even there for.

My generation understood what the World Wars had been about, and to a lesser degree, even the Korean Conflict, but Vietnam? There was no Hitler or Mussolini that we had to fear this time. It just seemed like it didn't really affect our everyday life at all or at least enough to justify sending so many of our friends and family over there to die. It just felt...foreign.

Since I had not been able to serve my country in Vietnam like a true patriot, as my father was quick to point out, I should at least serve it in the academic and working world. No matter what my dad thought, though, I just felt I was missing...something. Other than the occasional family vacation, I had never been anywhere or seen anything. A two-hour drive to the beach constituted a major event for me. I saw the Beatles and Elvis on TV and witnessed the tons of girls that were screaming and crying for them. All the kids on TV looked like they were having a good time. I couldn't relate at all. Elvis, John, Paul, George and Ringo were all small-town boys and here they were seeing the world. Girls were throwing themselves at their feet. What was I doing? Going to school all day and working in a factory at night just so I could get up and do it again for the next 50 years? No thanks.

I had always been artistic and creative and I had taught myself to play a little guitar, also to my father's chagrin, so when I heard about the "summer of love" and the "awakening" that was going on in San Francisco, it really appealed to me. That's when I said, "Fuck it," and packed up a duffel bag and my guitar. I grabbed a sleeping bag and bought a bus ticket.

Chuck W. Chapman

I had an old VW Beetle that I'd owned since I was sixteen but my dad forbade me to take it off on a "fool's jaunt to California" and truth is, it probably wouldn't have made it much past Georgia anyway, so I just decided to bus it. I thought about hitchhiking but my mom was worried about me doing that. I had to agree with her that I probably wasn't ready for that much independence yet anyway, so Greyhound it was.

Mom wasn't happy about my decision, but by the smile behind the tears, I could tell she knew that I had to do it. She sympathized with my plight, having lost a love at a young age herself, she acknowledged. She kissed me on the cheek and said, "Be careful. Your bug will be here when you get back." And I knew it would. Dad's bark was worse than his bite and I knew that once he got over his anger and disappointment, that he would be fine as well and that I would always have a home to come back to. I think that is what finally gave me the comfort and confidence to make a cross-country trip into the great unknown. I knew that if I ever really needed to, I could always go home, but I never did.

I slowly roused from my reverie to see Charlie three inches from my face. He was standing again but stooping kind of down and sideways to stare straight into my eyes. He wove his head slightly like a snake charmer, as he spoke.

"That's heavy man," he said with a twang that was Southern, but not *my* Southern.

"What?" I said, a bit confused.

"I don't blame you, brother. I wouldn't want to go over there either. The man is always wanting to take what ain't his. We just need to leave it alone. Ya dig?"

"Dig what?"

"Dig what I'm saying, man! The world doesn't belong to us, we belong to it. That ain't my water in Vietnam any

4

more than that's my water in the Pacific Ocean, so what's the point in fighting for it?" His logic made perfect sense to me and that was the first thing that had in at least the past month. He peered down the street as if someone was waiting for him and I observed a couple of skinny girls looking longingly back. "So. You coming or not?"

"Coming where?" I asked.

"Brother, you got a lot more questions than I got answers," he said, and started walking towards the two girls.

I stood and watched him go. The past two weeks had been a blur and I still wasn't sure what I was doing minute to minute, let alone day to day. I couldn't make a snap decision to just go off with some strange little guy I had just met, even if he did have an extra chick with him. That part was kind of tempting, I'll admit. I wanted to prove to myself, and to everyone else, that I could survive on my own, and so far I still hadn't done that. Isn't that why I came here in the first place?

About ten feet away, he stopped and took a few steps back towards me. "What's your name, man?" he asked.

"Billy. Billy Shepherd," I replied, and then added hastily for no reason at all, "from South Carolina."

"Billy, Billy Shepherd from South Carolina," he repeated. "Bill Shepherd. Bill….E…Shep…herd," he said again in a long, drawn out kind of way. Then, "Shep."

"I'm Charlie. Charlie Manson from the California Penal System. You take it easy, Shep," he called back over his shoulder as he turned and joined the girls.

I watched as they walked to the end of the street and were slowly swallowed up into the mass of people that seemed to multiply by the day. I had been letting my hair grow and was beginning to feel like I fit in at least to the casual viewer, but I still felt like an outcast.

I took another minute and looked in the direction they had left, half expecting them to be there motioning for me to "come on!" but they were gone. I picked myself up off the bench and headed to the part-time job I'd gotten, unloading trucks at a local grocery store. It wasn't enough for me to rent a place yet, but at least I was eating okay and could afford to stick a couple of bucks back. My boss would let me sleep over in his office if it was raining out, but so far, I hadn't needed to take him up on the offer. I was enjoying the freedom of sleeping in the park under the stars and nobody seemed to have a problem with it. At least not yet. Crazy how just a few months can change everything so dramatically that it could never be the same.

All in all, I was doing alright, but still, I hadn't found the peace and purpose that I somehow thought I would magically discover when I decided to come out west.

"What do *you* want?" Charlie had asked.

"Good question, Charlie. *Damn* good question."

CHAPTER 2

I spent the next few weeks going through the motions of life. I had come to California looking for something. Something.....different. But here I was, falling into the same routine as if I were still at home. I would work, eat, sleep, wake up and do it all again. It was time to move on. If I was going to be in the same rut as I was when I was living with my parents, then I may as well just go back home. At least there I had a warm bed and a hot shower every day.

Somehow though, I felt as if I had been drawn here. I felt as if God, the Universe, fate, I didn't know what to call it, but something wanted me to be where I was. That feeling was so strong inside me that I had no doubt in my mind it was true.

I had befriended a guy named Willie. He was about my age and worked on the docks with me. He often talked about driving to San Francisco on the weekends and asked if I'd like to join him sometime. The prospect was inviting so I said "sure," and the next weekend we loaded up my few belongings and headed the 15 miles or so down I-80 to the Haight-Ashbury district.

I thought Berkely was an adjustment, but the Haight was like driving into another world. There were people everywhere. All ages, colors, and styles were represented in a mish-mosh of sights, sounds, smells, and colors that somehow worked. It was my first real exposure to "flower power" and in that moment, it felt like my first real exposure to life. I just stood and looked around and felt a big grin ease across my face.

We didn't really have much diversity in my hometown in SC. Most people looked and acted like most other people and that was just the way it was. There were the white sections and the colored sections and rarely did the two meet. There were a few black kids at my school but they hung out together and the white kids hung out together and there were no conflicts. I couldn't even tell you their names.

At home, the issue of race wasn't even discussed. It was just a given. We were different. My parents weren't what I would call racist. I never heard a disparaging word about black folks one way or the other come out of their mouths, it was just that there was no communication at all. It was a different world we lived in.

Here in San Francisco, however, there were people of all ages, races, and creeds and they were all acting as if they belonged together and had always been together. The girls here were so much more...real. All the girls back home looked and dressed a certain way and wanted to come across as "good girls." I had never seen a woman without a bra, outside of maybe a *Playboy* magazine or my girlfriend Suzanne. She was the only girl I had ever seen naked or made love with. Here, no matter where you looked, there were boobs everywhere. No wonder kids were flocking to San Francisco.

The plan for my life was all in place. I was going to go to school, get a job, marry Suzanne, and join a bowling league with my best friend, Lee. Suzanne and I were going to have two kids, a boy and a girl, and buy a house halfway between her parents and my parents and live happily ever after. Until Suzanne went straight to the University of South Carolina, where I really didn't want to go, and I went to Tech School, and Suzanne met Todd, the back-up quarterback. She dumped me via a "Dear Billy" letter on the same day that Lee got his draft notice and left for Vietnam. Just a few months later, I was a pallbearer when Lee was shipped home from Vietnam in a box.

So, here I was in the Haight and everything I had heard was true and this was where I needed to be. At least for now. Willie had dropped me off on the corner, smack in the middle of everything. He told me he would be back at the same time, same place tomorrow, but I already knew that I wasn't going back to Berkely. When he came back the next day, I told him, "You go ahead man, I'm staying here for a while."

"Had a feeling we'd lose you here, Billy," he said, and with a grin, handed me a piece of paper. "There's my number, man, you change your mind and want to come back, just give me a call."

"Thanks," I said, and stuffed the paper into my pocket, but I was pretty sure I would never use it.

Willie drove off and there I was, starting over again, but I had a real sense of calm. That was weird for me, considering I had no job, no place to stay, and about 30 bucks in my pocket, but it just felt right.

CHAPTER 3

"Is that a guitar?"

"Huh?" The question jilted me out of my daydream. I looked down into the eyes of a girl who was maybe 5'3" and had the brightest smile I had ever seen. She wore a lacy headband with daisies tucked into it to attempt to hold down the mass of auburn curls. "Uh, yeah." I said.

"Play me something," she said. She took me by the hand and led me to a grassy area on a corner that was uninhabited. She sat down on the grass and looked up at me expectantly. Wow, those eyes. Holy cow, I could lose myself in those eyes and never come back.

"Sure. What do you like?"

"Cute guys with guitars," she replied.

I laughed and sat down in front of her and carefully removed my old Fender acoustic from its canvas bag. It had been a 16th birthday present from Lee.

"Since you're never gonna get laid, here's something to do with your hands," he joked.

"That's a pretty guitar," she said.

"Thanks, I really like it. It's been my only friend for a couple of months now."

"Well, not anymore. Now I'm your friend, too," she said in a little girl sing-song voice that melted me even farther, "I'm Terri."

"Billy. Billy Sheph…"

"Shhhh…" she cut me off by putting her finger to my lips.

"No last names. Billy is fine. Family names limit our identity. We don't have to be someone else, we can just be who we are. You're Billy and I'm Terri and that's all we need."

"Sounds good to me," I said, starting to strum some chords.

I started playing *Last Train to Clarksville* and her eyes lit up even more. A couple other girls and a few guys made their way over and sat down and it became a mini-concert and sing-along, with everyone throwing out their suggestions and if I even half way knew them, I would play and sing and everyone would join in and sing along. I had never had the kind of camaraderie that I felt just singing with this group of strangers. I played until my fingers were so sore I couldn't go on. That night I had the best time since…well, in longer than I could remember.

As the crowd began to disperse amid compliments of "that was groovy, man," and "you're pretty good," and "good times, brother," I felt that yes, I was beginning to find what I was looking for. The music. The music moved me, and through the music, I could move others.

"Come on," Terri said as she stood up and brushed the grass from her cut-off jean shorts. She had a peace symbol sewn on to her left butt cheek and a *keep on truckin'* one on the right.

"Where we going?" I asked.

"I stay at my sister's house sometimes. You wanna come over?"

"Sure," I said, trying not to sound too excited. "Is she going to be okay with that?"

"Of course, silly!" she giggled softly, and started pulling me with her.

"I've got to put my guitar away and grab my stuff," I said.

"Mr. Responsibility," she laughed again, but stood and waited as I packed up, slightly rocking her hips back and forth with her thumbs in her pockets and that smile. My Lord, that smile.

We walked three or four blocks. Terri skipped cheerfully while I did my best to keep up and take in the sights along the way. The night air was crisp and exhilarating and I just wanted to breathe it in.

"Wait a minute," I said, pulling her to a stop.

"What's wrong?" she asked.

"Nothing. I just got here and I want a minute to take this in and enjoy the moment."

She smiled at me and put her arms around my waist, joining me as I gazed up at the night sky. The kiss came naturally and I didn't want it to end. Finally, she stepped back and looked at me.

"You sing really well. Did you come out here to be a rock star?"

It made me laugh. "No. I don't know why I came. Maybe it was to meet you."

She giggled and, pulling my hand, away we went, off into the warm San Francisco night while the city still bustled noisily around us. We turned down a dark alley between a pharmacy and a convenience store. Then up a rickety set of metal steps to a small, three-room apartment that at one time was probably housing for the store owners below.

The living area was sparsely furnished...a table with three mismatched chairs and an orange crate, a love seat which had seen better days, and a record player which sat on the floor. Tucked into the corner beside the record player was a single mattress on the floor. It was made up nicely, with a pretty blue blanket and a few throw pillows on top. It was the only thing that looked orderly about the place.

"This is my space," Terri said, and led me to the mattress. She patted for me to sit down.

"Are you into the Airplane?" she asked.

Before I could ask what that was, she pulled Jefferson Airplane's *Surrealistic Pillow* album out of a cardboard box full of records beside the bed and placed it on the turntable. The sounds overcame me. I listened to the Stones and of course The Beatles, what my old man called "hippie devil music," but this was something else entirely. She fumbled in her small purse for a minute and withdrew a joint and lit it. She took a big drag, then held it out to me.

"I don't smoke," I told her.

"I don't either," she replied. "Well, not cigarettes, but this is different. Come on, Billy, it'll make you feel good."

Looking into those eyes, how could I resist? After all, I had come to California to "break free" and experience new things, right? She held the hand rolled joint to my lips as I cautiously took a big drag. My throat instantly caught fire and my eyes started to water and I began coughing uncontrollably.

"First time?" she asked with a knowing smile.

"Yeah," I gasped.

"It's okay. You gotta start slower. Let me help." She took a long drag and held it, pulling my mouth to hers and as we kissed, she slowly exhaled the smoke into my mouth. "Isn't that better?"

It was better. Much better. Her lips and patience made my first dance with Mary Jane a very nice experience. We lied down on the bed as she pulled the chiffon tunic she had been wearing up and over her head to reveal the most perfect set of breasts I had ever seen. Granted, at that time, I had not seen that many, but in retrospect, I still believe they were almost perfect. We made love to the strains of Grace Slick singing *Don't You Want Somebody to*

Love, and at some point I fell asleep with Terri in my arms. This. This is what I wanted.

CHAPTER 4

I spent the next two weeks with Terri showing me around the Haight, introducing me to new people, places and things. She introduced me to a really cool guy called Father Mike. Father Mike was a Catholic priest at some point I think, but was now indulging in the sins of the flesh. We would stay at Father Mike's sometimes instead of going back to Terri's place and stay up until the wee hours of the morning discussing religion, philosophy and smoking grass. Father Mike was a far cry from Preacher Hudson at First Baptist back home, but honestly I probably learned more from Father Mike in that short time than I did in my whole life at First Baptist.

When we got hungry, she introduced me to the Diggers, a group of do-gooders that set up in the park and fed anyone who needed it for free. If we needed money for anything, I could always pull out my guitar and put a hat on the ground and end up with a few bucks without breaking a sweat. Those two weeks seemed as if I had found the paradise that I had been seeking. Then, almost overnight, everything changed. The peace and love quickly turned to fear, violence and confusion. One night a gunshot rang out and sirens filled the night. Before we knew it, the grass turned to LSD and the free dope turned to pay for dope and the Diggers declared the "Death of the Hippie" and stopped coming. People were hungry and strung out with no place to go. The cops, who just a few weeks earlier were looking the other way, now began rousting people off of the benches and out of the parks at night. As quickly as paradise was found, it was just as suddenly lost.

We were in Terri's sister's place one night when her seldom-seen sister, Judy (who I honestly think may have just been a friend), came in wiping her eyes. She had been crying and her dress was torn. She had a small trickle of blood dripping from her nose and her left eye was swollen. She was quickly followed by a large black man, who was yelling abuse at her.

"Bitch, when I tell you to do shit, you fucking do it! You got that?! And I don't want none of your lip!" he exclaimed as he stalked her across the room. He pursued her until he had backed her into the small kitchen area.

"Whoa! Hey man, why don't you calm down?!" I said instinctively, getting to my feet.

"Say what motherfucker?" He turned and looked at me with eyes bulging, seeing me and Terri for the first time. "Just who the fuck do you think you are?" he said, stepping briskly towards me.

"That's Billy. He's a friend of Terri's," Judy said meekly.

"I don't give a shit if he's Bobby fucking Kennedy! He ain't coming in my house and talking shit to me!" said the black man, hatred in his eyes.

As he came towards me, Terri stepped in front of me. "C'mon Leon," she pleaded. "Billy didn't mean nothing by it, he was just looking out for Judy."

"If Judy needs any looking out for, I'll do it! I don't need no jive-ass honky cracker fucking with me in my house!" railed the out of control monster I then knew as Leon.

I could tell something wasn't right. I had never seen Leon before in my life, but it was obvious that the dude was on a major tweak and that this was not going to end well for one, or both, of us.

16

Family Man

"Leon! No!!" Judy screamed and Terri just shrank back against the wall. Instinct took over. I grabbed the first thing I could find, my trusty Fender and, gripping it like my baseball bat in high school, proceeded to make grand slam contact with the side of Leon's skull. The big man hit the floor like a ton of bricks, the splinters of my beloved guitar drifting down around him. The thud of him hitting the ground was almost as sickening as the thunk of the guitar making contact with his juiced-up head. The same head that was now split like a melon and beginning to leak another dark stain onto the already-stained carpet. This one wouldn't easily come out.

"Oh shit! Is he okay?" I asked.

Judy, who was now kneeling beside Leon with a dish towel held to his head, looked at me stupidly. "Of course he's not okay, you asshole! You just bashed his head in with your fucking guitar!"

"But.....he was going to kill you," I stammered.

"We fight all the time," she answered.

"He pulled a knife on me!" I protested.

Judy looked at the switchblade as if seeing it for the first time. She picked it up, closed it and wiped it on her pants. She then held it out to me. "Here. Take it. Now go."

I stood, looking dumbfounded. I had just defended myself, her, and Terri, and on top of that, had just destroyed my most prized possession and primary source of income. I looked to Terri for help but she just stood there, chewing on her bottom lip and staring at the floor.

"You should go, Billy." Terri finally said, barely audibly.

Leon began to moan quietly. Well, that was a relief. At least I hadn't killed the bastard.

"Here, take the knife. Maybe you can trade it for a new guitar," Judy said and pushed it into my hand. I looked

17

from one to the other, Terri refusing to meet my gaze. Finally, in disbelief, I took the knife, stuck it in my pocket, grabbed my bag, and split. Paradise lost, indeed.

CHAPTER 5

I was out on the street with no place to go, no guitar (well, I still had the neck, but little good that was gonna do me.) There was nothing in my pocket but some spare change and a switchblade that came from God-knew-where and had been used for God-only-knew-what. In such a short time, the streets didn't feel safe anymore. The Haight felt a lot less like peace and love and a lot more like, well....hate. Where I once had no qualms about just lying down on a park bench and going to sleep, now that was out of the question. I tried Father Mike. He always welcomed all comers, but when I went to his place, he wasn't there. Someone new had moved in and the new tenants had no idea who Father Mike was or where he may have gone.

I thought about my old pal Willie, the one who brought me here, but his number had disappeared long ago. A bright neon sign shone like a beacon and called to me like a sign from God. "Pawn," it flashed in blood red neon letters with "We Buy Anything of Value" in blue underneath. In white, neat, hand lettering on the store windows, "TVs, Guns & Knives." Surely the knife in my pocket would be worth a few dollars. Not enough to replace my guitar like Judy suggested, but maybe enough to rent a cheap hotel for a night or so, and just as importantly, I would be rid of it. The last thing I needed would be to get arrested with that in my possession. My luck it had probably been used in a murder or something.

I needed some time to regroup, find a job doing whatever I could until I came up with a plan. The Terri trip was fun, but I should have known that it wouldn't last forever. I felt like an idiot, but at the same time, living in the moment was so perfect. It was the most carefree feeling I had ever experienced. Until it wasn't.

I walked into the pawn shop and looked around. The wall on my right was full of guitars and I naturally gravitated towards it. I admired all of the instruments and felt another pang over my broken Fender as I gazed at a similar one hanging there. I looked at the tag. $65.00. It may as well have been $600. Well, at least I knew what I needed to come up with to replace it.

"Can I help you?" A gray-haired man in his 50s sporting a huge walrus mustache was watching me suspiciously from behind the counter.

"Um…yeah," I said, reaching into my pocket. I glanced around nervously, then pulled the knife out and placed it on the counter.

"I would like to sell this," I continued.

"It hot?" he eyed the knife warily, taking out a pair of glasses to examine it more closely and turning it over in his hands.

"Um….no. A….friend gave it to me," I said, semi-truthfully.

"I don't mean it is stolen. I mean has it been used in a crime?" said the Walrus.

"Oh. No. I'm sure it hasn't. She wouldn't do anything like that," I said.

"She?" He looked at me even more doubtfully.

"My friend. The one who gave it to me. It was a gift. For my birthday. I don't know why, I guess she just didn't know what to get me." So much for half-truths. I was in full out liar mode now.

Family Man

Walrus flipped open the blade and brought it to his nose and started sniffing. I didn't know what the hell he expected to learn that way. I was about ready to tell him to stick it up his ass and see how that smelled when he looked up.

"Smells clean," he said.

"I think it's new," I said, on a lying roll. "It came in a box but I threw it away."

"Too bad," said Wally, "it'd be worth more that way."

"Yeah, I wanted her to think I really liked it and was going to keep it so I tossed the box."

"Hmmm. Well, what's she going to think now?"

"Doesn't matter," I said. "We broke up."

"Ahhh," he said knowingly. "Fifteen bucks. I could've done 20 with the box."

"My luck," I frowned. "I'll take it." He counted three $5 bills out on the counter and I took them and stuffed them in my pocket.

"Pleasure doing business with ya, kid," said Walrus, not even trying to sound like he meant it.

"I'm gonna look at your guitars for a minute," I said, making my way back to the wall of instruments.

"Help yourself, but I ain't got nothing for $15.00. I can do layaway though."

"Cool. Thanks." Hmm. Layaway a new guitar or rent a roach-infested room for a night or two? The choice was tempting. About that time, the bell on the door chimed and another customer walked in. He was about my age and sported a full shock of dark hair straight off a Beatles record. He even looked a little like Paul McCartney.

"How you doing, Bobby?" said the talking mustache.

"Pretty good, Wally. Yourself?"

Son of a bitch. The dude's name really was Wally.

"Can't complain," said Wally the Walrus.

"Good to hear," Bobby said as he made his way over to where I was standing and pulled a white Fender Stratocaster off the wall. He plugged it into a small amp and started playing. Damn! The dude was good! He played for another couple minutes before he looked up and saw me standing there slack-jawed. Bobby flashed a Hollywood smile at me and said, "Sorry, man. Were you about to play?"

"Not after that," I said.

"Aww, I ain't nothing special," he said with a grin, but he actually seemed to mean it.

"Sounded pretty good to me."

"You play?" he asked.

"I strum some, but nothing like you," I answered.

"Well, pull one of those babies down and let's jam," he said. "Don't worry about Wally, he's cool." Bobby had obviously seen me look towards the counter where Wally was now indeed being "cool."

"I gently lifted the Fender acoustic off the wall. I figured if I was going to be out-classed, at least I was going to stick with an instrument that I was comfortable with and hopefully I wouldn't look too bad.

"Just start strumming and I'll riff over you," Bobby said.

I started just a basic G, C, D chord progression and Bobby jumped in seamlessly. We jammed for a good fifteen or twenty minutes and I felt myself actually beginning to smile. Music always seemed to be a cure for whatever ailed me.

"Groovy," Bobby grinned. "Don't sell yourself short, man. That was cool. You ever play anything else?"

"No," I said, "I've never even played an electric, only an acoustic."

Bobby reached up and pulled a black Fender bass guitar off the wall and plugged it in. He handed it to me as he took the acoustic back and returned it to the wall. "Just play the root notes and then feel the groove and do what it tells you to do," he said.

He started the rhythm this time and looked up and nodded at me to join in. It took a few minutes, but after I got the hang of it, like he said, I could feel the groove. I was no Paul McCartney, but I began to experiment with different notes and filled in when Bobby started playing some lead lines. It didn't sound half bad. After another twenty minutes or so, he stopped and flashed me that grin again and started nodding.

"Not bad, not bad at all!"

"Thanks," I replied.

"You looking for a band?" Bobby asked.

"Wow. I've never really thought about it," I answered, "but my guitar is broken right now."

"I mean bass. Hard to find bass men," he said, "and you are a natural."

"Thanks man, but I don't have a bass. I've never even tried one before."

"Hell, that's easy. Wally, hook my man here up with a bass guitar and amp," Bobby yelled across to Wally.

"Do you like that one?" he asked, turning his attention back to me.

"Well, yeah, I guess. It felt good, but I'm kind of broke right now, man. I'll have to save up some dough."

"Don't worry about it. Me and Wally go way back."

"My credit good here, Wally?" he yelled back across the room.

"$125, Bobby," Wally said without looking up.

"A hundred bucks next week," countered Bobby.

"$120."

"$110 it is," Bobby called out and winked at me.

Wally rolled his eyes but his lack of response made it clear that they had a deal. Bobby rolled up the cord and stuck it in the back of the amp. He handed me my (or was it our?) new bass guitar. He hung the Strat back on the wall and picked up the amp.

"I'll give you a hand carrying this," he said.

"Bobby, this is super cool of you, man, but I'm walking and I've got to find a place to crash. I would love to play with your band, but honestly I've got to find a job and a place to stay first."

"Have you got a driver's license?"

"Umm, yeah."

"Then dude, it's your lucky day." he said. "I've got a little extra room at my place and it just so happens that my landlord is always needing to have errands run and is down with dropping a few bucks for it." He seemed to have an answer for everything and just like that, my basic needs were met.

"Well, how can I refuse?" I stated.

"That's what I'm talking about!" Bobby said excitedly as we approached a red convertible Mustang at the curb. He loaded the amp into the backseat.

"This is nice! Is it yours?" I asked.

"It is today," he said cryptically, getting into the driver's seat.

I carefully placed my new guitar in the back seat and climbed into the passenger side. "Man, I cannot thank you enough," I started. I then realized I had just formed a band, took on a new job, acquired a roommate, and hadn't even introduced myself. "I'm Billy. Billy Shepherd," I continued, offering my hand. Bobby looked at me again with that teen heartthrob smile and reached over and shook my hand.

"Bobby Beausoleil," he smiled, floored the Mustang, and away we went.

CHAPTER 6

Bobby drove like he put no value on life whatsoever. Not his, not mine, and not the other people on the road. He took the curves at twice what any rational human being would have considered a safe or reasonable speed. I was grateful that I hadn't eaten all day because whatever it was would have been all over the Mustang's interior by now. I held on for dear life and prayed that if I survived this ride with Bobby that I would never, under any circumstance, ever get into a car with him again. It was of course a promise I failed to keep, but I did make it a point to drive whenever possible if we rode together after that.

Bobby looked nonplussed, as if he were just out for a Sunday drive, with the wind whipping through his hair and his right hand on the steering wheel while his left arm hung casually out the window. I was relieved when we finally arrived at a house that looked like it had been cut into the side of a hill at 964 Old Topanga Canyon Road. It was a red shake-sided two-story house with wooden steps going up the side facing the road.

"This is it," Bobby said, as he opened his door and grabbed the gear out of the backseat. I sat still for another few minutes trying to reclaim my stomach. Bobby proceeded to walk to a white door on the lower level.

"You coming?" He turned back to me and sat the amp down, reaching for the door knob.

"Yeah. I.....was just admiring the view," I lied, trying to buy time for my stomach to settle.

He looked around, admiring the view. It was as though he was seeing it for the first time. "It is gorgeous, but don't get too used to it. Gary's great about letting people stay here, but it's a temporary thing. We'll be here a few weeks, a couple months at best."

"Hey, an hour ago I wasn't set up for more than a day, so a few weeks is a big improvement," I replied.

"Yeah, I never like to stay in one place for too long anyway. Know what I mean?"

"Sure," I said. Although I didn't know what he meant, I was learning quickly. Little did either of us know that Bobby's wanderlust would be coming to an end in the not-too-distant future. Unfortunately for him, he was going to be staying in one place for a very long time.

We went into the house in what I guess would be considered the basement. Bobby motioned to a room in the right rear and said, "That's yours, man. We haven't been using it at all."

I pushed open the door and was surprised to see that it was a pretty nice room. There was a double bed, already made up, with a dresser and a small closet. It was way better than I expected and a whole lot nicer than any hotel room that I could have gotten for my 15 bucks.

Bobby poked his head in the door. "I got an old lady that hangs out here some and occasionally some other people will come and go, but it'll mostly be just me and you, man, make yourself at home."

"You're married?" I asked, still getting used to the West Coast lingo.

"Hell no man! I just got a shack job that hangs for a few days here and there. She's real classy." He stopped to think a minute, "Come to think of it, I don't know, she might be married or something, what do I care?"

He laughed and walked out the door, giving me a moment to settle in. I sat my bag down and sat down on the bed. Wow, what a day. I laid back for a minute and must have drifted off. I jerked awake and sat up abruptly, seeing a round face peering in the window directly at me.

"Shit!" I said, apparently really loudly, because Bobby came rushing into the room.

"What the hell, man, everything cool?"

I brought my hands up and rubbed my face and pointed at the now-empty window. "Somebody was watching me through the window!" I said, still unsettled. About that time, the "somebody" appeared in the doorway. He was pale and looked almost sickly, strange for someone in California. He had a sparse crop of blondish hair that was beginning to thin and he was holding a large gray cat.

"Oh, this is Gary. It's his house," Bobby explained as Gary just kind of gave me a strange smile.

"Gary, this is Billy. He's going to be crashing here for a while. I told him you could probably use him to make some deliveries or something," Bobby continued the introductions.

"Oh yeah. Sure. That will be great." Gary spoke so softly that I could barely hear him.

"Welcome, Billy. Make yourself at home. A man can never have too many friends. I'm Gary Hinman," he continued, "if you need anything, I'm right upstairs." The cat was chewing on Gary's arm but he didn't seem to notice.

Gary turned and left without another word. He struck me as odd, but he seemed nice enough. He was also supplying me with a roof over my head and a way to make a little money, so who was I to question him? Gary left the front door open behind him when he left, so Bobby went to shut it and I followed.

"Sorry man," I said, "but he scared the shit outta me."

"It's cool," Bobby answered. "Gary's a good cat, but he's a bit of a creeper. I've seen him watching through the windows while I was getting it on before."

"Wow! Really?!"

"Yeah. Hell, I guess watching gets him off or something, I don't know."

"And that doesn't freak you out?"

"It did at first, but then I figured 'What the hell?' He wants to watch, I'll give him a show," Bobby laughed. "Between you and me, I think the only pussy he's interested in is that damn cat, if you get my drift."

"You mean he's queer?" I said, incredulously.

"That'd be my guess," Bobby said nonchalantly. "But what the hell, man? Leaves more chicks for me and you, right?"

"Yeah, I guess," I replied thoughtfully, and that was the last time we talked about it.

CHAPTER 7

The next few weeks spent at Bobby's were magic. We would spend hours many evenings playing music. No schedule, no rehearsals, just sitting and playing. I did several odd jobs for Gary to help with my part of the rent, small repairs around the house, trimming some of the vines that were growing up the wall. I rarely saw Gary, though; he was either gone or giving music lessons. Gary was an incredibly talented dude who played and taught drums, piano, trombone, and even bagpipes. It was rare not to hear some sort of music drifting down from above. Bobby always gave me my assignments and Bobby always approved them. It was like Gary was there, but he wasn't there. I got the impression that he was quiet and valued his privacy and that was fine with me. Gary seemed like a nice enough guy but I really never got to know him. I'm not sure if anybody ever did.

Sometimes Bobby and I would ride into town and pick up girls or occasionally he would just bring a couple home. The whole scene out here was so different. Sex was casual and free. We would hang out, smoke a little grass, and then pair up. Usually they would stay for a day or two and then we, or at least I, would never see them again.

I did several gigs with Bobby around Los Angeles. Nothing extremely significant and usually we even performed with just a makeshift group that Bobby or one of his friends put together and didn't even use a name, but sometimes we used names of bands Bobby had used in the past, most often The Orkustra.

A few weeks into my stay at Topanga also brought me to doing some of the "deliveries" that Bobby mentioned Gary might want me to do for him. Bobby came downstairs with the keys to Gary's VW van and a small envelope. He opened up a map on the small kitchen table and used his finger to draw out a route. "Gary needs you to take this for him. Guy's supposed to give you 30 bucks. You keep 5 and bring the rest back and I'll give it to Gary."

"Sure. Okay. What is it?" I asked.

"Billy, sometimes it's better just to not ask questions," Bobby advised.

I didn't have a great feeling about it, but I also knew I wasn't exactly in the best place to be making waves. "Tell me this. Is it illegal?"

"That's a question," Bobby grinned, then, "not exactly, but I would recommend driving like you do and not like I do." With that, he guided me to the door. "You need the map?"

"Yeah. I'm still learning my way."

He handed me the map and patted my shoulder. "You'll be fine," he smiled. "Just remember not to speed."

That was the first of many deliveries that I made for Gary, and I suspected for Bobby as well. In addition to Gary's acumen for music, I also learned that he had a chemistry degree. He was putting it to good use to enhance his, and my, income by producing tablets of mescaline, an organic psychedelic drug, that he somehow derived from peyote or cactus. The chemistry was over my head, but apparently it was skirting the recently-passed law making LSD illegal. Bobby promised I wouldn't get in trouble as long as I played it cool and played dumb. I figured my naturally blond hair might finally work to my advantage.

CHAPTER 8

Fate plays funny tricks. On one of my excursions for Gary, I delivered 100 dollars' worth of mescaline to an apartment on Franklin Avenue in LA. The black man who answered the door was a big dude. I instantly had flashbacks to my encounter with Leon at Terri's place but when I mentioned that I had a delivery from Gary, the man's broad smile put me at ease. I made several trips to the apartment over the next several months and each time I was made to feel welcome. Some of the shipments were several hundred dollars, so it was obvious that he was a dealer and not just a casual user, but he always struck me as cool and laid-back. Unlike some of Gary's customers who I wanted no part of, Bernard Crowe made me feel at ease and would sometimes ask me to smoke a joint or have a beer with him. On probably my third visit as he was ushering me out, he placed his big paw on my shoulder and said, "My friends call me Lotsapoppa. We cool, Billy, so you can call me that, too." On a trip I would make later, I would hardly allow myself to even look him in the face.

This went on for a couple of weeks and I fell into a sort of routine. Do some chores or deliveries for Gary, smoke some grass, play some music with Bobby. I was making decent money and having a good time with Bobby, who was getting to be a good friend. I was hanging out with whatever girl happened to be around for a day or two and generally just taking it easy and enjoying life. That path was about to be altered dramatically.

I had just come in from my delivery. Ironically, I think it was to Lotsapoppa, when Bobby met me at the door. "Man, you're not going to believe this shit!" Bobby said excitedly.

"What's up man?" I asked as I approached the door, I had been around Bobby for a while now and I didn't think I had ever seen him this excited.

"I met this cat at the music store," he began. "He was playing some far-out tunes man, and he wants to play with us! And get this. He knows quite a few heavy-hitters. He said he can score us a gig at the Topanga Corral!"

"That's far out!" I was almost as excited as Bobby. The Topanga Corral was one of the hot spots in the area and lots of celebrities and musicians hung out there.

"So let's get together and get something going," I continued. "When can he come over?"

"He's inside right now!" Bobby exclaimed. He gleefully ushered me inside.

I walked through the door and was surprised to see a familiar face. Sitting cross-legged on the floor and holding a guitar, surrounded by girls, was the bearded face of Charles Manson. Charlie didn't look at all surprised to see me.

"Ol' Shep," he said instantly with a big smile.

"How's it going Charlie?" I asked.

Bobby looked stunned. "You guys know each other?"

"We've met," I said.

"Oh, me and Shep here go way back. We're one soul," Charlie said. This was the first time I had heard him use the term but it wouldn't be the last. I did feel a kinship with Charlie even though we had met only briefly. Seeing him here again sort of felt like reconnecting with an old friend.

"Bobby says you want to play some music together," I said.

Family Man

"We *are* the music, man." Charlie said. "We don't play *it*, *it* lives in us and sometimes we can help *it* escape." I noticed that the girls, whom he had failed to introduce, seemed to hang onto his every word, admiring him as if he was Mick Jagger or something.

"Well, hell, let's jam," said Bobby, picking up his guitar. I went to get my bass.

Charlie said, "No man, we don't need that. Play the drums, brother."

"We've been working with me on bass," I countered. "I really haven't messed around with the drums any."

"It's in your soul, man, I can feel it."

Charlie then closed his eyes and played a set of imaginary bongos, making coordinating faces to match every beat. I couldn't help breaking into a smile when on the final beat he went, "Boom!" and opened his eyes. The girls giggled hysterically.

"Whatever you say, man," I said, and picked the set of bongos off the floor. I sat down across from Charlie. Bobby pulled up a chair and joined us.

Charlie's rhythms were crazy and I had a little bit of trouble locking in with him until he stopped and said, "Whoa, whoa, whoa, Shep man, don't look at my hands, man, look at my eyes. Listen with your soul. Feel the music here." He pounded his chest with his fist. "Don't think, *feel*."

Charlie started playing again and Bobby joined in with some soaring riffs over Charlie's rhythms. I looked into Charlie's eyes. Soon enough, I fell right into the rhythms as Charlie started to sing. If I thought Charlie's rhythms were crazy, his words went even further. It was like they just flowed from his mouth. I had never heard anything like it and I have to say, it was magical. We jammed for several hours and the girls sat there as if mesmerized.

"Damn boys, that was fun!" Bobby said when we had finished. I started rubbing my hands. I didn't realize how sore they were until we stopped.

"What do you think girls?" Charlie said, looking around at his fan club.

"Great," "Groovy," "Far out!" they all spoke over each other.

"This here's Lyn, Pat, Ella, Mary and Snake," Charlie said, nodding at the girls in turn.

"I'm done, man," Bobby stood up and headed to his room. Charlie nodded to the girl he had called Ella. Ella got up and followed Bobby into his bedroom. I looked wide-eyed after them.

"Which one you want, Shep?" Charlie asked. I turned back to him with what I'm sure was a completely stupid look.

"How about Snake, man? You like her?" Snake smiled at me. Damn, she sure was cute. She was the smallest of the girls and probably the best looking, but man she looked young. Snake gave a soft smile and raised her eyebrows as if to repeat the question.

"Um...yeah, sure," I stammered.

"Snake, you go show my man...Shep...here a good time, all right? You take care of my drummer now, okay?"

"Yeah, Charlie," Snake answered and stood up and smiled coyly.

Snake was maybe 5 feet tall and 100 pounds. She had short, brown hair and was wearing a white peasant blouse and tight shorts. She reached out and took my hand and led me to my room. It was still not even spring time, but it felt like Christmas to me.

The next week or two were almost a repeat of that first day. I didn't spend a lot of time around Charlie, as he kind of came and went. At night, we smoked a little weed, played a little music, and then I retired to my bedroom

34

with Snake. Most nights we made love, but sometimes she just wanted to talk. In bed she was definitely a woman, but out of it, she was very childlike. She said her name was Diane, but Charlie and the girls insisted on calling her Snake. She said Charlie had given her that name based on the way she moved in bed. I couldn't disagree with his assessment, but I could have done without hearing it.

I enjoyed my talks with Diane. She told me of how her parents had once been a normal suburban family until her dad decided one day that he wanted to "drop out" and join the hippie lifestyle. They sold their house, bought an old bread truck, and abandoned everything. They just drove around attending music festivals, smoking grass, and doing LSD. They had allowed her to do those drugs at a very early age; she thought maybe when she was around eleven or so. I thought back to how "straight" my parents were and how they would be appalled if they knew what I was doing now - and I was nineteen. I couldn't even imagine parents allowing their kid to experiment with drugs at eleven.

She went on to tell me how they had ended up at the spiral staircase house and that's where she had met Charlie. Her parents had stayed for a while but then wandered around and found themselves at Wavy Gravy's famous Hog Farm. After a while there, she had asked her parents if she could go back to the spiral staircase house to stay with Charlie and the people there. They had let her go. They even gave her a signed paper stating that she had been emancipated. She had been with Charlie and his group ever since.

CHAPTER 9

Each day was a new adventure. I came to realize that Charlie had a whole horde of women following him around. The first group stayed for a few days, then Charlie and a couple of the girls would disappear for a day or two, then he would reappear with a couple of different girls. The only constants seemed to be Lynette, who was rarely seen without Charlie, and Diane, who always seemed to be waiting for me. Until one day when she wasn't.

I came in from making one of my deliveries and walked into the living room where only Charlie and a couple of new girls were waiting. "Where's Diane?" I asked, looking around.

"Well, Snake had to slither on down to a different hole for a while," Charlie said, as the girls sitting beside him giggled.

"Is she coming back?" I asked.

"Who knows? Snake's a free spirit, she's still trying to find her peace, ya dig?" Charlie replied.

"But I…"

"Now don't you worry none, I brought you another hole for your snake to slither into," Charlie teased. Once again, the girls laughed as if he were Lenny Bruce, saying the funniest things they had ever heard.

"Now Sandy, here, she's a little quiet and inside herself. She might be a little too much like you to be a fit," he said gesturing to a girl with soft dark blonde curls and a cute, innocent face. "But Susie…she could show you a thing or two."

Family Man

I must admit, the girl with the straight brown hair and the dark eyes absolutely dripped sex appeal. I had never been to a strip club, but the girl in front of me appeared to be specially built for the job (which I found out later she actually had been). Susie stood up and pulled her shirt over her head, revealing an absolutely perfect upper half. She started to sway to imaginary music and stuck a finger in her mouth, sucking on it seductively until she worked her way over to me. She began gyrating up and down until she was at my crotch and reached out to unzip my fly. I put my hands down and pulled her face up to mine where she gave me a deep, passionate kiss.

"I don't think Shep's ready for an exhibition just yet, Susie. Why don't you all head to the back and we will catch you later," Charlie suggested.

Susie basically shoved me with her kiss back into my bedroom and showed me her idea of a good time. She was a little wild for my taste and a little rough even. Susie looked like a stripper and screwed like a hooker. I can't say that it was a bad experience, but I didn't feel the chemistry or connection that I had felt with Diane or Terri. It almost felt like she was doing a job, and although she did it well, her mind seemed to be elsewhere. She was all body and no heart. Sometimes initial impressions can be very telling and I found that to be true in this case. It was the first and last time I had a sexual encounter with Susan Atkins.

CHAPTER 10

The next few weeks were repeats of the past few. Jamming, deliveries, and whatever girl happened to make herself available. I preferred spending time with Diane, but had seen that the rule of the day was, "Don't get attached." Charlie, Bobby, and the girls had made that clear. It was a whole new world view for me. The carefree lifestyle that they were so immersed in did have its appeal. I wanted to try different things. I supposed that there were worse things than making love to a different girl every few days.

Across the street from the Topanga house, there was a wooded area and one day Charlie came up to me and asked me to take a walk with him. We walked through the woods for probably half an hour in silence before Charlie spoke.

"Shep," he said, "listen up."

"Yeah, Charlie, what's up?" I replied.

"A man's word is who he is. If your word ain't no good, you ain't no good, ya dig?"

"Yeah, man, that's how I was raised."

"No, forget how you were raised. Were you raised to fuck a different girl each night? Were you raised to smoke and bang and booka booka booka? That ain't what I'm talking about man. I mean who you are. Way down where it counts. Not what Mama and Daddy taught you, but what you taught you. What the trees teach you. They'll be here when we are gone, Shep, 'cause they are truth. They don't know how to lie, ya dig? Shhhh!"

Family Man

Charlie knelt down almost silently and motioned for me to do the same. I did so, a lot more noisily than he did, I must admit. Charlie looked a little ill at me before focusing straight ahead. "You see that fox there?"

I looked out where Charlie seemed to be looking, but didn't see anything. "I don't…" I started.

"Shhh!" he stopped me. We waited in silence for several long minutes until, sure enough, a red fox about the size of a small dog appeared from behind a tree probably 100 yards away. I didn't see any way Charlie could have seen it that far away and that long before I did, but there he was. I watched in amazement as Charlie reached out his hand and the fox cautiously made his way within a couple feet of us.

"Wow," I started to say before Charlie shot me a look. After a couple more minutes of checking each other out, the fox walked straight up to Charlie. He reached out and started petting it on the head.

"You see," Charlie said, as he continued stroking the fox like a pet, "this fox don't know nothing but truth. Every decision he makes better be true 'cause his life depends on it. He knows I'm his brother and brothers don't lie to each other. You dig what I'm saying, Shep?"

I didn't really get what Charlie was saying at that time but I nodded. I was still amazed at how the fox trusted him. I reached out to touch the fox's head, but when I got within six inches of him, he ran off in the direction he came from and disappeared into the woods. Charlie stood up without looking at me and started walking back to the house. About 10 minutes later he finally spoke again.

"The only real truth is in real love, Shep. The reason that fox ran off is because he knew you didn't love him, and without love, he can't trust your truth and that causes him to fear."

He didn't say anything the rest of the way home and neither did I. What he had said left me with plenty to take in and, honestly, I was grateful to spend the night alone.

After a night and morning of reflection, I did at least partially understand what Charlie was saying, and after a day of work and a night of music the whole incident became a distant dream.

CHAPTER 11

We called our band The Milky Way. I don't remember who came up with it, Bobby or Charlie, but one day that's who we were. Charlie, true to his word, got us a gig at the Topanga Corral. In fact, we did several gigs there and a few at some of the other L.A. area clubs. Charlie said a friend of his from prison had some connections and had put in a word for us. The response wasn't bad, but it wasn't really good either. Charlie's stream of consciousness lyrics confused people, I think. Honestly, I feel he was ahead of his time but it was so different and unique that club crowds didn't seem to get it. After a few weeks it just kind of fizzled out.

We all knew that The Milky Way had run its course but we had some fun, made some bread and became closer friends. One day Lynette came in and told us they were all moving back to the spiral staircase house and we were welcome to join them. If not, we could come see them any time and that was that.

A couple weeks later, Bobby met a guy named Kenneth Anger. He wanted him to write some music and star in a film he was doing called *Lucifer Rising*. He was going to give up the apartment at Gary's and stay full time in the other apartment he'd been renting closer to L.A. to work on the film. He said he was sure he could get me a part in the movie if I wanted in. It sounded cool, but I had never acted before. After hearing the premise of the Devil and mythology and New Age mysticism, I decided it was beyond me, so I passed.

"See what you can work out with Gary, man," Bobby said. "I'm sure he won't put you out on the street."

"Hey, I'll figure something out, it's cool. Chase that dream, brother!" I reassured him.

"We've had some good times, Billy. I'm always there for you, man. You get in a tough spot, you hit me up...deal?"

"Deal," I said, and the best friend that I had in California walked out the door and out of my life, but it would only be temporary.

CHAPTER 12

Before Bobby left, he graciously took the bass guitar back to the shop we bought it from, and swapped it for the Fender I was admiring when we met. It was one of the coolest things anyone had ever done for me and cemented Bobby's place in my mind as one of the best friends I've ever had. While I was disappointed when he left, he said from the beginning that this would only be temporary, and I couldn't fault him for pursuing the opportunity that he had been offered.

I stayed on at Gary's for a few more weeks, but it just didn't feel the same and, honestly, I wasn't crazy about being a mule for Gary's mescaline deliveries anymore. Gary was also really bad about inviting pretty much anybody to crash at the house and some of the people that I would come home and find there didn't feel right to me, not that I've ever been the best judge of character. Either way, I decided that it was time to try something new. But what?

I told Gary that I was moving on and thanked him for all he had done for me. He was gracious and understanding and told me I could crash there any time. We shook hands and he smiled at me as I walked away. That is the image of Gary that I choose to remember.

I finished packing my bag and was walking out the door with my new guitar slung over my shoulder. I was going somewhere but I didn't know where. I had no particular destination in mind. Then, the familiar shape of a big black bus pulled to a stop right in front of me. It was as if it had been summoned by my wandering mind.

"Looks like you knew we were coming," said Charles Manson from the driver's seat with a devilish grin. "Hop in." He opened the bus door, and with a grin of my own and a shake of my head, I climbed on board.

Charlie said he couldn't wait for me to see where we were going. He was almost giddy, like a parent on Christmas morning when the kids walked in and saw the presents under the tree. Susan was on the bus along with a new girl named Ruth Ann. Ruth was absolutely gorgeous. Dark hair, dark eyes and a tan complexion that looked just short of being American Indian. Susan must have seen me admiring Ruth Ann because she came over and sat beside me, blocking my view.

As Susan was wont to do, she started talking nonstop and hardly shut up the entire trip. She said for me not to call her Susan anymore because Charlie had given her a new name and she preferred it. I thought that she was kidding when she told me that her new name was Sadie Mae Glutz. I thought she was joking, but she beamed with pride and told me to only refer to her as Sadie from now on. Whatever. She continued to ramble and I had pretty much tuned her out until she said something about the Beach Boys and Charlie slammed the brakes on the bus, throwing us all abruptly forward.

"Damnit, bitch, can't you ever keep your mouth shut?" Charlie scolded and for the first time Susan, nay Sadie, sat back. She stuck her lip out in a pout, and stayed quiet for the rest of the trip, which was only a few more minutes.

I realized we were near the coast. I could feel the ocean breeze in the air. I had kind of zoned out during Sadie's prattling and had not really been paying attention. We turned off Sunset Boulevard and pulled onto a driveway between iron gates that were swung open wide. We drove through a small wooded area into a clearing with a large ranch-style house with a cabana and a pool. Charlie grinned broadly as he brought the bus to a stop at the end of the long driveway. Sadie had gotten over her pouting and also had a big smile. I could tell this was the "surprise" they had been keeping from me.

"Nice," I said, seeing that they wanted a response.

"Guess who lives here?" Sadie blurted.

Charlie shot a quick glance at her that put her back into pout mode.

"Elvis?" I said, knowing it was wrong, but not wanting to let Charlie know that Susan had given it away earlier and besides, I didn't know *which* Beach Boy. As big as the place was, for all I knew it could be all of them.

"Not hardly," said Charlie, "but not that far away. Dennis Wilson, Mr. Beach Boy himself."

"Wow, that's really cool," I said, meaning it. "I didn't know you knew The Beach Boys."

"Just Dennis," Sadie intoned.

"Dennis is the one to know," Charlie said. "Dennis has got his head on straight. He didn't chase all that rabi-dobi-goodo Hindu Raji, Baji bull shit. He knows where it's at."

Charlie exited the bus and we all followed. We went into the house and were surrounded by the lush trappings of stardom. There were four or five bedrooms, several bathrooms, white shag carpet, and gold records hanging on the walls. In the living room sat a grand piano and a harpsichord. I was blown away by it. Girls were lounging everywhere, most of whom I had met, but several new ones and a guy who Charlie introduced to me as Bruce.

Bruce looked at me suspiciously and I suppose I did the same to him. Strange how I didn't mind sharing the harem with Charlie, and even Dennis Wilson, 'cause…well, he was a Beach Boy, but Bruce felt like competition. After a while, we both figured out that as The Beach Boys sang, there were at least "two girls for every boyyyyyy….." But in this instance, our pheromones took over.

I looked around for Diane and Charlie obviously picked up on it. "She's in the guesthouse," he said.

"Who?" I said, playing dumb.

"Snake. I know you're looking for her," Charlie continued. "Shep, you gotta learn that you can't con a con man." He looked me in the eye intently for a good thirty seconds, and while I never broke his gaze, I did feel a bit intimidated. Damn if I was going to let him or Bruce see it though. "Go on out there," he finally said, breaking into an easy smile. "She'll be glad to see you."

I did and she was.

CHAPTER 13

The guest house was a smaller version of the main house. I spent the next couple of hours sitting by the pool with Dianne, catching up on the group's happenings since I had last seen them. She introduced me to Brenda and Stephanie and reminded me of some of the names to go with the faces I had met only briefly before. Mary was sitting on the other side of the pool playing with her new baby that they all called Pooh Bear. A lot had changed in such a short time.

I asked Dianne about the guy inside and she said his name was Bruce Davis. She said that he was okay after you got to know him. She reiterated that Charlie trusted him so we should too. I decided I would make up my own mind but that I probably had been too quick to judge and I would give Bruce a chance.

We wandered back to the main house where somebody had lit a fire in the large stone fireplace. The glass doors were open and every light in the place was on. A couple of the girls jumped up as headlights cut through the dark of the driveway.

"Dennis is back!" several said at once and ran out to meet him. Charlie and I followed and stood on the top step. A silver Rolls Royce pulled to a stop and Dennis Wilson stepped from the driver's door. He had a confused look on his face for a moment, taking in the crowd of people at his house. It was at that point that I realized that I was not the only one meeting Dennis for the first time. Patty and Ella, the ones who had jumped up first, went to

Dennis and got him by each arm. After a few seconds, a glint of recognition lit in his eyes and he remembered them. Later, I found out that he had picked the two of them up hitchhiking a couple of days earlier and, after spending the night together, they had told him about the rest of the group. He had invited them to bring everyone over sometime.

Whether Dennis had meant that literally or not, they had taken him at his word and here we were. After his moment of indecision, Dennis seemed to come to the conclusion that his invitation had been accepted so what the hell? He smiled and locked arms with Patty and Ella. He started for the stairs until he seemed to notice me and Charlie for the first time. Charlie took a step toward him and Dennis froze.

"Are you going to hurt me?" Dennis stammered.

"Do I look like I'm going to hurt you, brother?" Charlie answered. Kneeling down, he kissed Dennis' sandal-clad feet. Charlie stood and produced an LSD tablet, seemingly out of thin air, and presented it to Dennis. Dennis took the tab and popped it into his mouth and the party was on. Dennis realized that he had met Charlie before a while back at Gary Hinman's house. In minutes, the two were acting like lifelong pals. California was so much bigger than South Carolina but it felt like everybody here knew everybody else. I wondered if the Gods had smiled on me and finally made me one of the popular kids. If so, I figured they owed it to me.

Over the years, many people have reported that we "took over" Dennis's house and forced him from it. Nothing could be further from the truth. Dennis enjoyed his time with us as much as we enjoyed our time with him. I may not be able to say I played with The Beach Boys, but I can definitely say I played with *a* Beach Boy. If sex, drugs, and rock and roll ruled the day when I was staying with Bobby at Gary's house, they ruled the nights when we were with Dennis.

Dennis and Charlie became fast friends and musical collaborators. Dennis was in awe of Charlie's ability to just throw words out. Dennis would sit at the piano while Charlie strummed his guitar and sang and I would just do my best to keep up. There were times when Dennis would stop playing and listen, his head nodding and his mouth hanging open in wonder at Charlie's creations.

"That's it!" I remember Dennis yelling during one of our all-night music sessions.

"What's what?" Charlie answered.

"The sound, man! The sound we've been missing!"

While Dennis and his brother Brian wanted to push the band and explore the musical possibilities in front of them, his cousin Mike and the other members wanted to stay the course and keep playing the music they were known for. Brian and Dennis were the revolutionaries. They could see that the times and sounds were changing and they saw that as an opportunity to expand their creativity. Dennis saw something in Charlie's music that he thought could help take his band in that direction. He took us over to Brian's house one night and we spent hours recording Charlie's music. Brian had become virtually a recluse by this time and hardly left his home studio, which he considered holy ground. The fact that he allowed Charlie to record there says something about his respect for Charlie's music as well as his respect and affection for Dennis. Brian's wife turned her nose up at the "dirty hippies" that Dennis had brought into her home. Brian, however, was just as enthused with the freshness of Charlie's sound as his brother was and couldn't have treated us nicer.

CHAPTER 14

While many of our group would drift in and out of Dennis's house over the next few months, I stayed there most of the time. I loved being near the ocean, and I didn't want to miss a single opportunity to sit in on the jam sessions that could break out at any time. It wasn't just at Dennis'. It also happened at a lot of the other places we went with Dennis.

At some point during our stay, Bruce took off. He said he wanted to see Europe, so he went. It was after he came back that I really felt like I got to know him. I always wondered who funded that trip. It may have been Dennis, but if I had to guess, I would say it came from a place much darker. Charlie and I had begun to take walks on the beach or sometimes just around the property on a regular basis and during these walks, Charlie would sometimes say nothing at all. Sometimes he would say things like, "Breathe it in, Shep," and "This is our mother. Not a woman, but the sky, the trees, the Earth." At these times, he would spread his arms, throw his head back and just breathe. This is when I saw Charlie happy--when he could be one with nature. I tried, but I could never lose myself in Mother Earth the way he could. I always envied him for that.

During a few of these "walk and talks," Charlie told me things that really didn't seem to align with what I thought I knew. He said that Bruce had gone to Europe on a "vision quest." He was looking for God, but that he would only find Satan.

Family Man

"I've walked that road, Shep. That's where I met Susie. Bobby too. We were there at the beginning and saw the end."

"I'm sorry Charlie, but I don't get what you're saying," I said.

"Abraxas, man. I was there with Lavey when he started the Church of Satan. Satan my ass. I'm Satan just like you are, just like that owl is. I wasn't there physically but Susie was there, and Bobby. They told me about it and I experienced it. I met him once and read some of his book. Buncha horseshit to me. Susie said they was doing it on his altar, man. I said, I ain't got no time for that shit, ya dig?"

"Not really," I answered.

"He hired Susie to be some vampire and sit up naked in a coffin and shit. He's making a movie just like everybody else is."

I stayed quiet. Charlie had his own way of talking. He often covered what he was really saying with a lot of extra words.

"We didn't start this world. I learned that in prison. Scientology, Church of the Process, Church of Satan, Church of dick and dak and frak and booba dooba, man, it's all just music to me." He fired up a joint and took a big hit, passing it to me.

"My church is in my mind. I'm God, I'm the Devil, and so are you. Bruce goes over there and wants to learn the Process. The Process is in your mind, man. It's doing what you need to do for you. You see that spider over there?" He pointed to a beautiful web that had been carefully constructed between two tree limbs and the yellow and black master of its domain. "He sits there all day long. Hey now, all he is, is *now*. Everything is now. Look at that web, how fucking brilliant that web is, and you think we can comprehend that?"

51

A few days after Bruce left, Sadie, Ella, Patty, Stephanie, Mary and her son, the one Charlie named Sonstone Hawk, but most of the rest of us called Pooh Bear, took the big black bus and drove up to Mendocino. It would be a while before we would see them again. In the meantime, it was all about now. Dennis and Charlie almost seemed to be in a competition as to who could squeeze the most living into the shortest amount of time, albeit in their own unique ways.

The experiences and events went by so fast, and happened so often, that it is impossible for me to put a timeline on exactly what happened in which order during those months, but I remember them all. See, with Charlie, time seemed to both stand still and go quickly all at the same time. That was probably how I would define "now." It was as if everything happened all at one time and every moment was both the one before itself and the one after. Each was caught in my mind as a snippet in time. We rarely looked at clocks or calendars and almost no one had a watch except Dennis, who was a slave to his Beach Boys obligations.

CHAPTER 15

Charlie would make a trip to Mexico every so often. He always talked about the juju down there and was usually only gone for a week or so. I asked to go with him, but he just smiled and said, "Shep, you've got clean hands. Ain't no need for you to go getting them dirty on my account."

It was near the end of our tenure at Dennis' and while Charlie was gone on one of these trips, that I remember walking out to the guest house. I was looking for Dean Morehouse, a former minister and Ruth Ann's father. At the time, I'm sure the reason was important, but now, it escapes me. Dean was one of the oddest members of our group. He had been a preacher who befriended Charlie and gave him a piano. Charlie showed his appreciation by trading the piano for a bus and taking Dean's underage daughter with him when he left. Dean tracked Charlie down with the intention of killing him for "corrupting" his daughter, but instead ended up dropping acid with Charlie, then "dropping out" of society himself. Charlie's way with people never ceased to amaze me.

Dean had been staying with us for a few weeks and was usually at the guesthouse. I knocked and when the door opened, the man standing there with a towel around his waist was not Dean. Dean was 50-ish, overweight and balding. This guy was a couple years older than me and was built like a football player, which he had been.

"Is Dean around?" I asked.

"The old guy? Nah, I don't know where he is. Who wants to know?" the tall man said with an immediately recognizable Texas twang.

I immediately bristled at the jackass attitude of this guy. "Tell him Billy stopped by," I said

"Tell him yourself. I ain't your messenger service."

"What's going on?" Dennis and a couple of girls appeared from behind the guy. "Oh hi, what's up Billy?" Dennis said.

"I was just looking for Dean," I said, never taking my eyes off the big man as we engaged in a stare down.

Dennis broke in, "Chill out Charles, Billy's cool." The man grunted and turned away from the door.

"I think Dean went up to Terry's Place," Dennis said. "Don't mind Charles. He helps me out around the place sometimes and he doesn't trust strangers. He will be alright now that he knows we're cool."

"Yeah, whatever," I mumbled, with a bad taste still in my mouth.

"You ever been up to Terry's?"

"I think once but I couldn't get back there."

"Hang on a minute, let me grab my keys." Dennis disappeared into the house for a minute and I was left to replay my first meeting with Charles "Tex" Watson. Despite Dennis's optimism, Tex and I never really developed a much warmer relationship than that first meeting.

"You want to drive her?" Dennis asked, tossing me the keys to his red Ferrari.

"Hell yeah!" I said excitedly. It's not every day you get an opportunity to drive a Ferrari afterall. "But I don't know where we're going," I replied.

"I'll guide you," Dennis said, jumping over the door into the passenger seat.

"Then let's go!" I said, doing the same but not near as skillfully.

"Woohoo!" Dennis yelled, drumming on the dashboard as I whipped the car around and headed down Sunset towards Benedict Canyon.

I took the winding roads at speeds that weren't even close to the recommended limits, but the Ferrari was so smooth and built for this that I never even thought about it. Dennis had his head thrown back and eyes closed. He seemed to be okay with it, so why not? After riding with Bobby, this felt like a Sunday drive anyway.

The ride through the Santa Monica Mountains was exhilarating. As we neared the familiar area just before Benedict Canyon Road, Dennis motioned me up a hill onto an unmarked road that abruptly climbed a hill opposite of Bella Drive. Ironically, that unmarked road would soon become one of the best-known in the nation, if not the world. It was Cielo Drive.

We drove up an incline until we reached an iron gate bordered by rock columns and a wooden fence on one side and a steep hill on the other. "Press that button," Dennis directed me, motioning to a gate control panel on a pole to the left of the gate. I reached out and pushed the button. A bell rang and the gate began to swing slowly and silently inward. We drove through the gate and up a short-paved driveway, approaching the front of what looked to be a three car garage. It was my first of many trips to the residence at 10050 Cielo Drive. I would be back on several occasions. Some of the best times of the next year and a half of my life were spent there, and by far, some of the worst.

CHAPTER 16

We drove up the curving driveway and Dennis directed me to park in front of the two-story garage on the right. Just past the garage was a low, sprawling ranch style rock and wood panel house. It was painted a dark red and stretched out for what appeared to be the length of a football field. The long perfectly manicured lawn easily could have been used as such. There were some low hedges by the door spaced neatly in each direction and a stone walkway leading to the door of the home. Off to the left, a sparkling swimming pool glistened invitingly.

We got out of the car and were motioned over by a bare-chested strawberry blond man with a mustache. He was lounging beside the beautiful pool with an even more beautiful woman. "Dennis!" the man exclaimed, rising and grabbing Dennis's hand as he patted him on the back.

"How's it going Terry?" Dennis answered, then gestured to me, "You remember Billy?"

"I think we met briefly, but not officially," Terry said, and extended his hand. "Terry Melcher, and this is Candy," he said, nodding towards the bikini clad goddess on the lounger.

"Nice to meet you both," I responded. The woman looked my way and smiled softly, then went back to her business of sunbathing. "Candy" was Candice Bergen, a model and actress. If only the boys back in Carolina could have seen me then.

Family Man

"Shep is a friend of Charlie's. He's been staying at my place some. We've been jammin' some great tunes, man," Dennis continued.

"Ol' Crazy Charlie," Terry smiled. "You better watch yourself with that one, he's a strange cat."

"You're telling me," I joked back.

"So Shep here was looking to see Dean. He still back in the guest house?" Dennis asked.

"Yeah he's back there," Terry gestured down a gravel trail at the front of the property bordered by a white picket fence. There appeared to be a much smaller version of the main house at the end of the trail. "Or you can just follow the path around the pool here, it's shorter."

"Cool, thanks," I said, and started toward the guest house. "You coming?" I asked Dennis.

"Nah, man, you go ahead. I need to talk to Terry about coming over and listening to Charlie again," he said.

I knocked on the door of the guest house for at least five minutes and was about to give up when Dean came staggering to the door. I could tell he was so wasted that whatever I needed to talk to him about was now pointless. I just said I was checking to make sure he was all right for Ruth Ann. "Yeh," said Dean. "Wanna do a line?"

"No thanks," I said. "And you might want to take it a little easy, too."

"I'm good," he said, and fell backwards onto the floor. His snoring assured me that he was just unconscious and not dead, so I left him there and headed back poolside.

On the short walk back, I pondered just how far I had come in a short time. I went from being a small-town boy who had never experienced anything in life to sleeping with beautiful women and hanging out with rock stars and Hollywood movers and shakers. And I owed it all to Charlie.

Terry Melcher was the son of Doris Day and a wunderkind music producer in his own right. He had just produced two huge hits for The Byrds: *Mr. Tambourine Man* and *Turn, Turn, Turn,* and had worked with Paul Revere and the Raiders on their latest album. Mark Lindsey, the head Raider, had been staying at Cielo with Terry until recently. Dennis was convinced that once Terry got his hands on Charlie's music, that he could turn it into gold. I was just happy to be along for the ride. For all that could be said about Charlie Manson, his loyalty was never brought into question. Once you were in Charlie's good graces, you were bound for life. "Sounds good man, I'll get over there this week," Terry was saying as I walked up.

"Far out," Dennis answered. "Charlie will be stoked."

We said our goodbyes and exited the property. It was a beautiful location inhabited by beautiful people. At the time, I could never see myself ever having anything other than pleasant memories of Cielo Drive.

CHAPTER 17

Driving back down the canyon to his home on Sunset, Dennis was as animated as I had ever seen him. He really dug Charlie's music and he felt like he would be the one that would be seen as having "discovered" him. He would be known not only as the drummer of The Beach Boys, but as the man who turned the world on to the genius he called "The Wizard."

"Charlie's going to be as big as Dylan!" he raved. "Man, just wait until they get a load of Charlie's vibe!"

I was excited as well. Dennis had me convinced that Charlie was going to be the "next big thing." His brother Brian had used those exact words when talking about him and who knows? Maybe I could be a member of his band, or at least carry his luggage. The future looked as bright as the red, setting California sun.

Charlie was sitting on a rock by Dennis's driveway when we drove up. I noticed that most of the girls had come back. They had also brought along a couple of new ones. The ones that weren't bouncing around naked in the pool were lying topless beside it.

"Well if it ain't my two favorite rock stars," Charlie greeted us.

"Everything good down south?" Dennis asked knowingly.

"Very good," Charlie answered, breaking into a big grin, two baggies appearing in his hands like magic.

"Hell yes!" Dennis exclaimed, and started stripping as he went towards the pool. "C'mon Shep, let's party!" The next thing I saw was Dennis's naked ass diving into the water.

Charlie pulled some small white tablets out of one of the bags and tossed the other one over to Sadie, who started rolling and passing out joints with the grass that was in that one.

"You ever do acid, Shep?" Charlie asked me.

"Nah, I think I'll stick to grass," I said.

"Oh, come on Shep!" one of the girls said, then they all were chanting my name.

"Shep! Shep! Shep!"

Next thing I knew, a topless Diane and a new girl named Catherine Share, whom everyone called Gypsy because of her dark exotic looks, came and sat beside me. I openly admired Gypsy's naked body. "Open your mouth," Gypsy purred, pulling lightly on my jaw.

You think you've experienced peer pressure? Just try to say "no" when fifteen naked girls are all saying your name to encourage you to do something. I opened my mouth and extended my tongue as Diane instructed me while Gypsy eased my head back and placed the pill on my tongue.

"Just hold it there, don't swallow," Gypsy guided.

The little bitter pill dissolved quickly, but it must have been obvious that I was still feeling the aftertaste because Dennis tossed me a beer over and yelled, "Chase it down man!" I caught the beer and took a long drink as time began to move in slow motion. Charlie was playing his guitar and he and some of the others were singing but I couldn't hear the sound. Just as the shock of being deaf started to register, I realized that I didn't have to hear the music because I could see it.

The sounds were floating from the guitar strings in a rainbow of colors before racing off in all directions. Its beauty amazed me. There were colors I had never seen before. I was trying to name them when I noticed that tiny little men, maybe fairies, danced on the beams of color. They would disappear only to reappear on a different arc. I felt an intense feeling of calm and lay back in the grass. I stared up into the night sky which was erupting in a symphony of colors all its own. The men were there too, then gone. I watched as the sky turned to streaks of purple which were racing backwards and quickly collapsing themselves into a single exuberant pinprick of light a zillion miles away.

I was witnessing the dawn of creation! I sat up excitedly to share with my friends what I was experiencing, but they were gone. Where a moment ago the brightness was awe-inspiring, now only blackness prevailed. I was all alone. What if instead of the creation of the universe I had witnessed its destruction? What if I was the only survivor?

I felt something wet on my arms and looked down to see two long tongues tracing their way up towards my face. I followed the tongues with my eyes until I saw the faces of Diane and Gypsy on either side of me. It was them, but it wasn't them. Their skin had burned to a bright devil red and their hair was growing longer by the second. They were sitting in circles of flames that licked up in synchronicity with their flashing tongues. Huge white eyes bulged out of their heads before exploding into a yellowish goo that splashed hot and wet upon my face. I tried to push myself backward, but my hands disappeared into the liquid earth as their hideous lizard tongues began snaking towards my face.

I tried to scream but no sound came out of my mouth, only colorless butterflies. The butterflies immediately evaporated into the flames with screams of anguish. I wanted to get up and run but my body was concrete and would not respond to my mental commands. Suddenly, in front of me appeared a woman, floating in mid-air. It looked like Sadie, but I couldn't be sure. She brought me peace. I felt a floating calm until she threw her head back and large ram-like horns pierced through her forehead, severing the skin. She was naked and deathly white. Her belly began to swell from the early stages of pregnancy until ready to deliver in a matter of seconds. As her stomach continued to expand past the point of anything humanly possible, blood began to pour from the heavens like it was being spilled from a giant overflowing bowl. It ran down in slow motion until she was completely covered and it was dripping from her feet.

Next, two nude men floated up on either side of her in crucifixion style poses, with heads bowed down and arms extended. They may have been Charlie and Bruce, or maybe Dennis, I'm not sure, it was just obvious that they were extremely dead.

A demonic laughter echoed in my ears, ever increasingly louder and closer. A huge man, almost as tall as the sky, appeared before them. He was clad all in black and wore a hood. There was no doubt who he was. It was the man I met earlier today that had been called Charles. He had a huge scythe in his hand like the one held by the Grim Reaper and he started to chop mercilessly at all three of the bodies before me. The bodies of the rest of my friends began to rain down from the sky. Thunder and lightning exploded in my head. I felt the hot, sticky feel of blood on my face. I finally found my voice and screamed, "Who are you? Why are you doing this?"

The man turned toward me and when he smiled, a hundred bugs and worms fell from his huge misshapen mouth. "I am the Devil and I am here to do the Devil's business!" he yelled as thunderous laughter boomed from the heavens.

CHAPTER 18

I awoke with a start. Drenched in sweat, I sat up abruptly in bed.

"Shhh! Shh, quiet now," Gypsy said. She stroked my sweat-soaked hair and laid me back down. I willingly collapsed into the pillow and let Gypsy soothe my head.

"That was some trip you had," she remarked. "You scared the hell out of us."

"It was no day at the beach for me either," I replied.

"I'm sure. Just lie back down and rest, it's all over now."

"God, I hope so," I said.

"Your first bad trip?" she asked.

"My first trip period. And my last," I answered.

"It can be amazing but it's not for everyone," she agreed.

"It's definitely not for me." I said.

"Feel like making love?" she asked seductively, biting her lip.

"Stick your tongue out," I asked, almost afraid to see the result.

She looked at me quizzically, but did as I had asked. She didn't turn red and her tongue looked far more inviting than terrifying. I stared into her deep brown eyes and surveyed her golden skin. The terrors of the night melted away as quickly as they had come. I took her face between my hands, her tongue between my lips and had a far more pleasant segue into sleep this time than last.

The next time I woke up, I was in bed alone. I looked around and it took me a while to get my bearings. I was almost positive I had been in the main house last time I woke up with Gypsy beside me, but this time I was in the guest house. There were doors and passageways between most of the rooms in Dennis' house, but I wasn't aware of any secret passages to the guest house.

I heard movement and voices in the kitchen. It was at least two girls and a guy. The guest house, a guy.....damn it, it was probably Charles Watson. No way was I going to let him see me this disheveled. I took a quick shower and put on fresh clothes. At least now I wouldn't be setting myself up for his smart-ass comments.

I walked into the kitchen and saw Gypsy and Ruth Ann talking to a man but it wasn't Charles. This guy was a lot younger, a lot smaller and had a welcoming smile that set me immediately at ease. "Hey, Shep. I've heard a lot about you," he said, extending his hand, "I'm Paul Watkins."

"Hi Paul, how's it going?" I answered.

"Call me Little Paul," he continued. "I don't want to compare to you 'cause Gypsy says you're hung like a horse." I was taken aback until I saw his grin spread and Ruth Ann and Gypsy burst into laughter.

"I didn't say that!" Gypsy responded playfully.

"But I can vouch for it," said Ruth Ann.

I had no idea if Ruth Ann could vouch for it or not. If she could, I was hating myself for not being able to remember it. Jeez, I really had been out of it. I was also a little hurt that Gypsy hadn't said it, but it broke the ice quickly between Little Paul and myself. I instantly decided that I liked him. He was 17, a couple years younger than me, but could have passed for even younger. He had that fresh-faced, innocent look that I knew the girls would go crazy for and I wasn't wrong. It wasn't so long ago that I had that innocence. Who knew how quickly things could change for all of us?

"Where's Charles?" I asked, pretending to care.

"Tex? He left. He kind of comes and goes," Gypsy answered.

"He said he had to get back to work," added Ruth Ann.

"Really?" I said. I was legitimately surprised that the guy had a job, but who was I to talk? "What's he do? And why do you call him Tex?"

"He sells wigs," Ruth Ann began.

"And no doubt a few other things," Gypsy interrupted, "and there can only be one Charlie, so since he's from Texas, we call him Tex. Didn't you notice the accent?"

"Makes sense," I said, feeling kind of stupid.

"I call him asshole," Little Paul added.

"Oh stop!" Gypsy smacked at him. "There's enough girls for everybody. You boys are so territorial. Just 'cause you stick your dick in it, don't mean it's yours. Like Charlie says, we are all one soul and we all belong to each other!"

That conversation summed up the feelings of our group, about each other and about the tall Texan. With Tex, you either loved him or hated him. Most of the girls loved him and most of the guys hated him. What the girls saw as smooth and confident, the guys saw as brash and arrogant. There were times, however, when I could see the attraction and look past the bravado to see the real Tex, and he was just as lost and wandering as the rest of us.

CHAPTER 19

That evening, Charlie, Little Paul, and I were invited to come along with Dennis to a party at a home on Laurel Canyon Boulevard. We didn't know until we arrived that it was the home of Mothers of Invention leader Frank Zappa. The house was old and a bit rundown but you could see its past beauty and charm. I have no doubt that's why Frank had chosen to live there. It was a log cabin style home that was built right over the edge of a pond.

Dennis introduced us to Frank and his wife Gail. He then proceeded to rave to them about Charlie's music. As the night wore on, the house became host to a veritable who's who of rock stars of the time. Joni Mitchell and David Crosby came in and sat on a couch together for a while before disappearing into the night. Eric Clapton sat smoking by the fireplace. I don't think I heard him say a word all night. He mostly bobbed his head and gazed at the floor.

Charlie fit right in. In the midst of all these "stars," Charlie shone the brightest. By the end of the night, everyone was gathered around in a circle. Charlie played his guitar and sang while Stephen Stills of Buffalo Springfield and Mama Cass from the Mamas and the Papas clapped along and chipped in harmonies.

At some point, Frank set a microphone up in the middle of the room and recorded hours of the evening's proceedings. I could swear that I've heard snippets of that night's recording session show up here and there in

Zappa's music throughout the years but I doubt that he would have ever admitted it.

Much grass was smoked, many pills were popped and much alcohol was consumed, but lots of incredible music was made that night and I feel fortunate to have witnessed it. It had to have been one of the most amazing gatherings of talent in one house at one time in rock n' roll history. Most of the people that were there that night, I never saw again, at least not in person, but for better or for worse, Mama Cass Elliott became almost like a member of the family.

I'm not sure exactly when, but somewhere in the wee hours of the morning, we all piled back into Dennis's Rolls Royce and managed by a miracle to make it back safely to the beach house on Sunset Boulevard. We arrived just as the sun was peeking its way over the blue horizon, painting the Pacific Ocean with a beautiful blend of blues and pinks.

CHAPTER 20

For the next couple of weeks we partied like, and with, rock stars. There was another party at Zappa's cabin which included another all-night recording session. There was a party at Terry Melcher's place on Cielo where we hung out with Jim Morrison of The Doors, and several blowouts at Mama Cass' house. The same faces flowed from location to location, the rich and famous blending seamlessly with the down and out.

Morrison was a very cool, laid back guy who came across as shy and not nearly as self-assured as his stage persona. Honestly, I guess that applies to a lot of us. It's much easier to have a public persona that is different from the person you are away from prying eyes. I had met enough famous people at this point in my life to know this was more often the rule than the exception.

Jim's father was a high-ranking officer in the US Navy. Sometimes when Jim was spaced out on LSD and alcohol he talked about his father being a secret CIA operative who had experimented on him and his friends with LSD and heroin. He claimed that without the CIA, The Doors would have never become successful. I never figured out if there was any truth to this or just Jim using his crazy imagination.

Watching Jim and Charlie riff on their spoken word and freeform singing was something to behold. They got on really well, but after the couple of times at Melchers, I never saw Jim again. He would be dead less than two years later. They claimed it was heart failure, but Jim was only 27 years old. I often wondered whether his heart really failed or whether he had overdosed on alcohol and drugs. Somewhere in the far reaches of my mind, I also wondered if maybe there was some truth to those CIA rumors he always talked about and I wondered if maybe Jim knew too much for his own good.

CHAPTER 21

It was during these times that Charlie and I really started to get close. It took Charlie a while to get comfortable with people and let them earn his trust. Sure, he got close to the girls fairly quickly, but that was mostly for sexual purposes. He also liked to see what he could get out of each one of them. If it was sex, great. If it was money, also great. Cooking and cleaning were good too. He would study each girl and fit her into the place that would be most beneficial to himself and the group. Charlie liked girls. He liked them a lot, but he didn't respect them. Still, Charlie could always find a reason to keep a girl around. He was much more critical of the guys. You definitely had to serve some sort of useful purpose or Charlie would make it clear that you needed to move on.

The first night he asked me to go for a walk on the beach with him, I had a feeling I was getting my walking papers. I could not have been further from the truth.

"Shep?" he said.

"Yeah, Charlie," I answered, tentatively.

"I've been watching you," he continued.

Yep, here we go, I thought.

"Yeah?" I said.

"You're not like everybody else around here."

"How so?" I asked.

"Well, they need me. They're lost little birds who can't survive if the mama bird isn't there to drop the worm in their mouth, ya dig?"

I didn't answer.

"You, you're different. I could tell you to get your ass out of here and hit the road tomorrow and you'd be okay."

"I like it here," I replied.

"That's what I'm saying, man. All these others are here because they don't have anywhere else to go and the world would eat them alive! If I don't look out for them, they'll just poof! They'd be gone and end up right back in the garbage dump I pulled them out of. But you...." he smiled a knowing grin and started nodding and pointing his finger at me. "You are a survivor, like me. Now you come from your perfect home and I didn't have no home. The jailhouse was my home. The judge was my father, but still-- you have that perfect home and you could say, 'Fuck you, Charlie' and go back there anytime you want, but you stay here. I know the broads are here but you could get pussy wherever you go, and I mean the high-class kind that spits on people like me and Sadie and Patty, but you're here."

"You're my friends, Charlie. I feel like I belong here way more than I ever felt like I belonged at home. I was lost, just like most of them, but you found me, and you helped me find myself. You're my family just as much as my folks are. You've shown me more of the world in just a few months than I have experienced my whole life. I want to stay here, Charlie."

"You think I'm asking you to leave?" He looked at me crossways and then turned on that Charlie charm again.

"I'm asking you not to leave, man. I can't do all these chicks by myself," he laughed.

"Damn, man, for a minute I thought you were trying to get rid of me."

His face then turned serious. It was amazing how quickly he could shift moods, personas, and appearances.

One of the girls had once referred to him as a chameleon and I really couldn't think of a more apt description.

"I was raised by the jailhouse, Shep, and one of the first things you learn in the jailhouse is to watch your back. The next thing you learn is to find somebody else to watch your back, but if you ain't damn careful, that person watching your back will turn around and stab you in it, you dig?"

"I would never…" I began.

"Don't say it," he cut me off. "Look me in the eye and tell me you're my brother."

Click, another flash and he had grabbed my arm and pulled me face-to-face with him. I sensed a new side of Charlie emerging. Somehow even though I was a good half a foot taller than him, he was looking me dead in the eye with an almost predatory look.

"I'm your brother, Charlie," I said calmly.

"Say it again!" he said loudly through gritted teeth.

"I'm your brother, Charlie," I repeated, raising my intensity to match his.

"Say it again!" He almost screamed, grasping my arms tighter.

"I'm your fucking brother, Charlie! What do you want?" I yelled in his face and boom.

He was calm, almost serene even. He stepped back and said very calmly and quietly, "You and me are brothers, Shep, don't ever forget that."

"I won't, Charlie." I assured him.

"Your word is your bond and your bond is your life, Shep."

"My word is my bond and my bond is my life," I repeated.

"There's always a wolf near the sheep," he said. "We gotta protect those sheep and you're the Shepherd. The

72

Good Shepherd. Now is the only thing that's real and now is all we got."

"We'll protect the sheep from the wolves," I assured him.

"Hell, I'm a wolf," he said, and let out a big howl that brought five naked girls running almost instantly from out of nowhere.

Charlie was always a mystery. Every time I expected him to zig, he would zag. I smiled to myself and walked towards the ocean and the ladies. My only concern for the rest of the night was to try not to get sand in any sensitive places.

CHAPTER 22

If Dennis was away at a recording session or gone out on tour, he would give us free reign of his house and cars. After I had asked Dennis' permission at least five times for use of his Ferrari, he just threw me the keys one day. "Here, Shep, why don't you just use the Ferrari anytime you want and I'll tell you if I need it," he offered. "I prefer the Rolls anyway."

Dennis was just like that. He was the most giving person I had ever met, with the exception of Charlie, of course. Charlie didn't have nearly as much to give. What he did have, he would freely give away. Charlie didn't have much use for material wealth. He said if you were only in the now, that tomorrow didn't matter. I saw him give away cars, motorcycles, you name it. They held little value to him. Dennis was similar to a degree. He would even let the girls take the Rolls on "garbage runs." It had to have been a trip for people passing by to see three or four barefoot hippie girls piling out of a Rolls Royce behind a Beverly Hills supermarket to dumpster dive for food, but the girls did it several times a week.

As gross as it might sound, Lyn, Sandy, Sadie and Patty all became experts at going through what the high-end supermarkets had thrown away and finding enough good, healthy food to feed the whole group. There were always fresh fruits, vegetables, bread, and sometimes even meats, still packed in ice, that had been thrown away. They had been discarded simply because the packaging was damaged or maybe some of the items had a bruise or dark spot on them. Charlie even wrote a song about it called "Garbage Dump." He talked about how he could feed the whole world with the food that was thrown away every day in America. Judging by the incredible meals the girls prepared from what some other people considered trash, I believed him.

Even Dennis would eat these "garbage meals" though he could have afforded to eat at the finest restaurants. I guess he figured it would make up for him footing the bill for so many penicillin bills for the group, and occasionally for himself as well.

One day, I just wanted to go cruising and decided to take the Ferrari for a spin. It was always fun to see the reactions from people trying to figure out what movie star or rock star was behind the wheel. Even in Beverly Hills in 1968, a Ferrari still turned heads. For all I know, it still does. I can't say that I didn't enjoy the attention it brought me either. I always played it cool and gave a slight wave or nodded behind my sunglasses. I wondered who people thought I might be.

It had been awhile since I had spoken to Gary Hinman, so I thought I would take the short ride up Topanga to pay him a visit. He had really come through for me when I needed him and I just wanted to say hello and see how he was doing. Gary wasn't home when I arrived at the house on Topanga, but there were several people hanging out inside and outside the house. As usual, it didn't look like Gary was being very picky about the kind of people that he let crash at his place.

I didn't trust them around Dennis' car so I just asked a couple of rough looking dudes out front if Gary was around and when they told me that he wasn't, I split. I was concerned about the company my friend was keeping and hoped that he would be safe with these kinds of people hanging around. In hindsight, they weren't the ones I should have been worrying about.

CHAPTER 23

One evening when most everyone was gone, it was just Dennis and I and a couple of the girls sitting around the house. Dennis asked me if I could come outside with him. I could tell he was nervous about something so I agreed and followed him out to walk around the property. I had seen Dennis and Charlie do this multiple times and I had accompanied Charlie on jaunts around "the yard," a term he had held onto from prison, but I had never walked with Dennis. As was often the case, the peacock that Dennis kept as a pet followed us around as if eavesdropping on the conversation.

"Shep," Dennis began, "I need to ask you something."

"Sure man, shoot," I responded.

"Well, the Beach Boys are about to leave on a tour, and…." he paused. I gave him a minute but he didn't continue.

"Yeah. What do you need to say, brother?" I coaxed him onward.

"Well, it's just….well, my lease is about to be up on this house and I don't think I'm going to renew it."

"Oh." I could see where this was going. Our group was going to have to find new digs.

"I just don't know how to tell Charlie, man. What if he goes all crazy on me? I mean, I love having you guys around but my manager says I'm spending too much money and I need to get something smaller for just me, you know?"

"No problem, man. You know, I'm really kind of surprised that Charlie hasn't already decided to move on anyway. He'll understand, no sweat."

"You think so?" He sounded legitimately worried.

"Sure man, he'll be good. You've been awesome to us, brother. It's all gonna be cool."

"Damn, Shep, I hope so. I don't want to piss Charlie off. I love him, man."

"I know Dennis. He feels the same about you. It's cool. You want me to be there when you tell him?"

"Would you?" he almost begged.

"Yeah, man. No problem."

Relief washed over Dennis' face. As if on cue, some headlights stopped at the end of the driveway and Charlie got out of the car. He bent back in and said something to the driver and then started walking towards us.

"What's up Charlie?" Dennis offered meekly.

"What's wrong Dennis? Do you need us to leave?" Charlie immediately intoned, creasing his brow. Charlie had an uncanny ability to know what people were thinking just by looking at their face.

"Uh no, it's just…" Dennis looked desperately to me for help.

"Dennis' lease is up and he's been told by the band's management that he can't afford to keep this property anymore," I filled in.

"Well…." Charlie paused, "why didn't you just say so?" He finished with a smile.

"You're not mad?" Dennis asked.

"Why should I be mad?" Charlie answered. "You've been a good brother. We'll find a place. Sadie was just telling me about a ranch not too far from here that needed some hands. I'll go check it out. You need us to leave tonight?"

78

"No, no," Dennis responded. "I've got a few more weeks left on the lease. I'm about to go on tour. Stay until they kick you out for all I care," he laughed.

"That's all we could ask," I chimed in, and that was the end of the discussion.

Later, some people claimed that we drove Dennis from his house and he moved away to make us leave. The simple truth is that Dennis was going through his money faster than it was coming in due to his generosity and lifestyle. It was his management that forced him to leave his house, not us.

CHAPTER 23

For the next few days before Dennis had to leave, he and Charlie really kicked their creativity into high gear. It was at one of these late-night jams that Charlie wrote one of his most memorable songs and Dennis absolutely flipped over it. They had been jamming for hours and some cool stuff was happening but then it got quiet, like both were deep in thought. Charlie broke the silence by starting a song we had never heard before.

Pretty, pretty girl,
Cease to exist, just come and say you love me,
Give up your world, come on, you can be
I'm your kind, I'm your kind, and I can see
You walk, walk on, I love you, pretty girl
My life is yours, you can have my world
Never had a lesson I ever learned,
  but I know we all get our turn,
And I love you, never learn not to love you
Submission is a gift, give it to your brother
Love and understanding is for one another
I'm your kind, I'm your kind, I'm your brother
I never had a lesson I ever learned,
  but I know we all get our turn
And I love you, never learn not to love you
Never learn not to love you

We just sat staring at each other for a few minutes because we knew we had heard something special. Dennis asked me to write out the words while he went to his piano and started writing out the music. Charlie played it again with Dennis stopping him periodically. Charlie never wrote anything down and usually played and sang things differently each time. Dennis wanted to make sure this one was saved so it could be duplicated and recorded later. It would go on to become Charlie's first "hit." But that's another story.

CHAPTER 24

Several of the girls had gotten arrested for various charges up north at the start of the summer. Mainly, they were in trouble for sharing some pot with a couple of underage boys. Patty and Mary were among them so Charlie asked Dennis if he could help get them out. Unfortunately, his managers wouldn't give him enough money. Charlie said that we would try to raise the money, but so far we had had no such luck. Charlie figured they would be out by fall anyway, so it was no big deal. Now that we would be looking for a new place to crash, he thought they may just do better to wait out their time. The group had grown to the point where there were always between 15 to 20 of us around and supporting that many people wasn't easy.

What couldn't be provided by garbage runs, Charlie and I could usually earn busking on street corners to make up the rest. Several of the girls still had active credit cards that they had gotten from their parents. We could always hit those if times really got tough. Still, there was no extra money to get anyone out of jail, especially when the charges were minor and they would be getting out soon anyway.

I think it was Sadie, but I know one of the girls had mentioned an old movie ranch and horse farm that might be available to give us a place to stay for doing some chores around the place. Charlie and I decided to check it out.

Family Man

I had never met anyone that could have the effect on people that Charlie did. Sometimes people would just give him things. A guitar, a piano and in this instance (and several others) a car. This time it was a 1960 Buick LeSabre. It was pretty beat up and the driver's door wouldn't open from where it had been wrecked, but Charlie was talking with the owner one day and the guy told him if he wanted to ride home with him, he would give him the keys, and he did.

Charlie and I climbed in the front of the old Buick, while Sandy and Lynette hopped in the back seat. We made the trek out to the end of Topanga Canyon Boulevard and up the Santa Susana Pass through the twisty and windy narrow blacktop road until we reached 1200 Santa Susana Pass Rd.

Turning off the main road felt like we had driven into a time warp. There was a big oval corral with several dozen horses roaming about. Stables and a dirt street ran right through the middle of a wild-west-style town. "Spahn's Movie Ranch" read an old faded sign with red painted letters. The main street consisted of a stretch of old wooden buildings complete with a jail, a saloon, and a cafe. Spaced along in front of the buildings were hitching posts for the horses and a boardwalk. A couple of cowboys were walking along the street as we slowly drove by. I half expected one of them to pull out his six-shooters and draw on us.

"You all just need to be moseying along now, if'n ya knows what's good fer ya," I expected one of them to say at any moment. They just ignored us.

Charlie came to a stop at a small bungalow a little past the end of the boardwalk. The house had obviously seen better days. "This must be the place," he said, crawling out the driver's window. "Shep, you and Sandy stay here," he instructed. "Lyn, come on in with me."

Lyn hopped out and I stayed put. I looked around to take in my surroundings as Charlie and Lynette went inside after a brief knock on the wooden screen door. I still felt as if we had crossed into the Twilight Zone. If not for the solid feeling of the old Buick around me, I may have thought I was having another bad drug trip. The place easily could have been something out of the 1860s instead of the 1960s but in its own way, it was beautiful.

The Santa Susana Mountains rose up in the distance and I could smell the eucalyptus in the air from a nearby grove of trees. There were hills and dales and large boulders spread around the property. I knew right away that Charlie would love this place as would most of the rest of our group. It played right into the whole "give up yourself and become one with nature" vibe that Charlie was always espousing. I lost myself in the scenery until I heard the front door shut and saw the childlike excitement on Charlie and Lyn's faces.

"We got us a ranch!" Charlie beamed, as he leaned into the car.

Lyn was climbing into the back seat, her enthusiasm a little more tempered. "He said we could stay for a while, at least," she elaborated.

"Good deal!" I answered.

This would be a far cry from the luxuries we had at Dennis' but it would be an adventure. Luxury was immediately forgotten. I was looking forward to the next stage of my own, and everyone else's self-exploration.

CHAPTER 25

Before we moved out of Dennis' pad and before he left to go on tour, Dennis introduced Charlie to Gregg Jakobson. Gregg served as a talent scout for Terry Melcher. Though Terry had listened to Charlie informally a few times, he wanted Gregg to come over and check Charlie out in a more private setting. He asked Gregg to really listen closely. He was then to report back to Terry what he thought about pursuing a recording arrangement. Terry obviously respected Dennis' opinion, but Gregg was his right-hand man. If Gregg thought Terry should give Manson a shot, then it would probably happen.

Gregg had called ahead to Dennis and set up an informal audition. Dennis didn't tell Charlie exactly what was going down, but he had made sure that everyone else was either gone or occupied so that there were only a few of us present: Charlie, Dennis, Gregg and me.

"Charlie, I've been telling Gregg about your songs and he wanted to come listen to you. You mind playing a few for him?" Dennis asked.

"Well, I usually like to have some of the girls around," Charlie answered nervously.

"Me and Shep can join you on some harmonies," Dennis urged.

"Sure," I added. "It'll be like the old days with Bobby."

Charlie picked up his guitar and started to strum and then sing a few of his songs. Gregg was blown away. By probably the third tune, Gregg told him that he was going to report back to Terry and recommend that he set up a time to come hear him in person.

"Terry's heard my music," Charlie told him.

"He's heard it at parties and with a lot of people around. He's never been able to just sit back and listen." Gregg explained. "Now that I've heard it like this, I think Terry's really gonna dig it."

Gregg hung around for a couple of hours and enjoyed the companionship of the girls by the pool. He smoked a few joints and promised that he or Terry would be in touch soon to set up a recording session.

After Gregg left, I expected Charlie to be as excited as I was. In contrast, he was unusually quiet. "Charlie, this is cool, man, you're getting your shot!" I told him excitedly when he asked me to take a walk with him later that evening.

"Ya know Shep, I just got out of prison. I don't know if I want to get put in another one," he answered.

"What do you mean?"

"Well, you see what Dennis has to deal with? People telling him where he can live, who he can be friends with, when he has to be somewhere and how long he has to stay there?"

"Yeah, but I thought it was your dream to have your music heard?"

"You've heard it. Dennis has heard it. The girls hear it and sing along. Maybe that's enough."

"Maybe, but you can't pass up this opportunity. You owe it to Dennis for going to bat for you."

"Listen Shep, I don't owe nobody nothing. The only person I got to look out for is me!"

I was surprised by the sudden shift in his tone. "Fine man, do what you want to do. You want to go, go. You don't, then don't."

"You going in there with me?" His mood shifted right back.

"In the studio?"

"Yeah. I'll need some support. If you can play and maybe Dennis can play..."

"Sure man, if that's what you want, you know I'll be there," I said, trying to temper my excitement.

"You're my brother, Shep." He put his hand on my shoulder.

"I'm your brother, Charlie." I returned the gesture.

We walked in silence the rest of the time. When we got back to the house, Charlie said, "Let's make an album, Shep." I nodded with a smile and went to bed that night with a newfound optimism.

CHAPTER 26

Dennis left to go on a tour that was going to keep him away for a few months. During this time, we began the move to Spahn Ranch. Charlie and I also began deciding which songs he should play and I helped him write down the words so that he could do them consistently.

Gregg Jakobson spent a lot of time at the house with us. Gregg was over almost every night, encouraging Charlie's playing and songwriting, doing some drugs, and having sex with a girl or two, not necessarily in that order. Gregg, like Dennis, was convinced that Charlie was going to be "the next big thing" and that once Terry got a hold of his songs, he was going to have a string of hits.

Charlie didn't really seem to care about having hits, he just wanted to get his music out so that people could hear his message. I really dug Charlie's tunes but I wasn't sure that I understood his "message." I just enjoyed the music and I told him so.

"You have to listen with your soul, Shep!" he would tell me. "You can't just listen to music with your ears, you gotta listen on a spiritual level, ya dig?"

"I know what you're saying, but don't you think most people just dig groovy music and don't really look for a deeper meaning?" I asked.

"They don't have to look for it, man. They will hear it here!" he said tapping his forehead. "They will get it in thought. They'll hear it in their soul. It's not for their ears, it's for their minds! I'm telling them the same thing I've always told you. The same thing I tell all my children,

88

every one of you, every day. Love your brother. Love the world you live in. Let go of your ego. Die to self so that you can become one with the soul! One soul!" He held up one finger.

"I get it brother, but I just don't know how many other people will. I just don't want you to be let down if most people don't look that far."

He was undeterred. "The ones who need to hear it will hear it. They have to be tuned in to the thought. The ones that matter will understand. If I think it and I sing it, then it is. They will feel it in their soul and they'll do what's right."

There was really no point in arguing with him. When Charlie got something embedded in his mind, or in his "thought" as he referred to it, to him it became reality and there was no changing it. After all, when you had people like Dennis Wilson, Gregg Jakobson, and Neil Young encouraging you, what weight would a Southern kid named Billy Shepherd's opinion hold? All I could do was sit back and enjoy the ride.

Tex Watson was back staying in Dennis' guest house. He was beginning to ingratiate himself to most of the group. Little Paul and I were the only ones that still seemed to be wary of him, so I thought that maybe I had judged him a little too quickly based on one brief encounter. I made a real effort to get to know Tex over the next couple of weeks and he seemed to make an effort as well. His awe shucks Texas schtick became a bit more authentic and I could see how people could be attracted to him. While I can't exactly say that we became great friends during this time, at least it felt like we had become a lot less like enemies. A few weeks later, when Dennis' lease expired and his manager came to kick everybody out of his house, most of us had already relocated to Spahn Ranch and Tex came with us.

CHAPTER 27

Over the next few months, most of our group made the transition to Spahn Ranch. Spahn Ranch was owned by an 80-year-old man named George Spahn. At one time, the ranch had been a hotbed for the nearby Hollywood film industry. Episodes of television shows like *Bonanza* and *The Lone Ranger* had been filmed there. Along with those, dozens of movies and TV commercials used Spahn as a backdrop. Unfortunately, as the popularity of Western themed entertainment waned, so did the cash flow of the ranch. It had fallen into a state of disrepair and was now mainly being used to offer a nostalgic location for horseback rides. It also attracted the occasional tourist, wishing to get a glimpse of old west life or to just enjoy the scenic views of the trails.

Mr. Spahn, who insisted that we all call him George, had been blind for the past 6 years. Although he got up every day and dressed the part of the big-time ranch owner in his suit jacket, slacks, white shirt, vest, tie and cowboy hat, he was little more than a figurehead. The ranch was really run by his business partner (and former lover) Ruby Pearl. Ruby was a red-haired fire plug of a woman, she was a good 20 years younger than George. They relied on a ragtag group of cowboys and ranch hands who mostly came and went at their own convenience and worked or not as the mood struck them.

George may have been blind but he was still a sucker for a pretty girl. He was especially fond of Sandy and Lyn, who George renamed Squeaky because of the high-pitched squeal she made when he would playfully run his hand up her leg. When they offered to clean his house, prepare his meals, and give him some female companionship in exchange for letting them and a "few friends" stay at the ranch, he enthusiastically agreed. He also agreed to let the rest of us stay rent-free in exchange for helping with repairs around the place, feeding and grooming the horses, and cleaning out the stalls.

Most of the girls, and a few of the guys as well, would serve as guides for the tourists that would come in on the weekends to take horseback rides on the trails. The biggest part of the cowboys had no problem at all with us taking over this part of their job because most of them disliked dealing with the tourists anyway. They would rather have their weekends free to spend drinking or to just kick their boots up and relax. And then there was Shorty Shea.

Shorty was one of the ranch hands that would come and go regularly. He was a Hollywood stuntman and it was not unusual for him to disappear for weeks at a time. He would then reappear, bragging about all the death-defying stunts he had performed for whatever movie he had been in. I never really heard why they called him Shorty because he was over six feet tall. All I could figure was maybe he had a really small dick, but then again, why would anyone want to be known by that? Shorty never fooled around with any of the girls, so I couldn't get confirmation one way or the other on my theory from any of them.

Shorty always appeared to be looking at us crossways and acted suspicious of everything we would do. If he saw a different car around, he was convinced we stole it (which was often true.) If there was a new girl around, he would assume she was under age (again, often true.) He was convinced we did every drug on the planet (partially true, but none of his business.) Anyway, Shorty made it obvious that he didn't like hippies around the ranch. Charlie told him that we weren't hippies, we were "slippies" because we had slipped through the cracks of society, but he wasn't amused. He always wrinkled his nose up like he smelled something bad every time Charlie went near him. I could feel the bad blood between them and it wasn't pleasant. Although Shorty was usually cordial to me, he was never what I would call friendly. Most of us felt more comfortable when Shorty went away for a while.

CHAPTER 28

There was another group of people already living in the big farmhouse when we moved onto the ranch but they mainly kept to themselves. They were nice enough to let the girls use the kitchen to prepare our meals and all of us could use their bathroom so we coexisted well enough. As our group swelled to 30 or so full-time members along with a few others that would come and go, sleeping quarters on the bus and the movie set were getting a little tight. Charlie worked his magic and traded the bus to the other commune so that we could move into the farmhouse. They had been looking for a way to take their whole group to Oregon anyway, so the big black bus worked out perfectly for them and having full run of the farmhouse made things much easier on us.

Not long after the move to Spahn, I was reacquainted with my old friend Bobby Beausoleil. Bobby had bounced around a few places but had found his way to Spahn and back to the group. He had brought a couple of new girls with him, most notably a real looker named Leslie Van Houten. Leslie had been a homecoming queen and it showed. After her parents had divorced, she had decided, however, that the straight-laced lifestyle wasn't for her and had started experimenting with marijuana. That had led her to leave home and move in with her sister who introduced her to Bobby. She had been hanging out with him and his crew for a while and they had now found their way here. Bobby was kind enough to introduce Leslie to his good friend Shep and for that I was grateful.

Leslie was a beauty and was very soft spoken and sweet. We would often sit and talk for hours in the evenings before finding a spot with or without the group, for some love making. Leslie became one of my favorite girls. No one ever really paired up. Charlie discouraged us from becoming regular couples because he said that could create jealousy and cause discord in the group. He wanted us all to share equally with each other and abandon our egos. Still, I had my favorites and Leslie quickly became one of them. I also still enjoyed spending time with Dianne, Ouish, and Gypsy. Some of the guys would always want a shot when a new girl showed up, but that was enough variety for me most of the time.

George welcomed the attention that the girls gave him and the much-needed cleaning that they gave his house. He also appreciated the reports that Ruby Pearl gave him about how well the guys were taking care of the horses and how well we were keeping their stalls repaired and cleaned out. The stories that came out later about how we moved in and took advantage of an old blind man were completely false. George enjoyed the girls' company and his home and business were in a lot worse shape when we arrived than they were when we left. We even helped out financially by taking up the last tenants of the farmhouse's rent. We continued to pay him the same $40 a month that they had been giving him. All the pictures that the police released that were published after everything had gone down showing how we had lived in "filth and squalor" failed to mention that those photographs had been taken *after* the police had tossed the place and destroyed everything. The girls did a great job of keeping our living and sleeping quarters clean and we kept the outside neat and organized.

It was strange how it all worked out, but everyone just pitched in and did what needed to be done. If a horse needed grooming, someone did it. If a stall needed mucking out, a few of us chipped in and got it done. It really was communal living at its best and our own little Utopia.

Dennis came out to visit fairly often and Gregg was almost a constant fixture. In fact, on one trip he brought the news that he was working on getting a recording session set up for Charlie at a real recording studio with Terry Melcher producing. The drugs and the love making hit an even higher peak than normal that night. We were all over the moon with excitement about the fact that the world was finally going to get a chance to hear Charlie's music.

CHAPTER 29

Brenda and Squeaky took a convertible that Charlie borrowed from someone and drove up north to pick up the girls who had just gotten released from jail. It was a happy reunion to have Mary, Patty (who was now going by Katie), Ella, Stephanie, and a now very pregnant Sadie, back in the fold. They even went down to San Francisco and picked up little Sonstone, who had been being fostered by Charlie's parole officer, Roger Smith.

The next few months were some of the best times of my life. Living at Spahn Ranch made me feel like Peter Pan must have felt when he found Neverland. By day, we would take care of the horses or fix a fence. Oftentimes on the hot days, we would take a break to take a dip in the cool waters of the nearby creek. In the evenings, we would pretend to be cowboys and indians or cops and robbers or sometimes even pirates scouring the land for buried treasure. Between the fact that we were living on an abandoned movie set and the abundance of nature surrounding us, our imaginations were our only limitations. Throw in a little weed, mushrooms, or LSD and those imaginations became virtually limitless. We could do whatever we wanted to do and be whoever we wanted to be.

Charlie would often point out things that we would all just simply overlook. He would stop whatever we were doing and have us take the time to observe a lizard sitting on a windowsill or a swarm of honeybees building their nest. He would patiently explain to us, as if we were his children, how we should study and appreciate the intricacies of a spiders web and he would admonish us not to do anything to disturb it in any way or to tear it down because the spider has just as much right to live and have peace in her home as we did. Charlie even said the mice and bugs that often shared our living spaces were not to be harmed because they all served a purpose in the will of God and in the balance of the universe.

Almost everyone who didn't already have a nickname on the ranch soon acquired one. Some of this was so we could be prepared in case we were arrested. It always helped to have an alias on hand but it was also to help us release ourselves from our egos and to erase any bad memories or programming that we didn't want to keep. The more we could recreate ourselves, the freer we could be, Charlie advised. Many of the girls were given their names by George, some of us, like me, by Charlie and some of the group just picked their own names. Ella became Yeller, Brenda became Brindle (although everyone knew her as Nancy), Ruth Ann became Ouish, Leslie became LuLu, and so on.

A couple of girls had gone hiking one day up in the hills at the back of the ranch and came back talking about a wild man they had seen while on their walk. He was staring at them from behind a big rock and when they spotted him, he took off running. Randy Starr, one of the ranch hands, often told tales of a wild runaway boy living in the hills and eating grasshoppers and bugs or something. We all thought it was just one of Randy's stories. The girls now swore that it was true. A couple days later, sure enough, here comes Charlie walking with a tall, dirty, young blonde boy that Gypsy and Ella identified as the wild man. Although he was barefoot and shirtless, he was talking calmly with Charlie and introduced himself as Steve Grogan. While Steve didn't exactly strike me as the

97

brightest bulb in the box, he was far from being a wild boy, thus laying yet another of the cowboy's legends to rest. The girls took an instant liking to Steve and because of his shyness and backward ways, they started calling him Clem. Clem instantly fit in. Especially with the drug use. He was an avid user of just about any drug he could find. Because of this, Charlie christened him with another name: Scramblehead.

A girl named Juanita came by the ranch to go for a horseback ride one day and by the end of the evening, Charlie had convinced her to stay. He also had talked her into giving him her brand-new Dodge camper van. It was none too soon either. A few days later, Dennis had been visiting us and had driven his Ferrari. While Dennis was enjoying the company of a few of the girls, Clem and Little Paul had decided to take his car for a joyride. Clem, who had very little experience behind the wheel of any car, much less a speed machine like the Ferrari, took a corner too fast and totaled Dennis's ride. They came walking up the road and told Charlie what had happened. Charlie had to break the news to Dennis. Charlie then gave him Juanita's van to make up for it. It was a somewhat less than equal trade, but as was always the case with Dennis, he took it all in stride and drove off in the van, like somehow he'd gotten a fair deal.

CHAPTER 30

More people than I can remember came and went during the time we were at Spahn. Some of them would only stay for a few days, like various members of the Straight Satans Motorcycle Club, some would stay for a few weeks, some would stay a day here and there, like Diedre (Didi) Lansbury, daughter of actress Angela Lansbury, and some would just stay. Some of the more notable of these was Straight Satan Danny DeCarlo, who the girls quickly gave the name Donkey Dick Dan (for obvious reasons), a guy named Christopher Haught, who became known as Christopher Jesus or more commonly Zero, and Catherine Gillies, who George christened with the name Capistrano, which we shortened to Cappy. Cappy was a cute, freckle-faced blonde who quickly became a favorite of most of the guys in the group, including myself. Zero was a cool, laid back dude who really didn't say much, but he had no problem chipping in on his part of the workload so we all got along well with him.

Danny served as treasurer for the Satans and had recently gotten divorced. Ready to take full advantage of his new freedom, the ranch was a haven for him. He became very popular with the girls and he couldn't get enough of them. Charlie liked having a Straight Satan with his colors on his back hanging around the ranch to discourage rowdy outsiders from causing trouble or trying to horn in on the girls.

A couple of other girls joined us around this time that I never really got very close to, although I didn't mind doing my due diligence of welcoming them to the group by spending a few nights with each one. They were Madeline Cottage, known as Little Patty or Crazy Patty - and with good reason. Sherry Cooper, a real cutie, and Barbara Hoyt, a quiet, attractive brunette with an affinity for wearing granny glasses that masked her true beauty.

Bruce Davis also reappeared from his European trip to rejoin the group. I guess his trip across the pond mellowed both me and him out because we became fast friends and brothers after his return. The awkwardness of our first meeting was long forgotten and neither of us ever even thought about why we had been wary of each other in the first place. Not only with Bruce, but also with Tex did I notice that the move to Spahn seemed to smooth out the rough edges of our relationship. I could only attribute the brotherhood that grew out of those first meeting clashes to the fact that all of us were becoming more one with each other and the minimizing of our own personal egos.

Tex had plenty of eccentricities, but as I got to know him, they became more things that I admired him for or appreciated in him. Still, something about him never allowed me to completely let my guard down. He was an excellent mechanic and there was no shortage of junk cars and farm equipment around the ranch that needed repairs. While Little Paul, Clem and I were more comfortable tending to the horses, Charlie, Bruce, and Tex were right at home working on all the vehicles. They would work tirelessly for days at a time on cars and trucks that had been sitting for years. On rare occasions they successfully brought them back to life. More often than not, they had been left abandoned for so long that too many parts had been stolen or simply rusted to the point that they were beyond repair.

After a hard day's work, we would often sit around a fire at night and listen to Charlie play guitar and sing. Sometimes Bobby and Clem and I would join him and sometimes we would just sit back and listen as he sang or told stories. He would share tales from the jailhouse and lessons and secrets he had learned along the way. He became our de facto leader simply because of his age and life experience. He was 10 to 15 years older than almost all of us with the exception of TJ, Dean and a few of the bikers, and none of them were around all the time. He had also lived a far more adventurous and exciting life than we had. He wanted to pass on the knowledge he had gathered throughout his life along to his children he said. Most of us sat rapt and paid attention as we were eager to learn from him. Nobody was required to sit in on Charlie's circle, but if you did, you had better pay attention. Nothing pissed him off more than one of the girls giggling or talking or the guys screwing off during his talks. He made it real clear that if you didn't want to listen, then you should just get the hell out of his circle. He would frequently say so in far less polite words. I saw him more than once slap a girl or throw something at one of the guys for not being attentive. You could always not come at all or get up and leave, but disrespect was inexcusable to Charlie.

It was during these evening talks that the subject of an impending race war would come up. Charlie had witnessed in prison how each race formed its own gang and didn't associate with each other. He had seen more than his share of fights and violence between the racist gangs in prison and foresaw it happening on a larger scale. He pointed to the recent riots just a few years ago in Watts and the fact that they were occurring in big cities all over the country. He reminded us how the blacks were fighting the cops and burning their cities to the ground. He said that he had heard some of the black prisoners in his cell block talking about how it was their time to rise up and take over and that the white man had been in control for too long. He was also concerned about the new Black Panther Party and how they had started carrying guns openly. They were a constant presence in the city streets and their frequent clashes with the cops was concerning.

This talk of an impending black/white Armageddon scared the hell out of us of course but Charlie said that we shouldn't be scared, we should be prepared. One of the ways he suggested for us to prepare ourselves was for us all to have knives and learn how to use them. Charlie also said we should find another place to stay because Spahn might be too close to the city of Los Angeles. He was concerned that it could become unsafe if a full-scale war were to break out. He said we should look for a place out in the desert that would be so remote that we couldn't be found and hide out there until it was safe to come back. This was "the hole," a jail term for solitary confinement, and also the "bottomless pit" so often referred to that we were supposedly looking for. We found these things. They were simply known as the Barker and Myers ranches. These terms were figurative for a secluded hideout. They were never meant to be taken literally. The girls filled in fantastical details about chocolate rivers and gumdrop trees and whatever just as a way to make it sound like a place we would want to go, instead of a place we would be forced to go. Tex suggested it might be a good idea for us to start acquiring some vehicles that we could strip and turn into dune buggies to handle the rough terrain of the desert. He said Volkswagen Beetles would best serve this purpose since they were already fairly basic and known for their durability. By "acquire" based on our finances, it went without saying that for a large part of them he meant "steal."

Someone had recently brought the newly-released eponymously titled album by The Beatles (that soon came to be known as *The White Album*, based on its stark white cover) to the ranch and we all really dug it. We listened to it over and over. Charlie said that The Beatles were really tuned in to what was going down and that if we listened really closely, we could hear messages in the music. He said that they had put hidden meanings in their songs to help prepare the tuned-in people and their fans to be aware and know what was about to happen. He explained that there were lots of clues in that album but we would probably have to smoke some grass or drop some acid to really connect with them. Over the course of the next few weeks, that was exactly what we did.

CHAPTER 31

As the talks of Armageddon continued and progressed, we gave it a name: Helter Skelter. Notice I say "we." That's because that's what we as a group decided to call it. I'm not even sure who brought it up although I'm pretty sure that it wasn't Charlie. Somebody said: "That sounds like Helter Skelter, man," and that's what we called the coming Armageddon from that point on. *Helter Skelter* was a Beatles song that talked about either a British amusement park ride or chaos and confusion, according to which Beatle was telling the tale. It sure sounded more like chaos and confusion to us and Charlie said that was exactly what was going to go down once the war started. In fact, all we had to do was look around us to see that it was already coming down. He said even if the blacks didn't rise up, we still needed to be ready because confusion was already going on all around us, couldn't we see it? We could. You would have to be blind not to. Anyone who had spent more than a few minutes around the Haight could definitely see it. The best thing we could do was to get away from society as much as we could and get attuned to nature like God had originally intended. In addition to that, there was a line in the song *Helter Skelter* that said: "look out! It's coming down fast!" Charlie said this was The Beatles warning us that we didn't have much time, so we better get prepared fast.

There were some other songs that were thought to contain messages too. *Blackbird* talked about the black man "spreading his wings and learning to fly" and that he "was only waiting for this moment to arise." *Piggies* told of the rich, white establishment who would be taken down by the black man while they were getting all fat and richer before they knew what hit them and espoused that they "needed a damn good whacking." *Rocky Raccoon* told us to read Gideon's Bible to know the details of what was coming and that it would "help with our revival" after the war was over. The craziest song on the album was *Revolution 9*. It had all kinds of messages in there including sounds of war and people screaming and just all kinds of wild stuff. Charlie said it also referenced Revelation Chapter 9 in the Bible where it talks about the beast and the Antichrist and angels breathing fire. Now I had grown up in church but they rarely talked about Revelation. It was always a mystery to me, so at the time, this made as much sense as anything I had ever heard before. It's easy to look back now and see this as folly, but in the uncertainty of the 1960s what with the Vietnam War and civil unrest, it actually made a lot of sense.

As Tex suggested, we started building dune buggies to facilitate quick and effective transportation in the desert. The plan was to have at least 10 or 20 of them available. We could hide or bury tanks of gas at strategic intervals and locations so that we would always have a ready supply. Cappy said that her grandmother owned an old ranch out in the middle of Death Valley. She said the ranch hadn't been used in several years and she was sure that we would be allowed to use it for a desert headquarters.

Charlie was really pleased by these suggestions. It was another example of groupthink, in that once an idea was hatched, the group as a whole would formulate a plan and put it into action. We were truly becoming One Soul. We worked together as a team for a common goal. This thinking was not what got us into trouble. It was when that one thought got shattered by individual actions and ambitions that the trouble started. For now, we were functioning as one and it was a beautiful thing. Although Charlie thought we had a little time, it was best that we go ahead and start making these preparations. After all, Helter Skelter was coming down fast.

CHAPTER 32

Even though Shorty Shea was never a real fan of our group staying at the Spahn Ranch, most of the other ranch hands seemed to be okay with it. Johnny Swartz gave us permission to use his yellow and white 1959 Ford anytime we needed it, which was probably more than Johnny himself used it. Randy Starr, the self-proclaimed "Famous Movie and TV Stuntman" (all one had to do was look at the words painted on the doors of his beat-up old pickup truck to confirm the claim) let us use said pickup truck on occasion. Juan Flynn, a tall cowboy from Panama, practically became a member of our family. We never referred to ourselves as "The Family" mind you. That was created by the news media and the district attorney as part of the media circus to come. We did think of ourselves as a family, however, so it was an apt description. There were other ranch hands that came and went and there were a few like Cowboy Benny and Cowboy Larry that were friendly and accommodating to us, but never took part in any of our extracurricular activities. It was during one of these activities that Charlie and I reached what I came to see as a pivotal point in our relationship. We had eaten dinner an hour or so earlier and I went to take a walk down by the creek. I often did this just to step away from everything and enjoy the quietness of the evening and the beauty of the ranch. It was a world unto itself. There were mountains, deserts, forests, brooks and streams all within a few minutes' walk. Lots of us did this regularly. It was truly an awe-inspiring setting when you actually took the time to enjoy it.

I had just returned from my walk and was strolling up the boardwalk when I heard the sounds of group sex coming from the Rock City Cafe building. Figuring there was always room for one more, I opened the door and stepped inside. This was no ordinary orgy however. Usually the girls far outnumbered the guys so there was always room to find a willing partner. Not this time. Charlie, Bruce, and a couple of the ranch hands were all sharing one girl, and when my eyes met the eyes of the girl, my heart hit the floor and I got nauseous.

The glassy, drugged-out eyes that oh so briefly locked with mine, belonged to Terri. I had not seen her since that night in the Haight when I had to leave the apartment after trying to protect her sister from her maniac boyfriend. Every bit of the heartbreak, pain, and confusion came rushing right back. I didn't see any recognition in her eyes and though I realized she was stoned out of her mind, I think that made it hurt even more.

I suppose I must have inadvertently made some sort of noise because Bruce and Charlie both looked in my direction. I just turned and walked away, feeling a hollow burning inside. Charlie, zipping his fly, caught up with me near the end of the boardwalk.

"Hey, hey, hey. What's up, Shep? You okay, brother?" he asked, reaching out and grasping me by the elbow.

"No! I'm not fucking okay!" I exclaimed angrily.

"Whoa, whoa, whoa, now," he brought me to a halt.

"I used to….to…know her," I tried to explain.

"What the hell's your problem, Shep? She's just another broad, just like all the others. We share them all, you know that!"

Family Man

"Listen motherfucker!" I began, and before I got any farther, there was a knife at my throat.

"I could cut your damn throat!" Charlie hissed at me, inches from my face.

"Go ahead," I responded calmly. I closed my eyes and extended my arms. I then leaned my head back, exposing my throat to his blade. After a few moments, I opened my eyes to see Charlie in the identical pose. He was backed up 6 feet away from me and stuck the knife up in the ground between us. I lowered my arms and just stared at him. He held the pose for a good five minutes before lowering his arms and meeting my gaze.

"Are you my brother, Shep?" he asked calmly.

It took me a minute as I surveyed this guy who was a half a foot shorter and a good 50 pounds lighter than me. He had just held a knife at my throat before I knew it. I took a deep breath.

"I'm your brother, Charlie."

"No broad is ever gonna be as important as that."

I held his gaze. I didn't say a word, I didn't need to. I knew Charlie could see the pain in my eyes.

"It really hurts you that she's here, doesn't it?" he asked.

"Yeah," I said after a moment. "It does."

"Then she's gone," he responded.

The next morning he told me that he had bought her a ticket and put her on a bus home. I didn't ask him where that was and he didn't tell me. I never saw Terri again.

CHAPTER 33

The cowboys often hung around with us and told stories. One evening, we overheard some of them talking about a place just down the road in Box Canyon. It was called The Fountain of the World. They had what we would now call an open mic night, sort of a talent show I guess you could call it, every weekend where anyone that wanted to could come and perform. A group of us went up one weekend to support our friend Cowboy Larry, who went every time he could to thrill the listeners with his jokes and adventurous Western tales.

The Fountain of the World was a religious community that was built around a natural fountain that had long since run dry. There was a grouping of mostly adobe style dwellings around the fountain. Some of these were inhabited by monks and the rest by some elderly ladies. It was a beautiful and fascinating area with an even more colorful past. Much of what was attributed to Charlie and "The Family" in a few years would actually be derived from the history of The Fountain.

A man named Krishna Venta started a religious sect in the 1940s at this location. Because of the natural fountain that sprang forth on the land, he called it The Fountain of the World. Venta obtained the land around The Fountain, which was only a few minutes' drive from Spahn Ranch, in 1948 after deciding that he wanted to start his own religion. He called it WKFL which was an acronym for Wisdom, Knowledge, Faith, and Love, but it was most often referred to as The Fountain of the World. Venta claimed to be Jesus Christ. He would often perform mock crucifixions of himself where he would be strapped to a wooden cross. He predicted an end of the world level race war where the blacks would rise up and conquer the whites of America. The only white people left would be the WKFL followers who would have grown to 144,000 by that point. Krishna Venta and his followers would then conquer the blacks and would proceed to build a new world based on the concepts of equality, justice, and peace. Krishna Venta would then be allowed to take his rightful place on the throne as the world's new messiah. Krishna Venta was killed when two disgruntled members of his cult used dynamite to blow up the building he was in at the compound. Ten people died in the explosion including the bombers, Venta, and two of his children.

While I do think that Charlie was influenced some by this story, especially in his future founding of his ATWA (Air, Trees, Water, Animals) Foundation, he was far from the one most influenced by it. That honor would have to go to Little Paul Watkins, who told this story almost verbatim, only substituting Charlie's name where Venta's should have been when he testified against Charlie at his murder trial. I never really understood why Paul had told that story. He knew that it wasn't a story about Charlie and his beliefs, it was a simple rehashing of the Krishna Venta history. Anybody who lived in the area had heard it all before. By the early 1970s the Fountain of the World cult had ceased to exist.

CHAPTER 34

When we got back to the ranch that night and after almost everyone had gone to bed, I asked Charlie if we could have a walk and talk. He agreed, so we walked along the boardwalk and over near a couple of old cars that he and Tex had been working on.

"What's in your thought, Shep?" he asked me, leaning against a rusty front fender.

"Have you ever been to The Fountain of the World before?" I asked him flat out. I could tell by the sly smile that played across his face that he knew exactly where I was going with this.

"Have *you* ever been to The Fountain of the World before?" he reflected back at me. He was good at answering questions with the same question.

"Charlie, you know I haven't."

"What makes you think I have?" he asked, knowing full well why I had asked.

"Don't bullshit me, Charlie. We're brothers, remember?" I challenged him.

"Yeah, I remember. What do you want to know?"

"How much of Helter Skelter did you pull from that Krishna Venta story?"

He grinned even bigger and started to shake his head slowly. "You're pretty sharp, Shep. Venta was a tuned in dude. He saw what was happening way before anyone else."

"How much of it do you believe?"

Family Man

"Helter Skelter is confusion, man. Don't you see that it's coming down fast?"

"You know what I mean, Charlie. This race war stuff. The end of the world. Do you really buy it?"

"Buy…...buy. Buy die, brother can you spare a dime? You know, Shep, it doesn't really matter what I buy. What matters is what I sell. You put old George on a dollar and people expect you to bow down and worship him, ya dig? Those children back there were throwaways. Those people put their kids in the garbage cans and the trash piles and I pick them up and clean them up and tell them they're beautiful. Nobody wanted them just like nobody wanted me. I was just a tramp walking around in San Francisco and the kids came up to me and said 'we want to ride with you,' and I said 'well, hop in.' I learned to take care of myself. It's survival, man. We all do what we can to survive! Now I gotta teach those children to survive. And you too! Cause there's a world out there, Shep, that don't care about you and me and those children. They care about chasing that dollar. They'll grind you into the dirt and spit on you and then ask you why you're dirty and tell you they don't want to look at you. I've seen what the black gangs will do to a white man when they get the chance. I've seen them jump a Jack when he's mopping the cellblock. He ain't doing nothing but what the man told him to do, and they jump on him and stab him 50 times with shivs before the guards can get there and ain't no reason but because he was white and didn't have his own gang to protect him. I've seen his blood so thick on the floor that it runs into a whole 'nother cell block. I've seen that blood dried between the cracks in that concrete floor to remind others, 'Don't fuck with us, Jack!' I've seen the hate in their eyes and I know what they would do to my girls. If my children know how to use a knife, they can defend themselves! If it takes it having a name to get it

113

through their heads, then I'll give it a name! I'd die for every last one of you and the only way any of us will survive is if they'll die for me, and for you, and for each other! You see that don't you? I'm not selling no race war. I'm selling fear, 'cause fear means awareness, and awareness means survival, and I'm gonna do whatever I can to survive and you better too!" he ranted.

"So I guess that means that you knew about Venta before tonight?" I summed up.

The calm, thoughtful Charlie had returned. He stroked the hairs on his chin. "I spent a couple weeks at The Fountain awhile back. Me and a few of the girls. It wasn't my scene."

"So you dug the story but not the scene." I concluded.

"You might could say that," he admitted.

"I did say it. Would you say it?" I asked again.

"I guess I would, Shep. What does it matter?"

"I'm not sure it does," I countered. "I just wanted to hear you say it."

"I won't lie to you, Shep," he stated. "I'm a lot of things but I'm not a liar and I'm not a snitch. You look out for brother and you tell the truth. You live by those two principles and nothing else much matters."

"You can count on me, Charlie," I assured him.

"I believe that, Shep. You know the truth. Don't prove me wrong."

"I won't," I promised. I walked back to the ranch house leaving Charlie still leaning against the fender.

Leslie was in the kitchen when I got back. "Where have you been, Shep?" she asked. "It's late."

"Hanging out with Charlie. Just screwing around, I guess."

"Everyone else is asleep. You want to screw around with me?" she teased, taking my hands.

114

"I think I would enjoy that," I answered, cozying up to her.

"I'll bet you will," she assured me, and I most certainly did.

CHAPTER 35

Charlie often talked about how life is a big circle and that there is no beginning and end, no life and death, there is only now. Now is the only thing that's real, he always said. Something happened the next day that makes me think of that often. Sometimes, no matter how big the world may feel, you seem to always encounter the same circle of people regardless if you try to or not. Maybe fate really does play a part in everything and we really do move in small circles.

There was a group at the stables getting ready to go out for a ride when I heard Sadie call out to me. "Hey, Shep! Can you come give me a hand with this?"

"Sure," I answered back and trotted over to where Sadie was trying to help the riders mount up their horses.

"I can't get this saddle to tighten down," she whined. "Can you try to get it?"

"Go ahead and take care of the others," I told her. "I'll get this one for you."

"Just my luck," said the lady waiting for her horse to be readied. "This kind of stuff always happens to me."

I looked up at her for the first time. Soft blonde curls hung loosely over the milkiest white shoulders I had ever seen. She was wearing a striped halter top held up by spaghetti straps and tight jeans tucked into what were obviously brand-new cowboy boots. The outfit was completed by a spotless white cowboy hat. Her perfect makeup and pouting lips were accented by perfectly manicured fingernails. She was a city woman wanting to

116

play cowgirl for the day, but she was terribly ill-prepared. Nevertheless, I was smitten.

"Ahh, no big deal," I told her, "these straps are just stubborn sometimes. The real problem is that if you don't cover those shoulders, you're gonna get burned to a crisp out there."

"Really?" she frowned, genuine concern registering on her face. "I don't have anything else with me to wear."

"Here," I said, taking off my shirt and handing it to her. "Put this on. You don't have to button it up or anything, you just need to cover those shoulders."

"Thanks," she smiled, taking the shirt and pulling it on. She tied a small knot at the waist. "That better?"

"Wow," I breathed, thinking how much better my shirt looked on her than it did on me.

"What?" she said with a soft laugh that sounded like a gentle breeze through the trees.

"Oh, nothing," I blushed. "And those boots. Your feet are gonna be killing you by the time you get back."

"Gosh. I guess I don't know much about horseback riding. I don't have any other shoes with me."

"Well, my boots won't fit you," I laughed, "so just look me up if you need a foot rub when you get back."

I cringed at my own terrible attempt at a pick up line. She cocked her head sideways and commented that she just might hold me to that. I figured that I would never see her again. Worse, that she would probably complain to one of the girls about me flirting with her. If Ruby Pearl or George Spahn got wind of it, they would tear me a new butt.

I showed her how to put her foot in the stirrups and push her way up onto the saddle. She looked terrified. I reassured her that she was on a calm horse. I explained to her that the girls always describe the riders to George and he personally picked which horse best suited each of them.

I told her that George had never been wrong and that she would be fine. That seemed to strengthen her resolve a bit.

"Thanks for all your help. You've really been sweet," she looked down with a smile.

"My pleasure, ma'am," I responded with my best John Wayne imitation.

"Sweet and funny. I'm Vicki," she said.

"Shep," I smiled. "You better get going. Your group is about to leave you."

"Will you be here to help me get off of this thing when I get back?" she asked.

"Do you want me to?" I tried to hide my surprise.

"I'd like that," she answered.

"Then I'll be here."

"Good," she smiled.

"Come on!" Sadie yelled, stopping the group about 25 yards away, "Is she all ready to go?"

"All good!" I replied, giving her the thumbs up.

I made it a point to hang around the stables awhile before I expected the riders to come back in. I also made it a point to have showered and shaved. I had not done a lot of work since then so that I wouldn't be all sweaty when Vicki returned. Even the winters in this part of California could be pretty hot and today was one of those warm days. I would guess it was in the high 80s. Over the past year or so, I had gotten pretty good at gauging the temperature.

As if on cue, the tour group crested the small hill and rode toward the stables. "Well, look at you," I smiled up to Vicki, "you look like you're all ready for the rodeo."

"Not quite, but at least I didn't fall off," she laughed, "and look at you! You clean up really well."

"Awww shucks ma'am," I grinned, helping her dismount from the horse. "How are those feet?"

118

"Sore as hell," she confided, putting her hand on my shoulder and alternately rolling each ankle.

"That foot rub offer still stand?"

"Anytime," I beamed.

"How about tonight? My boss is having a few friends over to his house. Nothing fancy, just wine and snacks."

"Sounds great," I said. "I'll have to see if I can round up some transportation."

"I can pick you up. Where do you live?"

"Here," I answered a little sheepishly. She looked around the ranch, a little skeptical.

"There's a farmhouse down the trail a bit that some of us share," I explained.

"Oh, okay. So I'll pick you up around…" she looked at her watch and did some figuring in her head, "…7:30? It's not far, maybe 30 minutes."

"I'll be here waiting with my spurs all polished."

"You're really cute."

I could feel myself blushing.

"See you then!" She gave a little wave and hurried along, with a little limp, to catch up to her friends. I didn't really expect to ever see her again, but what do you know? 7:30 came and sure enough, she showed up.

CHAPTER 36

Vicki was there at 7:30 sharp and looked absolutely gorgeous as she rolled up in a silver Corvair convertible. She had the top down. Her hair was tied back in a ponytail to keep it from blowing in her face. She smiled a big smile that was so warm and contagious that I couldn't help but return it.

"Ready to go?" she asked, pulling the car to a stop beside me.

"Yeah. I've been standing here for half an hour," I replied.

"What do you mean?" she asked, checking her watch. "I am perfectly on time."

"Yes you are but I guess I was just anxiously awaiting your arrival."

"You are *so* cute," she beamed.

"You ain't too bad yourself ma'am," I countered, once again channeling the Duke.

"Well are you just going to stand there all day grinning like a goose or are you getting in?"

"Can I still grin after I get in the car?"

"Of course. I'm not sure that I could stop you. I haven't been able to stop myself all day."

"Can I make goose noises?"

There was that laugh again. My heart fluttered and I took my place in the passenger seat beside her.

"Nice ride," I complimented, admiring the Corvair. "These are really neat cars."

Family Man

"I like it. Jay pays me well, so I figured why not treat myself? It's nice to put the top down and enjoy the breeze and warm air on a day like today."

"It is," I agreed. "So Jay is your boss? You know my gig, but what do you do?"

"Oh," she laughed lightly again and I heard the fluttering of angel's wings. "That's right. I'm a manicurist. I do nails fah da stahz," she finished in an exaggerated fancy accent and broke into another laugh, just to emphasize how pretentious she thought that sounded.

"Oh yeah? Is Jay a star?"

"Not really. He's been in a couple of small things but he's best known as the hairdresser to the stars. He does Paul Newman, Warren Beatty, all the big stars. He even flies out to Vegas every three weeks to cut Frank Sinatra and Sammy Davis, Jr.'s hair."

I was genuinely impressed. "Wow, that's pretty cool," I surmised.

"That's where we are going tonight. Jay is having a little get together. Nothing fancy, just a few close friends and business associates."

"Are you sure that a bumpkin like me is gonna fit in with all these Hollywood types?"

"You'll do just fine. You're from the South, right? Jay is originally from Alabama. They're really down to earth. I was nervous around his friends when I first started working for him, but they're not really that different from anybody else."

"I've hung out with a few music people and most of them are like that."

"Oh? Who do you know?"

"Dennis Wilson from the Beach Boys is a friend. I know Frank Zappa and Mama Cass, and I've met Jim Morrison from The Doors."

Chuck W. Chapman

"See? You're used to hanging out with rock stars. Movie people aren't that much different. We even have some mutual friends. Jay cuts Jim Morrison's hair and I've done Mama Cass's nails, so there."

"That's cool." I still wasn't that confident. I felt like there was a pretty big gap between rock stars and movie stars, but what did I know?

"I'm really glad I met you today, Shep. I was going to be the only one going tonight without a date. Maybe it's karma."

"Perhaps fate smiled on both of us," I offered.

She slowed to a stop at a traffic light and turned herself to face me.

"I think it did," she agreed.

She leaned over and gave me a light peck on the lips that was well on its way to becoming more. Unfortunately, we were interrupted by the honking horn of the car behind us. She looked down, laughed that small, breathy laugh again and turned her attention back to the road.

"Mind if I ask you a question?" I said nervously.

"Sure, whatever you want," she answered.

"It doesn't really matter, but is Jay….you know…"

"What?"

"It's just that I haven't been around any and I've heard…"

"Spit it out, Shep. I have no idea what you're talking about."

"I was just wondering if Jay was, well...queer."

She burst out into laughter. "Good lord, no! Jay is about as far from queer as you could get. It's rare to see him with the same girl more than once or twice. Jay is a real ladies' man."

"OK. Good, I was just wondering. I mean, I just wanted to know what to expect. I'm sorry. It was a stupid question."

122

Family Man

"No, it wasn't. I know where you're coming from, but you're safe. You don't have to worry about Jay trying to take you away from me tonight."

We laughed together and enjoyed the rest of the ride. After the recent experience with Terri, I was concerned if I would be able to feel comfortable with a one on one relationship with a woman anytime soon. Everyone at the ranch belonged to everyone. Even though that arrangement did have its upside, I was still an old-fashioned boy at heart. It was nice to have a girl that you weren't expected to share with all your friends.

It was easy to feel comfortable with Vicki. She had a light, fun personality that just made me feel a warmth inside. She was not at all hard on the eyes either.

"Here we are," Vicki interrupted my thoughts as she turned onto Easton Drive out in Benedict Canyon.

"Wow." That was all I could say as I took in the sight of the Bavarian style mansion. The high-peaked roof reached high into the sky, casting its shade over the creme paint with the brown wood plank accents. A quartet of gargoyles graced each of the beams extending above the entryway.

"It is a bit over the top, isn't it?" Vicki commented.

"It's amazing. Now I feel even more out of place."

"Jay likes to flaunt his wealth, but he really is a nice guy. I promise you will like him. For that matter, they're all nice. They are people, just like me and you."

"I'm more worried about what they're going to think of me."

She turned to face me and put her arms around my neck. "Shep, you are one of the nicest, sweetest guys I've ever met. I like you for who you are. That you cared enough to give me your shirt to keep me from getting sunburned is one of the most considerate acts that I can imagine. Once I tell them that story, you will have won

123

them over for life. Be you. Be the guy that I counted the minutes until I got to see again."

I looked into her eyes and saw eternity. We finished the kiss that we had started at the red light before we were so rudely interrupted by the honking horn. "Okay," I took a deep breath and let it out slowly. "As long as I'm with you, that's all that really matters."

She put her arm through mine and we walked towards the door. "Yes it is. It's all that matters to me too," she assured me, and she reached out and rang the bell.

CHAPTER 37

The door was answered by a short, good-looking man with perfectly styled dark hair. I could tell that the clothes he was wearing probably cost as much as Vicki's car, and more than I probably had in my pocket in my entire life. He gave Vicki a quick peck on each cheek and extended his hand to me for a firm handshake.

"I'm so glad your friend could make it. Jay Sebring," He introduced himself.

"Billy Shepherd. Nice to meet you, Mr. Sebring, thanks for having me."

"None of that Mr. Sebring stuff, it's Jay. Please come in."

I noticed Vicki looking at me funny and I realized that she had not heard my real name before. She only knew me as Shep. Hell, I'd been called Shep so often lately that introducing myself as Billy felt kind of strange even to me.

"Everyone calls me Shep," I added.

"Then Shep it is," Jay welcomed. "Have a seat, make yourself at home."

"Thanks. It's a beautiful house," I said. "I really like Bavarian architecture, and those gargoyles on the beams are an exquisite touch."

Jay seemed impressed that I knew the words, let alone the meanings. "It was built in the 1920s," he explained, walking us through the entryway and into a large wood beamed living room, "but it's been marvelously maintained and I agree, the gargoyles are quite exquisite. They are hand carved and face to each directional point on

125

the compass. They are said to resemble the biggest Hollywood stars of that era. Of course, they're also supposed to ward off bad luck and they've been falling down on that job, but I'm being rude. Let me introduce you to my other guests."

"Don't get him started on the house," Vicki warned. "He won't talk about anything else all night."

Amidst Vicki's comment and the laughter, it brought forth, Jay gestured to a man and two women sitting on a plush wrap around sofa. "This is my secretary Carlene McCaffrey and her boyfriend Joel Rostau," he referenced the man and woman to his right and then the woman on his left, "and my good friend Sharon Tate." I wasn't aware until later in the evening through the course of our discussions that Sharon Tate was a movie star, but I had no trouble at all believing it. She may have been the most physically perfect woman that I had ever laid eyes on. With her long blonde hair, shapely legs, soft lips and big brown eyes, it was as if God had decided to construct the perfect woman and she was sitting right here in front of me. While the other ladies in the room were very attractive in their own right, Sharon was simply stunning. Had I not been so enamored with Vicki, it would have been all I could do to not just sit and stare at Sharon.

Once we all exchanged our pleasantries, Jay had his butler, who he introduced as Amos, bring out some wine. He was dressed in the tux and tails that you would expect and behaved professionally. Nevertheless, he still gave off the vibe of being more like Jay's friend than an indentured servant. Amos proceeded to pour glasses for all of us. Jay and the girls discussed the planned opening of his third salon location for a few moments while the rest of us sipped our wine and listened in. Sharon talked about her upcoming movie roles and about an upcoming trip to London that she was planning to take with her husband. I was plenty content to just sit back, drink some wine and listen to stories about these people's fascinating lives, but eventually the conversation came around to me.

"We've been talking about ourselves this whole time," Jay interjected. "Tell us about you, Shep. What do you do?"

He opened a small wooden box on the table and withdrew from the contents the necessities for rolling a joint. He then slid the box around the table for each of us to help ourselves to its contents.

"I work out at Spahn's Movie Ranch. I guess I would be considered a ranch hand."

"That's where we met," Vicki added. "Shep was so sweet. He helped me with my horse *and* he gave me his shirt to keep my shoulders from getting sunburned."

Her comments appeared to win me points with the ladies that were present.

"Spahn Ranch…" Joel said thoughtfully. "I think I've conducted a little business over at Spahn."

"Is that so?" I asked.

"Yeah. Well, actually my partner has," he continued. "Eugene Massaro. You know Geno?"

"I don't recognize the name, but a lot of people come through there," I answered.

"You ain't missed much," Joel laughed. "Anyways, we've had some dealings with a guy named Charles."

"Charles Manson?"

"Nah, that don't sound right."

"Oh, Charles Watson. Yeah I know Charles. We call him Tex."

"Yeah, Watson, that's him. Come to think of it, I have heard 'em call him Tex."

"What kind of business are you in?" I asked him.

I was curious because I didn't know about Tex having a business other than the wig store and he hadn't been

127

there in quite a while as far as I knew. On top of that, Joel didn't exactly strike me as a wig salesman.

"I have a little…." he paused, "…vending machine business. Drinks, cigarettes, some….other things." Joel broke into a big smile and everyone laughed. It was obvious that he had made an inside joke and that I was on the outside.

"Well, what do you say we partake in some of those other things?" Jay announced, rubbing his hands together as I was let in on the joke. He walked to a cabinet built into the wall and opened a door. He withdrew a small, golden box from the cabinet and brought it to the table. Removing the lid, he produced a baggie of white powder. Flipping over the lid revealed a mirror attached to the back. He measured out the cocaine onto the mirror and sorted it into six straight lines with a single edge razor blade. These also came from the box along with a short gold-plated straw. Jay took a line up each nostril and passed it to Joel. He and Carlene did a line each and slid it over to me and Vicki.

"I'm not much of a user," I said. "I'll pass."

"Oh, come on, Shep," Vicki urged, "just do half a line. That's what I do. I don't use very often either."

Vicki did her half a line and then passed it to me. I did my half as I'd seen her do. It burned like hell and I decided I would add cocaine to LSD on my list of shit to stay away from.

Sharon politely declined and, after finishing off the last line himself, Jay put his kit away.

"This is some good shit!" Joel exclaimed.

"They don't call him the candy man for nothing," Carlene chimed in.

"I thought that was Sammy Davis, Jr.," I said, trying to make a joke.

Family Man

"Where do you think he gets his shit?" Jay asked, and we all had a good laugh.

CHAPTER 38

As the evening wore on, the conversation turned back to Jay's house. He insisted on giving us the grand tour, even as Carlene and Vicki complained that they already knew the drill. It was quite clear that Jay loved the house and that he enjoyed showing it off. It was also easy to see that he enjoyed talking about the dark history of the place. He readily admitted that it was one of the main reasons that he had purchased the house to begin with.

The house was the former home of actress Jean Harlow and her husband Paul Bern, a producer at MGM studios. Jean Harlow was the original Hollywood "blonde bombshell." On Labor Day in 1932, Bern committed suicide in the house by shooting himself. He and Harlow had only been married for two months at the time. Bern's ex-wife, actress Dorothy Millette, a former inhabitant of the house, jumped from a ferry and drowned three days after Bern's death. Harlow herself only lived another five years, dying at the age of only 26 from acute kidney failure.

In addition to those deaths, another previous tenant had committed suicide in the house, although Jay wasn't clear on the details of that one. Yet another had accidentally drowned in the pool in the backyard. Years later, a maid would kill herself by hanging in the house. Jay proudly pointed out each of these locations as he told the stories. Although Vicki had undoubtedly heard all of this before, I still saw her shiver as Jay went into the details.

Sharon had not accompanied us on the ghost tour, choosing instead to remain on the sofa in the living room.

Carlene had stayed behind to keep her company. She explained that she had taken Jay's tour enough to have it memorized. We all returned to join them in the living room for a final drink before we headed out. Jay said that Sharon had her own experience in the house and encouraged her to share it with everyone. Sharon was reluctant to do so, as the event had really affected her, but after fifteen minutes or so of goading by her still hyped up fellow party guests, she gave in.

She explained that this had happened three or four years ago when she and Jay were dating. She had stayed the night and sometime between midnight and 2 a.m., she was awakened to see a small, bearded man standing beside the bed. She turned to wake Jay, but he was no longer in the bed beside her. When she turned back, the man was gone. Terrified, she jumped out of bed and started down the stairs. Halfway down, she screamed as she saw the body of a man who looked like Jay with his throat slashed. He was hanging suspended by a rope from the ceiling. As instantly as it had appeared, the apparition was gone. She went into the kitchen to fix herself a drink. There, she encountered Jay doing the same. He claimed to have seen and heard nothing, not even her scream. Sharon was convinced that she had seen the ghost of Jean Harlow's husband, Paul Bern. Jay could never talk her into spending another night in the house. After four years, she still refused to be in the house alone. Jay appeared to find the whole situation amusing.

"Wow, Jay, aren't you afraid that there is a curse or something on this place?" I asked him. "I mean, that's a lot of death to be associated with one house."

"Not at all," he smirked. "And besides, if so, good enough. I want the whole world to know about it when I go." His friends told him not to worry, all the heads in Hollywood would be crying for him when he was gone.

After a few more minutes of small talk, we all said our goodbyes and went our separate ways. In less than a year, the house could add two more deaths to its list of former inhabitants. Even more prophetic, Jay would get his wish.

CHAPTER 39

Even though it was after 2 a.m. when we left Jay's house, neither of us were tired. Vicki attributed it to the effects of the cocaine. If I was this wired after just half a line of the stuff, I figured that Jay would be awake for the next two weeks. Vicki asked me if I would like to go out to the beach with her and watch the sunset. At the time, it sounded like the best idea I had ever heard. We spent the rest of the night walking on the beach, talking, and getting to know each other better.

"I'm surprised Jay never made a move on you," I said.

"He did. I knew I would just be a conquest though. His reputation far succeeded him. Sharon is the only girl he's ever really loved, the rest were just games to him. I didn't want to be a toy and I had no desire to be tied up and beaten."

"You gotta be kidding me?"

"No. That's his thing. I don't fault him for it. He only does it with willing victims, it's just not my thing. I drew the lines early on and he's always respected them. We are friends and colleagues, nothing more."

"I'm glad to hear that. I feel intimidated enough already. What if I couldn't tie my knots as tight as him?"

"I'll have nothing to compare it to. I'm sure your knots will work just fine."

I wasn't sure if she was kidding or not, but it brought me some comfort. It also showed me that no matter how many famous people I met, I could never be a real part of their world. Even their hang ups were more exotic than mine.

When she dropped me off at the ranch at around 6 a.m., my plan was to spend most of the day in bed. Mondays at the ranch were usually fairly slow. There were very rarely any tourists and we didn't have specific duties on our schedule. We all just did what needed to be done. If someone needed a day off or a recovery day it was never any big deal. Of course, just my luck, this day was not a usual Monday. I had barely settled into bed and drifted off when I was awakened by the excited voices of Cappy and Brenda. They were talking all over each other so it was hard to get the message that they were trying to relay. Somewhere in the squabble I was able to understand that Charlie had been looking for me all night and that Gregg Jakobson and Terry Melcher were coming soon. I roused myself up and splashed some cold water on my face and proceeded to get dressed again. Charlie was waiting for me on the boardwalk. He appeared to be a little agitated but his enthusiasm was nowhere near that of the girls.

He asked everyone to leave us alone so that he and I could have a walk and talk. On the walk, he explained to me that Gregg and Terry had come by last night to inform him that they had arranged a recording session for him this evening. He said that he and the girls had been up half the night singing and practicing the songs that he was planning to do.

"That's great, Charlie!" I encouraged him. "Everybody's been waiting for this for a long time!"

"Yeah," he agreed, "but I don't know if we're ready.

"What do you mean? We've been doing these songs for over a year! You couldn't be any more ready."

"Are *you* ready?" he asked pointedly.

Family Man

"You know I am, Charlie. I could play these songs in my sleep." I refrained from telling him that that was practically what I was going to have to do if he didn't let me go back to bed.

"Where were you last night, Shep?"

"I was with Vicki, the girl I met yesterday here at the ranch. I told you about that, remember?"

"Oh yeah….city girl. She got any money?"

"I don't know. She's got a job and a car and rents her own place so I guess she does okay."

"She gonna come stay here?"

"She's got a place, Charlie. Besides, I don't think she would do well here. Like you said, she's a city girl."

"Yeah," he nodded thoughtfully. "You gonna leave us and go back to the city, Shep? You gonna go off with your rich girlfriend and leave us to do all the work around here?"

"You know I'll do my share," I countered. "Tex goes off with his girlfriends all the time and you don't give him no shit."

"Tex, rec ruth kabob roth vantage bobsnabagoogoob!" he stormed. "Tex ain't the one I count on to have my back, Shep, you are! If I can't count on you to have my back, then you just need to head on up the tracks with your hot shit girlfriend, ya dig?"

"This isn't about me, Charlie, you know who I am," I tried to calm him, "why don't you tell me what's really going down?"

"They shoulda give me more time. They showed up yesterday and tell me that today I need to play every note right and Terry's spending his money and Dennis and ooba na gooba black mack spix an stacks and you expect me to be calm?!"

135

I put my hand out to try to settle him down some. He was jumping around like he was the one that had done the cocaine.

It may come as a surprise, but Charlie tried to keep hard drugs away from the ranch. He had no problem with weed, LSD, mushrooms, and things like that, but he was against drugs like cocaine. He said that hallucinogens expanded your mind while hard drugs just fucked with your mind. There was rarely a shortage of some kind of drug around almost all the time. Marijuana was always readily available and there was LSD at least two or three times a month. Very few people had an issue with Charlie's ban on hard drugs. There were a couple of exceptions however.

Tex and Sadie kept a baby food jar hidden underneath a loose board on the boardwalk. If Charlie had known about it, he probably would have chewed both of their asses and made them get rid of it or make them leave, but as far as I know, no one ever told him. He did catch Tex with speed a few times and raised hell at him. In fact, that very morning he had made Tex leave the ranch for trying to get some of the girls to do speed with him. I heard him and Charlie yelling at each other and then saw Tex storm off, jump in his truck and peel out, but he would be back. It might be a few days, it might be a few weeks, but eventually he would tuck his tail and want to come back and Charlie would give in and let him. He would give him the third degree and tell him never to bring that shit back on his ranch, but Tex would do whatever he pleased anyway. Thanks to my conversation with Joel the previous night, I was pretty sure that I knew where Tex was getting his supply. I figured that he was skimming his own personal stash from the drugs he was getting from Joel and Eugene to resell. I also wondered if he was sharing his proceeds with the group. I seriously doubted it.

Family Man

Charlie had finally calmed down enough to tell me that Gregg was supposed to come by and pick us up later that evening and take us to the studio. Charlie was adamant that we all get together and go over everything again. Although I felt that this was totally unnecessary, I went along with him because I knew that was the only way that he was going to let it go and be happy. We all got together and practiced for the rest of the day. My fingers were sore and some of the girls complained that their throats were hurting but we kept going until Charlie finally decided that we were ready.

CHAPTER 40

Gregg arrived that evening to take us to the studio. He told everyone that they would have to follow him if they wanted to come along because he only had so much room in his car. He was trying to discourage tagalongs because he knew that transportation for the group could be hard to find sometimes. The girls quickly lined up Johnny Swartz's '59 Ford to use for the trip. Bobby would drive and six or seven of the girls piled into it. Charlie, Squeaky and I rode with Gregg. Charlie asked about Dennis and said we needed to go get him to come along. Gregg assured him that Dennis would be at the studio waiting for us to arrive.

Gregg was unusually quiet on the drive to L.A. No one else seemed to notice, but I could tell that something was making him uncomfortable. When we arrived at the studio, I learned what it was that had been bothering him.

We all unloaded from the cars and followed Gregg up a set of stairs and into the suite of Gold Star Studios where Dennis and Terry Melcher were waiting. Terry introduced us to a guy named Steve Vesper. He explained that Steve would be the engineer for the session and explained Steve's duties. This was the first thing that began to throw Charlie off his game.

"Now wait a minute," Charlie started. "Nothing against Steve here, but Terry you said you was doing the session."

Terry explained to him that Steve would be the one giving the instructions, but he would only be doing and saying what Terry told him to. Terry explained that if he were doing the engineering, it would distract him from being able to listen as closely. It would make it more difficult for him to fulfill his role as producer efficiently. This seemed to appease Charlie, at least for the time being.

"All right. Where do we set up?" he asked.

"Not we, Charlie, just you," Terry told him. Gregg noticeably stiffened and began to rock back and forth nervously. So this was the source of the discomfort that I had noticed on the way over.

"What do you mean? We been practicing all day and it's sounding real good," Charlie protested. "And now you wanna throw this at me? No, no, nah, nah, nah. I want to do it the way I planned."

"When you're making a record, Charlie, it's up to me to decide what we need to do to make sure everything sounds the best that it can," Terry explained. "Now you go into that room and get your guitar tuned up. Everyone else has to leave."

"Wait a minute. Now see here, the girls are my backup singers, and Bobby and Shep are my band..."

"Not here they're not," Terry told him calmly.

"And what about Dennis? He's my...." Charlie continued.

"I'm sitting this one out, Charlie," Dennis piped up. "Terry's calling the shots here. He's got a great drummer for you."

I could see the conflict building in Charlie and could see that the whole session was about to go up in smoke.

"But they don't know my songs, I ain't got time to be teaching them my songs...."

"They know the songs, Charlie. These are some of the best musicians in the business," Terry persisted. "I've already had the charts printed out for them and they've been practicing them."

"But they ain't been practicing them with me!" Charlie said petulantly, like a child not getting his way.

"You're going to have to trust me on this one, Charlie. We don't have room in here for everybody and we need to get to work," Terry insisted.

Charlie looked around with a mix of frustration and anger, finally relenting and telling the girls to head on back to the ranch and that they could come back and do their part later he guessed. I don't know if he thought that would happen or not, but it seemed to work. The girls were disappointed, however I'm sure that they also could feel the tension in the air and they didn't want to upset Charlie any further. We all started to head back out to the car when Charlie asked Terry if Bobby and I could stay.

"They can hang out in here if they want as long as they can stay back and be quiet," Terry relented.

"I'll go ahead and run the girls back," Bobby volunteered. "These things can take a while and no use them having to wait outside for all that time." Bobby had some experience with this sort of thing so Charlie didn't question him.

"Shep?" he said to me in a quiet voice, reminding me of a wounded animal. It was the closest I'd ever seen Charlie to asking for a favor, so I told him that I would stay. Bobby nodded to us and left. I was kind of glad that he had asked me to stay. Even though I wouldn't be playing, I was still interested to see how everything was done. I had never been in a real recording studio before and I was fascinated to view the process of how a record was made. Charlie seemed to calm a little but he had been caught off guard and taken out of his comfort zone. I wondered why Gregg or Dennis had not talked to him about this and told him what to expect. They knew Charlie well enough to know that he liked to feel like he was in control of his situations and that he would not respond well if he was cornered. If they had told him this a week or maybe even a day ago, it would have given him time to get it in his thought, as Charlie would say, and come to terms with it. As it was, it put both Terry and Charlie in an awkward position that could have been avoided.

Terry walked Charlie into the studio and introduced him to the people that would be playing with him on the recording. Whatever Terry said to him, it did seem to calm his nerves a bit. The joint that Terry pulled out and handed him I'm sure was a help as well.

The musicians that Terry had hired to play with Charlie were some of the best in the business according to Dennis. He said that they had played on records by The Byrds, The Mamas and The Papas, Paul Revere and the Raiders, even The Beach Boys. He figured they had probably played on every hit record of the past ten years. I turned my attention from my conversation with Dennis to see Charlie gesturing adamantly for me to come into the studio. Although I could see the frustration on Terry's face, he nodded for me to come on in.

"I didn't feel right, you know, you sitting there while I was playing with these cats without you meeting them," Charlie said.

To appease Charlie, Terry gave me a quick introduction to each member of Charlie's studio band: keyboardist and bassist Larry Knectel, drummer Hal Blaine, and guitarists Jerry Cole and Mike Deasey. Mike made the mistake of telling Charlie that his guitar was out of tune and picked it up to tune it for him. Somehow the favor was taken as an insult by Charlie, who forever after referred to Deasey as "the blue-eyed oriental." These guys, along with a few other L.A. session musicians, collectively came to be known by several names but most popularly as The Wrecking Crew. In some form, they ended up providing the backbeat for numerous hit songs throughout the 60s and 70s. We exchanged hellos and then Charlie stated that he wanted me to remain in the studio with him while he recorded.

"That's not how it's done," Terry began.

"That's how it's gonna be done this time," Charlie insisted.

Terry took a deep breath and let it out slowly, trying to control himself.

"Shep. Please try to be as quiet as possible," Terry relented, choosing to pick his battles. I assured him that I would try. Terry excited the studio and went back into the control room to start the session.

From the minute they started, I was glad I had been replaced. It was obvious that these guys were pros. It was also painfully obvious that Charlie wasn't. He kept stopping for no reason. He would start in the wrong key or change the chord structure in the middle of the song and sing different words. Terry constantly had to stop the recording and ask him to start over.

"Charlie, you've got to play everything the same way every time!" Terry stressed.

"Sometimes when I'm playing, I'll think of a better way to play them," Charlie stated.

"You should have thought of that way a month ago, it's too late to change them now."

"That ain't how I play. If I decide I wanna do something different I just do it," Charlie protested.

"I don't care how you play them on the ranch, but in here you have to play them just like you wrote them," Terry explained.

"No, no, no, now, listen. I'm playing my songs my way!"

"Fine, Charlie," Terry said, finally giving up. "You play whatever you want to play and I'll figure out a way to make it work."

142

Family Man

Terry finally decided to just let the tape run and stop interrupting him. He would even leave the control room and go out for a smoke or a bathroom break. I wished that I could have done the same. The session lasted for what seemed like forever. Charlie kept playing songs that none of us had ever heard before and then 30 seconds in would stop and ask Terry what he thought.

"We didn't come here for you to write new songs, Charlie. We're here to record the songs you've already written, remember?"

"But what if these are better?"

"Save them for the next album then."

Charlie went back to the songs that he came to do but he still kept changing them. He refused to tune his guitar when someone would tell him it was in tune with what was in his head, saying that it was in tune with what he was in his head. After more than 12 hours, Terry finally said that he thought he had enough to work with and that we could go. The relief from everyone in the room was palpable.

"If I need anything else, maybe I can bring a crew out to the ranch," Terry said, his hand on Charlie's shoulder as he walked us to the door. Dennis followed us outside to Gregg's car for the trip back.

"You have to listen to what your producer and engineer tell you when you're in the studio, Charlie," Dennis tried to explain, albeit too late.

"They don't know my music, Dennis. You and Shep know my music. You gotta be part of the soul to feel what I'm playing. Terry shoulda let you and Shep play instead of all them guys I don't know."

"Those guys are better than us, Charlie. Terry knows what he's doing."

"My band is just as good," Charlie insisted.

"Goodnight, Charlie," Dennis replied, giving up the argument.

"I did good, didn't I, Dennis?"

"Yeah, Charlie. You did great," Dennis said with a smile. "It's going to be a groovy record."

Dennis patted the top of the car in a "so long" gesture and an exhausted, red-eyed Gregg drove us back to the ranch. I fell asleep in the back seat of Gregg's car and woke up there late the next morning.

CHAPTER 41

The next few weeks at the ranch buzzed with activity. There were the preparations to move at least part of us to the desert alongside the excitement created by Charlie's recording session. Terry had also sent Mike Deasey back with a mobile recording unit to try to get Charlie and The Family Jams, as he had begun calling the group of us who played and sang with him, in more of a relaxed and natural setting for him. Unfortunately, Charlie still held a grudge against "the blue-eyed oriental," so the sessions didn't go as well as I'm sure Terry had hoped. Charlie and Mike butted heads constantly with Mike finally just giving up. After listening to those recordings, Terry and Gregg came up with another plan. He had the idea of doing a documentary of Charlie and the rest of us and what it was like to be living on a commune at the ranch. They thought it would be a great companion piece to air on television before the release of Charlie's album. Everyone thought it was pretty cool that we were going to be on TV. Everyone but Charlie. Charlie said that we were trying to get away from society and he was afraid that the publicity would make more people come to the ranch to gawk at "the television hippies." Charlie hated the word "hippie" though. He explained that we weren't "hippies," we were "slippies," we were trying to slip away from society and we would work to earn our keep. Hippies were lazy and dirty and expected a hand out. That didn't describe us at all. Finally, Gregg convinced him that it would all be done low key and not only would it be a great promotion for the record, it would also be a boost to George by bringing more business to the ranch. Charlie would probably be in the desert by then anyway, so what did it matter? Charlie begrudgingly said ok, but he would prefer it to focus more on the family than on him. Gregg said that they could make that work and that Charlie's music would be playing throughout the film. When the record came out it would be a big boost to sales.

"It's all about chasing that dollar, ain't it Gregg?" Charlie asked him.

"Yes, Charlie. That's how the music business works. If no one makes any money, then there's no point in doing it."

"What about just for the music?"

"You can do it for the music, Charlie, but if you want Terry's help or anyone else's help, they're gonna have to make money. Not everybody lives on a ranch or in the desert. Most people have rent to pay."

"Maybe they should all live in the desert. Maybe their lives would be happier if they didn't spend their lives worshipping a piece of paper with ol' George on it."

"Maybe so, Charlie, but that's not the way it is for most people and never will be."

Charlie shook his head and walked off mumbling to himself. Gregg turned to me and asked if that meant they could do the filming or not. I told him that it was a yes. If it had been a no, it would have been perfectly clear. Since Charlie had left him hanging, it meant that he would let them do it and then complain about whatever bothered him about it at the time.

"You know him better that I do," Gregg laughed. "But if he throws us off the ranch when the film crews show up, I'm blaming it on you."

"Fair enough," I answered, and Gregg went back to tell Terry that the deal was on.

146

Family Man

Business at Spahn was picking up on the weekends even before any publicity push coming from the documentary and prior to the album being released. Lots of women had stopped coming to the ranch when the cowboys were leading the rides because of their unwelcome advances and lewd conduct. Once word got around that young girls were leading the rides, women were much more comfortable coming and men...well, they had heard that young women were leading the rides so that enticed them to come too.

Ruby Pearl had asked Juan Flynn to become the ranch manager of sorts. She claimed she was getting too old for the job and half the cowboys didn't listen to her anyway. Everyone had always pitched in and done what needed to be done, but it did help with organization if everyone had a specific job assigned to them, especially on the weekends. It didn't change things that much and Charlie and Juan functioned well most of the time. Charlie felt that staying busy was good for the mind and body, so he had no problems with Juan deciding the jobs. Juan pretty much knew what everyone liked best and what they did best, so it was a smooth transition.

There was one incident that stood out though. Juan was expecting everyone to work but things had slowed down for the day and Charlie decided we needed some "soul" time. This usually consisted of everyone sitting in a circle in the saloon, smoking grass and doing LSD. Charlie said this helped draw us closer together and helped us all become part of one soul. Not long into the soul session, Juan came bursting in and demanded to know why everyone wasn't working. Juan and Charlie then got into a face to face shouting match. The Panamanian cowboy was almost a foot taller than Charlie but when Juan threatened to kick Charlie's ass, Charlie stepped back, calmly lit a match and held his hand over it. We all sat in stunned

147

silence, hearing the sizzle of skin and smelling the stench of burning flesh. Charlie, however, appeared unfazed by it.

"Do what you will, brother," Charlie told Juan, still holding his hand to the flame. "You can't hurt me. There's no such thing as pain. Pain is just a thought."

Juan backed down and stormed out the doors. Charlie shook out the match, took his place back in the circle and picked up talking right where he left off, as if nothing had ever happened. By the next day, he was back twisting wrenches on the cars and I never even saw a scar. There were a few other incidents that happened around this time that stand out in my mind.

Tex had been staying in the guest house of what was soon to be Terry Melcher's former house on Cielo Drive for a couple of days. Dean had lived there for a few weeks and Tex had gone to spend a few days until Charlie cooled down and let him come back to the ranch. Dean had a court date coming up for a minor drug charge. Terry loaned Tex and Dean his car and credit card to make the trip for his sentencing. Terry was moving out of the house and into his mother's cottage out on the beach. The owner of the home, Rudy Altobelli, had told Dean that he would have to leave as new tenants were going to be moving into the main house and Rudy himself would be coming back to live in the guest house. Considering Dean was about to take up residence in the county jail, it wasn't much of an inconvenience. Even when Tex and Dean were living at the ranch, they tended to stay in tents or in one of the outlaw shacks away from the rest of us. Once Tex came back, he buried himself in a top-secret project of his own for several weeks. He had started hauling truckloads of wood up the pass a mile or so every chance he could get. No one knew what he was working on but we all chipped in and helped him by throwing the wood over a big embankment down to him. He worked on this project alone for the better part of a month before finally inviting us all to come witness his creation. We had to go down a hill and follow a path for a couple hundred feet to see that he had built a big bunker type structure between two large concrete bridge supports. These were anchored in solid rock that Tex had meticulously dug out. He smoothed the rock by hand and finished it with wooden walls. The building was big enough that we all could fit in it at the same time comfortably. We called it the "In Case Place." It was a secret place that would be there in case we needed it for any reason. It was an impressive feat, especially considering that Tex had built it completely alone.

Also notable was the birth of Sadie's baby. We all assisted in the birth in one way or another with Charlie performing the actual delivery. Sadie named the baby Zezozose Zadfrack Glutz simply because she liked the sound of it. To say that Charlie or anyone else could ever control Susan "Sadie" Atkins is just plain wrong. Susan was always her own woman. She came and went as she pleased, as did all of us that wanted to, and she didn't take any crap from anyone. It frustrated most of us to no end that Sadie was such a loose cannon. It also earned her my respect that she played by her own rules and had no problem changing those rules whenever she felt like it. As to Susan ever being "mind controlled" by Charlie, I think Charlie himself said it best one night while we were sitting around the fire.

"Spirit is a power that can't be controlled," he explained. "I don't move it. The two ways to lose it are when I try to use it, and when I fear and fight against it."

CHAPTER 42

Very few of us were looking forward to the trip to the desert. Charlie told me that it was just to be a much safer "in case place." He swore me to secrecy for fear of no one else wanting to go, but said that not only could I return to Spahn after two weeks, but that he would be returning soon himself. He explained that he wanted to use the Myers Ranch out in the desert as an outpost, or colony, if you will. He said that if things got too hot around Spahn or if Helter Skelter started coming down too fast, that we would need a place to escape to. We might not even need it, he confided, but like the knives, it was better to be prepared.

"New starts now," he explained. "We got to look at all the bad thoughts, fears, and doubts in order to see the good." He always had a way of making no sense make sense.

Shortly before the desert trip, a young, skinny boy named Brooks Poston appeared at the ranch. He jumped right in and started doing chores including mucking out the horse's stalls. He was such a natural fit that everyone just assumed that someone else had invited him to join us. Eventually, we came to find out that no one there knew him before. While many of us distrusted him after learning this, Charlie accepted Brooks right off, saying that Brooks "needed to work himself out, just like the rest of us."

I had to give Brooks credit, he wasn't afraid of hard work. He was the skinniest, whitest dude I had ever seen, but he didn't let that stop him from shoveling horseshit all day long in 100-degree heat like the rest of us. Working in the stalls did keep the sun off of his pasty skin at least.

Brooks was an odd, quiet guy that generally kept to himself. The first LSD trip that I remember him taking went even worse than mine had. I only hallucinated seeing blood, carnage, and my friends being drug to hell, Brooks legitimately thought that he had died. He lay completely unmoving on a sofa in the farmhouse for five straight days. We could see him breathing and his wide-open eyes would occasionally blink. Otherwise, we would have probably thought he was dead too. When I use the term "unmoving," unfortunately that did not apply to his kidneys or bowels. He pissed and shit himself every single one of those days, yet continued to lie deathly still in his own excrement. The smell emanating from Brooks was even worse than that of the horse stalls which he helped to clean out. After almost a week of this and everyone's efforts to snap him out of his funk, someone went and got Charlie. Charlie calmly walked in, knelt down beside Brooks and told him that since he had been doing such a good job cleaning up after the horses, that he guessed we would have to clean up after him but that he was tired of him messing up the furniture. Charlie proceeded to take off his vest that all the girls had embroidered and made for him and held it up in front of Brooks.

"I'm gonna put my vest in under you," Charlie told him. "So if you have to shit, you're just gonna have to shit on my vest. And Brooks, you *know* how much I like this vest." Brooks blinked his eyes a few times then immediately got up and went to clean himself up. I've heard some people describe this as one of Charlie's "miracles." Truth is, Charlie had studied up on psychology and influencing people while he was in prison, and more importantly, Brooks knew what would happen to him if he shit on Charlie's vest.

I had agreed to accompany Charlie out to the desert to scope out Cappy's grandparent's place with the understanding that I was coming back to Spahn at the first available opportunity. I had been seeing Vicki as often as I could lately. I didn't want that to end because I had disappeared into the desert and had no way to communicate with her. Charlie gave me a speech about "opening my thought," and I reminded him that had my "thought" not been opened, that I would not have agreed to go out to the Myer's Ranch with him to begin with. That seemed to placate him. I made a quick phone call to Vicki to tell her that I was going out to the desert to look at some property with Charlie. I figured I would be gone for a couple of weeks but I would call her as soon as I got back to Spahn and we could pick up where we left off. A group of us boarded a big green school bus that Charlie had wrangled up somewhere and set course for the Myers Ranch.

CHAPTER 43

It took almost three hours in the bus to make the trek through the Panamint Valley. Cappy acted as our guide, telling Charlie where to turn as we made our way over more and more rugged terrain. We made it to the end of the road, at least the end of the paved road, and turned onto a dirt road to head off deeper into the desert. Just after turning onto the dirt road, we came upon what had once been a small mining town. We decided to stop and look around. The town, if you could call it that, was Ballarat, and it consisted of one building that was still in use. What had once been a bustling stop for gold prospectors, now boasted a population of three. The single business left was a small store with a cafe counter. I bought a Coca-Cola because I figured it would be my last opportunity to drink anything besides water for the next couple of weeks. A couple of the girls purchased candy bars before we all climbed back on the bus and drove off.

The road was so rough that we had to stop several times to re-secure our belongings back to the top of the bus. It also gave us some time to stretch our legs and rest our backs. The rough ride was taking its toll on all of us in stiffness, bumps, and bruises. There were lots of big gulleys cut into the side of the mountains that looked like dry river beds. Cappy explained that these were called "Washes" because during heavy rains, the canyons were prone to flash flooding which in turn created rushing rivers that would wash rocks, debris, and even large boulders down these areas at high speeds. She said that we

153

had to be careful not to get caught in these areas during rainfalls because a person could be swept away in them in a heartbeat.

We eventually arrived at a mountain that was too rugged and steep for the bus to surpass. Cappy said that we would have to walk the remaining seven or so miles to her grandparents' ranch. A collective groan went up from the group. Having little choice, we unpacked the supplies from the top of the bus and started lugging our bags up what she identified as Goler Wash. I wasn't sure how she could tell one wash from another but she knew her way around this barren wasteland and led the way with confidence. Once we had reached the top of Goler Wash, the land changed dramatically. It was a lot easier to traverse. It leveled off into a series of small hills and valleys. We soon came to a group of buildings that Cappy called the Barker Ranch and just past that, maybe a quarter mile farther, we reached our destination.

The Myers Ranch was built by Cappy's grandfather, Bill Myers, in 1932. In addition to the main house, there were several outbuildings and an in-ground swimming pool that had been hand made with rocks and concrete. There was a natural spring above the property which gave us access to fresh water. Unlike the barren areas we had journeyed through to get here, plants and bushes on the property were plentiful. The place had not been used in years so it took quite a bit of cleaning. The guys did the outside work while the girls dusted, washed and scrubbed everything inside. When we weren't working, we all took time to explore and enjoy the desert. Charlie acted as if he had found Nirvana. He loved the quiet and isolation of the place. For miles in all directions, there was nothing but open land. At night, we would just sit still in the darkness and listen to the sounds of nature. Charlie would identify each animal as it made its way across the desert floor. He recognized owls, coyotes and rattlesnakes. I was amazed at how someone who had spent half their life locked inside could be so in tune with nature. He would tell us how to avoid the snakes and the wildlife and instructed us on how to behave if we encountered them. Animals seemed to speak to Charlie in a secret language that only he and they could understand.

The nearby Barker Ranch had also been uninhabited for a number of years. Naturally, we had to go there and explore it. It was bigger than Myers and consisted of more buildings. There was a stone house, a bunkhouse, sheds, livestock corrals and a stone swimming pool. The houses were beautifully constructed of multi-colored rocks and beams made from railroad ties. Inside, there was a stone fireplace, cabinets and a sink which provided a small trickle of running water. I could admire and appreciate the rustic beauty but I still looked forward to returning to Spahn. At least there, we were near civilization. If Charlie wanted a place where the law, the blacks, or anyone else couldn't find him, I felt that this was it. On a return trip, Charlie later tracked down the owner, Arlene Barker, and asked for and was granted her permission for us to stay there sometimes. He gave her a gold Beach Boys record for compensation. I think Charlie would have been perfectly satisfied if we had all gone back and just left him out here all by himself.

In retrospect, I wished that is exactly what we had done.

CHAPTER 44

Juanita came up a couple of weeks later to replenish supplies and to let some of us swap out. Those of us who wanted to stay at Myers could stay and those of us who wanted to return to Spahn could go back and let a new group come up. I had agreed to come up to Myers as a favor to Charlie and for an adventure, but I was more than ready to get back to the Spahn Ranch and to Vicki.

I'm not sure how or when he did it, but somehow Charlie had managed to get Juanita's van back from Dennis. She drove the van up to bring some more food and supplies and to let anyone who wanted to go back with her to come along. The van would not have made the trip as far as the bus did so those of us who were going back had to hike down to Ballarat to meet her. Bobby and Clem decided to stay in the desert with Charlie, so it was me and four or five of the girls who walked the 27 miles down to Ballarat. Brenda, Squeaky, Mary, and Gypsy made the trip with me and there were a couple of the younger girls that I didn't know that well. We left around noon and didn't get there until the wee hours of the night. It was a rough hike and we were all exhausted. The store was closed. Luckily, an elderly lady that lived in a trailer behind it let us use one of the wooden sheds to bed down for the night. She also gave us some drinks and snacks from the store. I was so beat that I don't even remember lying down.

When we got back to Spahn, Squeaky learned that George was behind on his taxes and was afraid that he might lose the ranch. Juanita called her mom and got enough to pay the taxes for George with a few thousand left over. Charlie came back a few days later and then left again to go right back to the desert. I was just glad to be back to what I now thought of as home.

While Charlie was gone, I learned that Dennis Wilson had taken *Cease to Exist* to The Beach Boys and they had decided to record it for inclusion on their *20/20* album. I was excited for Charlie and couldn't wait to tell him about it, at least until I actually saw the album and heard the song. Dennis had rearranged the song and changed some of the lyrics. He had also changed the title from *Cease to Exist* to the more innocent *Never Learn Not to Love*. If that wasn't bad enough, not only did Dennis not tell Charlie that The Beach Boys were recording the song, but he had taken full credit for writing it. Charlie's name wasn't even mentioned anywhere on the record. I hoped that I could talk to Dennis and get him to explain why he did that before Charlie came back, but the opportunity never presented itself.

CHAPTER 45

There was plenty of talk of a coming revolution in the late 1960s and it came from many circles. From students on college campuses to militant groups like the Black Panthers and The Weathermen, talk of anarchy was never far away from the public consciousness.

Helter Skelter was never a scene that Charlie ever wanted to speed up or encourage. It was something he wanted to avoid and escape from. Charlie was very respectful of the police and military. He said that once Helter Skelter started coming down and the culture devolved into one without the law and without Christ that there was "no sin that wouldn't be committed." This is why he wanted to have the desert hideout ready and means of quick escape at hand. Charlie never talked of starting a race war. Only of hiding from it once it had started. He felt that the desert gave us the best chance of escape and with that escape, the chance of protection. He started encouraging Danny to bring his Straight Satans brothers to the ranch with the promise of companionship with the girls. What Charlie didn't count on, was the drugs the Satans brought along with them and the fact that they would be rough with the girls on occasion. Most of the girls were fond of Donkey Dan but didn't care much for the rest of his crew. What positives the Satans brought in protection were far outweighed by the negatives they caused in public perception and abuse to the girls.

After the first of the year, Charlie came back to Spahn. I was hoping that I could have been the one to tell him about what Dennis had done with *Cease to Exist*, but someone had beaten me to it. Charlie, as you would expect, was incensed. He was pacing back and forth on the boardwalk like a caged animal.

"That son of a bitch!" Charlie fumed. "How could he fuck with my song like that?!" Dennis has sold his soul, man! I thought he was my brother and he sold me out for a dollar man?! You dig what I'm saying??"

"I get it Charlie," I said, trying to defuse the situation, "but why don't we talk to Dennis about it? Maybe they left your name off accidentally."

"Name? You think this is about my name? I don't give a damn about my name! It's my words, ya dig? In other words, he ripped the soul right outta my song and made it about fucking!"

"Let's go talk to him, hear his side of the story."

"There ain't no side. If he had eyes in his head and could see under the bed, he'd see that heads are lead and eyes are wood, but it doesn't really matter because rubber fingers are taking the hand off into the universe anyway."

I listened to him rant for a while longer until he calmed down and agreed to take a ride out to the beach with me to visit Dennis. Charlie didn't say a word for the entire ride to the Malibu beach house. I was flipping back and forth in my mind between hoping that Dennis wouldn't be home so we could avoid the confrontation and hoping that he would be so that we could get it over with. When we rounded the corner and rolled to a stop, I saw that it would be the latter.

It took a while for Dennis to open the door. I'm sure he was having that same internal debate whether he should acknowledge us or not. After probably a good five minutes, he opened the door slowly.

"Hi Charlie, Shep. What's going on?"

Dennis never looked up at us. He kept his eyes on his sandal clad feet as he spoke. Charlie pushed his way inside the house before he said anything. He then whirled on Dennis as if he were the interloper.

"I'll tell you what's goin' on," he began. "My song is what's going on. It's going on all them Beach Boys records, but it ain't *my* song that's being played!"

"I'm sorry about that, Charlie, but because of publishing and all, you know, I had to just put my name on it," Dennis stammered.

"Name?! You think this is about my name on some piece of paper and black plastic?! You stole my song and changed everything all up where it ain't even my song anymore. Do you know how that makes me feel?"

"I can pay you for it, Charlie, I just can't put your name on it."

"Money is all that matters to you ain't it Mr. Beach Boy?? I don't want your fucking money, I want my song put back like the way it's supposed to be!"

"That's the only way I could get it on the record. I didn't want to change it, but they made me."

"Made me, make me, maybe baby, cry baby cry, you make them change it then."

I was glad that there was a counter between Charlie and Dennis so that I wouldn't have to be the one that had to keep them separated. I feel like my presence made them both a little more comfortable although you could still almost cut the tension with a knife.

"Charlie," Dennis explained, "I've tried to tell you, that's not how the music business works."

"You telling me you can't take my song off that record?"

"No, Charlie. Once the records are pressed, it's too late to change it."

"Why didn't you tell me you were gonna put my song on there?"

"You were in the desert, Charlie. I had no way to tell you. I thought you would be happy about it."

I knew that this was not even close to the truth. Dennis would have had no problem getting the word out to Charlie even when he was in the desert. As far as I could tell, he hadn't even tried. Maybe Gregg had told him that Charlie couldn't be reached but I doubted it. I was pretty sure he hadn't talked to anyone else at the ranch. Charlie either believed him or figured that there was no point in dragging it out any further.

"Ya know," Charlie said slyly, "I think I will let you pay me after all. That song oughta be worth a couple thousand or so, right?"

"I don't have that kind of money on me, Charlie, you know that," Dennis protested.

"What does an old hobo like me need with cash anyway? I could use that motorcycle though," Charlie hinted, peering outside.

Dennis followed his gaze out through the glass doors to see the Triumph motorbike that Charlie was referring to.

"Sure. Take it," Dennis offered. "Is that fair enough?"

"A couple of those gold records would look good at the ranch. I mean, you took my records so I should get a couple of your records."

"Fine." Dennis pulled two of the multitude of gold Beach Boys records off the wall and handed them to Charlie. "Are we good now?"

Charlie looked around for a minute, trying to decide if there was anything else that he wanted to squeeze out of Dennis. "Yeah. I think that's fair for now," he agreed.

I could see the relief wash over Dennis's face until Charlie reached into his shirt pocket, pulled out a bullet and stood it up on the countertop. "But Dennis, I know you got a kid out there. You better be careful who you fuck with."

"Shep, grab our gold records," Charlie said, turning to me. "I'm gonna take a ride on my new motorcycle." With that, Charlie walked out, straddled the Triumph and sped off.

"What the hell did he mean by this?" Dennis exclaimed, picking up the bullet with a trembling hand.

"You know Charlie," I answered. "He has a flair for the dramatic."

"You tell him to stay the hell away from my son!" Dennis threatened.

"He was right here," I replied. "You could have told him yourself."

Dennis and I locked eyes for a minute before he picked up one of the gold records and started towards the car. I grabbed the other one and walked behind him. He opened the rear door and we carefully loaded the records into the back seat.

"Do you think Charlie will still let me come to the ranch?" he asked, propping himself against the open driver's door as I started the car.

"He said you were good, Dennis, and besides, Charlie doesn't own the ranch, George Spahn does."

"So we're cool."

"We've always been cool, man. As for Charlie? You made it right. I think you're fine."

Dennis broke into a big smile that reminded me of the little boy he would always be. He shut the door and patted the roof a couple times, then he leaned his head halfway through the window.

"Thanks, Shep. See ya soon, man."

"See ya, Dennis."

Family Man

I drove away, pondering how Dennis could go from being enraged that Charlie would threaten his child to being hurt and worried that he might not be able to come back to the ranch in a matter of minutes. It was then that I thought I was beginning to understand the dynamic between Dennis and Charlie. Dennis was the boy who would never grow up. Conversely, Charlie was the boy who had to grow up before he had a childhood. They were both little kids trapped in grown men's bodies.

CHAPTER 46

What is a "family"? It's people who love and care for each other and work together for a common good, right? In that case, we were definitely a family. From the beginning of our time together, we came to think of ourselves as brothers and sisters. We lived together, we worked and played together and we cared about each other. That's where sometimes the terms "a family" and "The Family" get confused. We were "A" family to ourselves. Only in the media and to the prosecution were we "THE" Family. When I refer to our group as family, I am using it in that sense: a group of people that love and support each other, not as a proper name.

Early in the year, it seemed like our family was beginning to go its separate ways. Word had gotten back to us that George was thinking of selling the ranch. The advantage of Squeaky and Sandy being in George's house on a regular basis was that we could keep a good hand on what was going on around the place. One of the girls was almost always present, allowing them to listen in on George and Ruby Pearl's conversations. A neighbor had been pressuring George to sell for a couple of years, but he had really turned up the heat recently.

George never knew exactly how many people were living at the ranch but he had been told that having so many hippies and undesirables hanging around the place would decrease his chances of getting top dollar if he did ever decide to sell the property. Regardless, in their opinion it was just bad for business. Although I know he wasn't the only one, Shorty Shea seemed to be the loudest voice to try to get us to leave. Shorty wasn't even there himself that often but he was stubborn and set in his ways. If he didn't approve of something, he didn't think anyone should.

George was also upset over the fact that so many of the guys and girls were sleeping together out of wedlock and that so much sex was going on his ranch. This seemed especially hypocritical to me because George was married but lived separately from his wife. He had participated in a long term, well known affair with Ruby Pearl and had sired at least eleven children. Most of those children he wasn't even on speaking terms with. After a while, I suppose the negative talk must have gotten to George, because he and Squeaky had a big fight in which he told Squeaky to take her friends and get off his damn ranch.

While some of the group were already staying at the Myers Ranch, a large part of us were about to become homeless. Luckily, once again Charlie worked his magic and located a large one and a half story house on Gresham Street that came to be known as the Yellow Submarine House due to the yellow siding which reminded everyone of the Beatles song. It worked out great for a while though and it was fun to hear everyone walking around singing:

We all live in a yellow submarine, a yellow submarine, a yellow submarine.

The yellow submarine worked well because it was big and sat on a relatively large lot. It possessed a large living room that Charlie said would be a cool rehearsal space. We all never lived there though. In addition to those that had stayed in the desert, a few secretly remained at Spahn out back in the outlaw shacks. Then there was me and Tex Watson.

It had been a while since I had spent what could be considered quality time with Vicki. We had kept in touch and we had gone out a few times here and there, but between my time in the desert and her work schedule of going around from salon to salon for Jay, our time had become quite compromised. When I informed her that we were going to have to move off the ranch for a while, Vicki suggested that I come stay with her. I thought about it for maybe half a second before I jumped at the chance. George had decided that even though he didn't want us living there, he would let a few of us continue to work at Spahn. He grumped that he couldn't afford to pay us, but that we could keep tips and a percentage of the money that tourists paid to go on the horseback tours of the ranch. That percentage was never nailed down and it varied day to day, mostly on George's mood. Still, it was enough to keep some change in my pocket. It also allowed me to chip in on some groceries, and prevented me from feeling like a complete freeloader at Vicki's place.

I didn't have a car of my own but I rarely needed one. It wasn't that far from Vicki's apartment in the Valley out to the ranch, so she would usually just drop me off in the morning and pick me up in the evening. If for some reason she had to go in early or work late, I could always hitch a ride to or from Spahn. Times were so much simpler back then and hitchhiking was a common means of transportation. That's even how we all met Dennis Wilson. Tex picked up Dennis hitchhiking, Dennis picked up Pat and Ella Jo, and the rest of us all met him through those connections.

I was looking forward to having so much time to spend with Vicki and the opportunity to find out how compatible we were with each other. There is a big difference between spending time with someone every now and then and being around them all the time. I think that's what made the family so special. There were so many of us, usually around thirty, give or take, yet we almost always got along well. That was a real advantage and big difference of communal living over "normal" society.

Tex had met a new girl and after what must have been one hell of a first date, he immediately moved in with her. This practically coincided with us having to leave Spahn, so it worked out well for him. It seemed rather insignificant at the time, but in retrospect this meeting would be the start of a domino effect. This would be the first in a series of events that would lead up to the beginning of the end of the family. A couple of days after we had all split up from the ranch, I was there working with the horses when Tex pulled up in his pickup truck. Tex and I never had a very close relationship so I was surprised when he gave a little whistle and jerked his head for me to come over.

"Hey Shep, come here, will ya?"

"Sure, Tex. What's up?" I answered, approaching the truck's open window.

"You doin' anything tonight?" he inquired.

"Not that I know of. Hanging out at Vicki's place I guess. Why?"

"Well, I just thought I'd see if you and your girl would like to come over and have a beer with me and my girl."

Tex had never asked me to hang out with him before. While our relationship was cordial, we had never exactly been chummy. We had kind of existed in the same place at the same time without ever really interacting with each other. I wondered if he had an ulterior motive but quickly scolded myself for the suspicion. I thought that it couldn't hurt and figured maybe he was missing the group. Since I was the only one around, he had decided to ask me. I still doubted that I was his first choice.

"I don't see why not," I answered. "We were probably just gonna watch TV or something."

"Groovy. See y'all then," he said.

He scribbled a phone number and address on the inside of a matchbook, handed it to me, then wheeled the truck around and drove away.

I stood watching through the cloud of dust until I saw his brake lights come on as he made the turn onto Santa Susana Pass Road all the while questioning Tex's motivation for the invitation.

CHAPTER 47

I informed Vicki of Tex's invitation when she picked me up that evening.

"Since when did you and Tex become such good pals?" she asked.

"Today, I guess," I responded.

"I was under the impression that the two of you weren't very fond of each other."

"Not really. I mean, we haven't been close but we've never had any real problems ethier. I think we're just very different people. Now that I think about it, Tex doesn't really seem to be close with anyone. He's kind of quiet and keeps to himself. Dean is the only one that I've seen him spend any amount of time with."

"Isn't Dean the other outcast?" she said with a glint in her eye.

"I guess you could say we're all outcasts, but yeah, probably them a little more than the rest," I laughed.

"Well, I'm all for drinking someone else's beer, so why not?"

"Then it's a date."

"Yes. It is. You've met most of my friends. It's time I met some of yours," she smiled.

"Even if we are starting from the bottom up?"

"Even if."

Vicki had a way of making me smile on the inside as often as on the outside. I liked that about her. Charlie made me think, a lot of the girls made me horny, but Vicki made me feel a warmth inside. She made me feel special in

169

a way that I hadn't felt in more than a year at least. We drove back to the apartment to change clothes and freshen up. A day of working with horses in the California sun, even in the winter, is not the aroma you want to spend the rest of the evening with. I called the number on the matchbook and a polite sounding lady answered. I told her that Tex had given me the number and invited us over. I was just calling to confirm that we would be there.

"Oh, Shep! I'm so glad to hear that. Charles has told me a lot about you," said the voice on the other end of the phone. The name Charles threw me for a minute. Everyone at the farm had called him Tex for so long that I had almost forgotten that his real name was Charles. Kind of like the fact that I was so used to Shep now that if someone called me Billy, I didn't even realize that they were talking to me.

"I'm looking forward to meeting you and your girlfriend," she continued.

"The feeling is mutual," I replied. It wasn't, exactly, but why be rude?

She asked if 8:30 or so would be convenient for us and I told her that would be great and we disconnected. The bewilderment must have shown on my face because Vicki asked me if everything was all right.

"Sure. Just the fact that she said Tex had told her all about me…..I don't get it," I puzzled.

"Maybe you made a bigger impression on Tex than you realized. You sure made a big one on me." She put her arms around my waist and kissed my lips.

"Hopefully in a much different way," I joked.

"Yeah. I'm not interested in one of *those* kinds of parties," she agreed, laughing.

We arrived at the Franklin Avenue address Tex had given me at around 8:15 p.m. It was located in the heart of the Hollywood Heights section of Los Angeles.

Family Man

Considering that it was still early on a Friday night, the area was hopping. After circling the block three or four times, we finally spotted a parking place near the front of the building that was being vacated by a dark green Jaguar and eased the Corvair into it.

The Franklin Avenue Apartment Complex consisted of a couple of rows of nearly identical two-story apartment buildings. The sign in front of one identified it as the Franklin Garden Apartments, which closely resembled the writing Tex had scrawled on the matchbook.

"These are nice," Vicki commented, "and in this area, they can't be cheap"

"Guess ol' Tex has found himself a sugar mama," I commented.

"So you two really do have a lot in common," she teased.

We took a flight of stairs up to the second floor. Tex met us in the breezeway with two open bottles of beer in one hand and one that was half empty in the other.

"Shep! Glad you could make it, c'mon in. Hey, she's even prettier than you told me," he said, referring to Vicki.

I couldn't recall that I had ever described her to him at all, but the smile on Vicki's face revealed that the flattery had worked so I didn't bother pointing out the discrepancy.

Tex led us to an open door a few feet away and we followed him into a neat, clean living space that had obviously been decorated by a woman. We followed him through the living room and kitchen area, then out a sliding glass door that opened onto a nice sized patio. A very attractive olive-skinned woman with long, dark hair sat with her feet propped up at an outside table with a canvas umbrella coming up from the center. She was wearing shorts and a lacy white blouse and had a beer bottle in her hand. I could tell that she was short even

171

though she was sitting down. Still, her legs had a nice shape and she was tanned and toned. I could see why Tex would be attracted to her. He handed the two bottles in his right hand to me and I passed one to Vicki.

"I'm Rosina," said the lady on the porch. "Forgive Tex for being rude."

Vicki introduced herself as she took a seat beside Rosina, added that it was a man thing and the two ladies clicked bottles. Tex and I remained standing.

"Helluva view ain't it, Shep?" Tex asked, finishing off the beer and going to a cooler at the corner of the porch for another one.

"That it is," I agreed. "What's that building over there?"

"That's The Magic Castle," Tex informed me. "It's a private club. They do magic and shit in there. We like to sit out here and watch all the magicians go in and out. It's so exclusive that they won't even let you in the door unless you can pull a rabbit out of your ass or something."

"Guess I'll just have to settle for the outside then," I replied.

"You and me both, buddy. Hey!" he exclaimed, as if an idea had just struck him, "what do ya say we burn one?"

"If you're supplying," I answered. "I don't have anything on me."

"Oh, don't you worry, Rosina's got the hook up," he bragged. "Best shit in town."

Rosina smiled and picked up what I had assumed to be her purse that had been sitting on the floor beside her. She dumped at least a hundred bucks worth of grass onto the table, then proceeded to sort and roll it.

"Fire away," I said.

We spent the next hour or so lounging on the deck, drinking beer, and smoking grass. There was a steady stream of tuxedo-clad men, almost all with a buxom beauty on his arm, going in and out of the Magic Castle.

"Bet it ain't no rabbit that he's pulling out of her ass," Tex commented at one particularly short skirted lady coming out of the club. Rosina smacked him playfully on the arm but didn't appear to be bothered by the remark. We had another beer and shared another joint as an awkward silence prevailed. I felt that I had fit in and been more comfortable around the rich folks that Vicki worked with than I did now. Vicki saved us by saying that we had enjoyed the company and had a nice time but she had to work early tomorrow so we had to be going. We stood and complimented Rosina on her place and thanked her for her hospitality. We were turning to go when Tex grabbed my arm.

"That was some good grass, don't you think Shep?" he asked.

"Yeah, man. It was great. I really appreciate it."

"You know, man, we had to buy a little more than we needed, so it'd be a help if y'all could take a little of it off our hands."

Son of a bitch. There it was. This whole ruse was so that Tex could try to sell some dope. I was about to say thanks, but no thanks when Vicki piped in.

"It is good stuff," she said. "Yeah. We'll take a quarter if that'll help."

"Good deal!" Tex exclaimed.

He went to the table and as if he had been watching the magicians practicing, produced a baggie from somewhere, hopefully not his ass, I thought, and sectioned off our share of the dope.

"You didn't have to do that," I whispered to Vicki.

She just smiled and gave me a peck on the lips. Tex delivered the goods and Vicki handed him two tens and a five.

"We appreciate that. It means a lot," Tex said, shaking my hand. "You need anything, you know where to come."

"Wouldn't go anywhere else," Vicki intoned sweetly.

I shot her a look and she responded with a little nudge.

"See you later. Nice meeting you!" Rosina called without turning around.

"Later, Tex," I offered and we headed back down the stairs. I took note of the fact that Tex didn't bother to see us to our car.

"That asshole," I exploded once we were in the car. "I can't believe this whole invitation was to sell us dope!"

"It wasn't all about selling dope," Vicki corrected, "it was about showing off his new girlfriend and his uptown digs, too. At least we got free beer and close to twenty bucks worth of grass for it."

I looked over at her to see if I had misunderstood what she was saying. I hadn't.

"Yep. He short changed us," she confirmed with a laugh. She shifted the Corvair into gear and we headed home while visions of punching Tex in the face next time I saw him danced through my head.

CHAPTER 48

After a few weeks, George had decided that he was lonely and missed our company. No doubt, he especially missed that of the girls. I was stocking some bales of hay when Ruby Pearl came rolling up in her truck. She stuck her head of flaming red curls out of the window and told me to get in, that George wanted to talk to me. I was concerned that he was going to inform me that he had sold the ranch or that he didn't want me around anymore. Therefore, I was majorly relieved to hear that not only was I welcome to stay, but that he wanted me to tell everyone else that they could come back as well. I gave him a quick "Yes, Sir!" and bolted through the front door to ask if I could borrow Ruby's truck so that I could inform the others.

Ruby was leaning against the fender with a shit eating grin on her face when I came out. She had known all along what George was going to say to me but had let me spend those long, painful minutes wondering about it. "Guess you expect me to let you use my truck to round up the rest of those freeloaders," she grumped. Then she gave a half smile and threw me the keys before I could even answer. That was typical Ruby Pearl. She liked to come across as tough on the outside but was really as tender hearted as they come.

Everyone was excited to be back at the ranch. In fact, we seemed to be given more freedom than ever before. Maybe it was because George had asked us this time instead of us asking him. Shorty was away on one of his movie projects or whatever it was that kept him away for weeks at a time, so there was no opposition to our return. Randy pretended not to care one way or the other but he had a glint in his eye that told us he was happy to see us. Ruby and the other cowboys always seemed to like us and it helped to ease their workload, so they were more than okay with it.

Juan and Mary and a few others who had stayed in the desert at the Myers Ranch came back near this time as well. Only Brooks and Juanita remained to look after the place and to keep it prepared should we ever need to escape there. Not long after, in the barren desert, Juanita would meet a gold prospector and end up marrying him. I don't know if any of us ever saw her again. Just goes to show that your love will find you, wherever you are.

That evening when Vicki came to pick me up, she saw that everyone was back at Spahn. She sat still in the car for a minute and then looked straight ahead as she spoke.

"You want to stay here, don't you?"

I took a few moments to collect my thoughts before answering. "They're my family," I finally responded.

"I've had a great time with you being there every night," she said. I saw a tear roll down her cheek. "But you're not ready. Not yet."

"Yeah, not yet," I agreed.

"Do you think you ever will be?"

"I do. Maybe even soon. Just not yet."

"I know. I've always known."

"Are you dumping me?" I asked, a lump rising in my throat.

She smiled and I melted. "You're not getting rid of me that easy," she laughed softly, wiping the back of her hand across her eyes. "Besides, I can't smoke twenty-five bucks' worth of grass by myself."

"Twenty," I reminded her.

"Twenty, then."

She leaned across and hugged me and I held her tight.

"Don't give up on me," I whispered.

"Not on your life," she answered.

We parted and looked at each other through damp eyes. I opened the door, got out, and shut it behind me.

"And Billy," she beckoned, leaning over to look out at me.

"Yeah?"

"I love you."

It was the first time she had said it and I was too surprised to respond. She hit the gas and left me standing in the middle of the road, looking after her.

CHAPTER 49

The next couple of months at the ranch were like going back in a time machine and reliving my childhood. Now that George had pretty much given us free reign, we were all more open and relaxed. We would do whatever work needed to be done and then we would play games. We were living on a movie set. It was easy to lose yourself in fantasy. one of the girls saw a snake crawl up under the boardwalk and mused, "Wow, I wonder what it would be like to be that snake?"

"If you want to be that snake, just do it," Charlie stated, matter-of-factly. Everyone just stood around staring at him until Charlie got down on his belly and started slithering around like the snake. He was wiggling back and forth with his arms flat against his sides and flicking his tongue in and out. We all got down and pretended to be the snake. It seems funny and childish now, and it was, but that was the point. Charlie said that the child was perfect and that we should strive to be like children. He thought that adults had screwed up the world and that it would be up to the next generation of children to fix it. The more of us that could become like children, the bigger a help we could be to that generation. Charlie stood up and watched as 8 or 10 of us slithered around on our bellies, laughing and having a high old time. Leslie and I were almost nose to nose, flicking our tongues at each other when Charlie brought his foot smashing down between us. The laughter immediately ceased and everyone stopped moving.

Family Man

"You see what happens when fear comes down? Now you know what that snake feels like when you come smashing into his home. All that matters to him is surviving right now. He don't think about what's happening tomorrow. You see why he wants to bite you? His fear is real, because his fear is now, and now is the only thing that's real to him."

He then dropped back to his knees, then his belly and went back to slithering around with the rest of us. Seeing things from the snakes' perspective and from his point of view really opened my eyes though. My lifelong fear of snakes became more one of respect and understanding. Live and let live took on a whole new meaning for me that day.

The entire ranch became our playground and we played lots of games. Sometimes we would pretend to be pirates. Oftentimes we would be cowboys, and still others spacemen. There was a lot of talk about putting men on the moon at that time so we would go to the very back of the ranch to some of the more barren areas and some of us would be astronauts and some of us would be aliens. The junk cars that were spread around made for excellent spaceships. I was raised by a very conservative, military father so I felt that I was expected to behave like an adult even when I was a kid, thus I relished these times. Charlie had been raised in reform schools and institutions, therefore he had never experienced a childhood at all. In quiet moments, often late at night and away from the group, he would share these memories with me.

"Shep, I didn't have a childhood. I went to reform school in '43, and I've been fighting ever since," he confided.

"I'm sorry Charlie, that must have been terrible."

"Nah. It was alright. A child don't know what terrible is."

"I still hate that you had to go through that," I said.

"It's okay. Now I'm born again. Every day I get a new start. When you start all over, every day is a rebirth. That's why I care so much for these kids right here. They're all throw away kids and I was a throw away kid."

"And that's why we all care so much about you, Charlie."

"You ain't like them, Shep, and you ain't like me. You're better than that, but I know your word is good and when your word is good, you're good."

"Thanks, Charlie, that means a lot."

We had many of those kinds of conversations. Sometimes Charlie would almost open up completely to me, but he would always stop just short of the whole story. We came up with our own characters for certain games and would use these characters again and again in different situations. Charlie was Riff Raff Rackus. Clem was John Jones from Minneapolis, who just came in from driving a truck. My creation was Dimwit Duffendorf, the dumb deputy from Dry Gulch. It was such an escape from reality that drugs were rarely even used during these times.

Not long after, the games turned a little riskier and a lot more serious. I think it may have been Sadie, a lot of the dumb ideas often were, or it may have been Pat, who brought up something called "creepy crawls." This was where you would dress all in black and sneak into someone's house late at night while they were sleeping, or sometimes during the day while they were at work. You wouldn't steal anything, but you would rearrange their furniture, hang a picture upside down or change their refrigerator items around. Just about anything you could think of to mess with people or freak them out was fair game. It was to instill fear in them and to raise awareness in ourselves.

Family Man

I went on a couple of the daytime ones when people weren't at home and it was kind of funny to imagine their expressions when they came home to see all their furniture turned upside down or rearranged. I only went on one of the night time crawls. It freaked me out to be in people's houses while they were sleeping. The object was supposed to be to freak them out, not ourselves, so I skipped the night time ones after that. Some of the girls really enjoyed them and were really good at them, because they never got caught. Almost no one bothered to lock their doors back then and during the summer, most folks slept with their windows open which allowed for easy access. This was not training for anything else as has been suggested, but was simply a game. It did however, give quite a few of the girls a certain confidence and comfort that would serve them well in the not too distant future. It would also be a big part of what brought them crashing down to earth.

CHAPTER 50

Danny DeCarlo had been a regular around the ranch for a while, but sometime around April or May he officially moved in. Not only did Danny move in, but with him came his huge cache of weapons, especially firearms. Danny had rifles, shotguns, carbines and even a submachine gun.

"What the hell are we going to do with a machine gun?" I overheard Charlie ask him.

"It's for protection," Danny answered.

"We don't need nothing like that," Charlie replied. And yet we were preparing for a race war? I don't think so.

Danny even had a mold to make his own bullets. He would spend hours producing hundreds of rounds of ammunition, only for us to go out and spend them in a matter of minutes.

While we had all taken to wearing a knife in a sheath, guns were a rarity until Danny moved in. The knives were for defense in the extreme case that we needed them, but even more so they were handy for everyday use around the ranch. I can't count how many times I used mine for cutting or untangling knots in a rope or removing a burr from a horse's mane or tail. It also came in handy to cut slices of apple to feed the horses or to trim small branches to clear a trail.

Once Danny arrived, the weaponry moved to a whole new level. He took over the front room of the bunkhouse and turned it into a gun depository. He also brought his motorcycle into the house and would work on it until all hours. I was a pretty sound sleeper, especially after a hard day's work. I usually slept in one of the trailers anyway, but it drove a bunch of the girls absolutely crazy. They would complain endlessly but their complaints fell on deaf ears. I think Charlie just liked having Danny around. He gave Charlie a sword that had come from the Straight Satans' clubhouse and Charlie absolutely loved it. He had Bruce weld a scabbard onto his favorite dune buggy just to carry the sword around in. He used it when we would play pirates and when he needed to clear a trail. He had Danny grind the blade constantly to keep it razor sharp.

I never thought of Charlie as violent although he could have a very quick temper, but weapons have a tendency to embolden people. This sword would soon come into play in a way that I never could have imagined.

Remember, time to us was relative. We had very few clocks or calendars at the ranch. It wasn't by any plan or order, it just didn't matter. Our goal was to live for the moment and in the now so there was no need for time-keeping devices. We came to tell time by the sun, the moon, and internally, and were usually pretty precise if we needed to be. It was also around this time, I can narrow it down to sometime in May, that Charlie acquired the now infamous .22 Buntline revolver.

Johnny Swartz had been fired by Ruby Pearl several months earlier for some unnamed offense. Whether it was George or Ruby having a change of heart, or Johnny coming crawling back to ask for his old job, I don't know. Regardless, he was back. None of us ever had a problem with Johnny and he had another set of wheels we could borrow, so his was a welcome return.

Also making his return to the ranch was the "famous Hollywood stuntman" Randy Starr. Randy claims that he had been away working on a new movie where he had made friends with an actor named Ron. (I never heard a last name). He said that Ron had been so impressed by Randy's stunt work that he had given him a nine-shot Hi Standard Buntline .22 revolver that had once belonged to Ronald Reagan. Reagan was a former actor who most of us remembered from the TV show *Death Valley Days*. He was also the Governor of California at the time and would later become the 40th President of the United States.

Randy was showing it off like a trophy. I had to admit that it was a beautiful firearm. The long barrel with its natural bluing and its polished wood grip looked like it could well have been the same gun that Reagan brought down the bad guys with on TV.

Charlie instantly fell in love with that gun. Every time that we would shoot target practice, Charlie would ask Randy if he could borrow the Buntline. After three or four weeks of Charlie asking to borrow the gun every day, Randy finally just told him if he liked the gun so much, he could just keep it. Charlie was elated. The Buntline became just as important to Charlie as the Satans' sword. It would figure even more heavily into the following few months' events.

CHAPTER 51

If I could pinpoint a time when Helter Skelter started coming down, it would have to be April and May of 1969. Things started happening so fast that it's really hard to wrap my head around them, even after all this time.

Helter Skelter by my, and our, definition, was confusion. It was never about a race war. The impending race war was just a small part of all the confusion that was coming down in the late sixties, both in the world as a whole and in our little section of it in particular. The fact that we thought we could, or that we would even want to, incite a race war is the idea of a madman. That madman was not Charles Manson, but the district attorney who would prosecute so many of my friends in the next couple of years.

I never once heard Charlie say that he wanted a race war to happen. He simply felt that it was inevitable. If Charlie had ever wielded the power that was attributed to him, he would have done everything he could to prevent such an event from occurring, not to assure or kick start its happening.

I'm not sure of the date, I just remember Vicki tearing into the ranch in the middle of the day and coming to me with tears in her eyes. She asked me if I could please come with her, and of course, I readily agreed. I had no idea why she was so upset until we got in the car and were back on the highway. She told me that Carlene was back at her place almost in hysterics. She hadn't wanted to leave her alone, but said that Carlene was afraid to come to the ranch with her. I didn't know why she would feel that way but I soon found out.

We arrived at Vicki's apartment to find Carlene still visibly upset to the point of shaking. She was also sporting a black eye and a badly swollen upper lip. I found it particularly odd when she asked if we were sure that we hadn't been followed or if anyone had come with us. I assured her that no one else had accompanied us and that I was pretty sure we had not been followed.

She said that Vicki had just picked her up from the police station. The previous night at Joel's place, two masked men had burst into the room and held both she and Joel at gunpoint. They had proceeded to take a large sum of cash from Joel along with quite a quantity of drugs, mainly cocaine and LSD. Joel argued with them and a scuffle had broken out during which Joel was shot. The bullet had gone cleanly through his foot and miraculously hadn't caused any major damage. However, Joel was left completely unable to defend himself, or her, at that point. Carlene had pulled at one of the men's arms while screaming at him to stop. The man jerked away and backhanded her, knocking her across the room and causing the injuries to her face.

Gratefully, it seemed that the men were only interested in the drugs and money as they made no further attempt to harm them. She and Joel were forced into two kitchen chairs back to back. The men then tied them together with rope before leaving. A neighbor heard the scuffle and gunshot and called the police. When the cops got there, quite a bit of cocaine was still in the house, resulting in them both being arrested. Joel claimed that Carlene did not know about the drugs being in the house. So after questioning her, they let her go. They took him to the hospital to get his foot tended to and then booked him on the drug charge. She didn't know when Joel would be released.

I listened to her tell this story, and while I then understood why she had been so upset, I didn't get what it had to do with me. It was clear that Vicki wanted me to be here for some reason, but I still didn't understand why.

"I'm sorry to hear that, Carlene, that's really crazy, but at least you are both okay," I said in my most comforting voice. She just nodded and fidgeted with a tissue that wasn't going to be much more help. "I'm sure that Joel will be out soon. It seemed like he had some pretty solid connections. I'm sure they will take care of him."

"That's not why I brought you here, Billy," Vicki cut in. I looked back and forth between her and Carlene.

"Well?" I asked.

She heard one of the guys call the other one Charles," Vicki filled in, "and she says that Charles had a Southern accent."

I felt a lump rise in my throat. Now I knew why Carlene had been afraid to come to the ranch. There were two guys named Charles there and they both spoke with a Southern accent. I knew where Charles Manson was last night and I knew that he had never left the ranch. I had no idea, however, where Charles "Tex" Watson had been.

"Joel knows Tex," I argued. "I'm sure he could have identified him, right?"

"He said that he's never met him. He said that all their dealings have been between him and Geno," Carlene answered. "On top of that, Joel wouldn't tell if he did know. He wouldn't want to lose the business connection."

"Even if Tex ripped him off?" I asked.

"I doubt it. He would probably figure he would make it back somewhere down the line."

I didn't know what else to say. I made some lame attempt to try to assure them that I was positive that Tex would never do anything like that. The problem was, it was hard to convince them when I couldn't even convince myself.

CHAPTER 52

When I returned to the ranch, I saw that Tex had wiggled his way back into Charlie's good graces. I was beginning to wonder if Charlie was afraid of him. It made no sense to me that he kept letting him come back over and over. Other than Susan's constantly outlandish behavior and stories, Tex caused far more issues and problems than anyone else. Susan was constantly ripping off, or pissing off, some guy then running to Charlie for help. Tex was the same. Police cars were becoming a common sight at the ranch and, more often than not, it was because of those two. Sometimes the girls would flirt with them and they would forget why they even came out. Other times, Charlie would have a chat with them and assure them that he would talk to Tex or Sadie, whichever the offending party was, and it would be enough to pacify them. I still didn't get it. Charlie would tell him he had to leave, then a few days or a few weeks later, he would be right back. One time, Tex even had his mother call the ranch and talk Charlie into letting him return.

Tex was leaning under one side of the hood of an old Chevy with Clem on the other when I walked up to them. "What's up Tex? How's Rosina?" I asked casually.

"Fuck if I know," he replied. "Last time I saw her she was running off to Mexico to get an abortion or something."

"Why didn't you go with her?"

"I ain't left nothing in Mexico."

"How about your friend Joel? Seen him lately?"

Tex straightened up and, wiping the grease from his hands onto the T-shirt that had been laying across the fender, looked at me sideways.

"Joel who?"

Tex was a terrible liar.

"Rostau. Hear y'all did some business together."

"I don't know no Joel Rostau. What you trying to get at, Shep?"

He took a step towards me and stood up to his full height. He may have had a couple inches and a few pounds on me, but damned if I would let him intimidate me. I stood my ground.

"I just got back from Joel's place. A couple of guys wearing masks beat him up pretty good. Even shot him through the foot and roughed up his girlfriend. Must have been some real assholes. I was concerned that maybe they'd be coming for you next. Just wanted to tell you to watch your back."

I could see his ire rising through the reddening of his face. He eyed me suspiciously for another moment or two before speaking.

"Yeah. I'll do that. Thanks."

"No problem. Always looking out for a brother," I smiled.

I could feel Tex's eyes boring into my back as I walked away. I didn't trust him half as far as I could throw him. I decided that I should take heed to my own advice and keep an eye on my own back as well.

Just then, Charlie drove up in Tex's pickup truck and I knew why Charlie had allowed Tex back again. He had given him his damn pickup truck.

CHAPTER 53

The parties were non-stop as spring gave way to summer. If Dennis wasn't throwing a party, then Frank Zappa, John Phillips, or Mama Cass were. Charlie had an old friend named Harold True, who lived over in Los Feliz on Waverly Drive. Harold threw some crazy parties. Oftentimes, Charlie and a few of the girls would end up spending the night because they were so zonked out. Harold's parties were always loud and rowdy and almost always resulted in his neighbors calling the police to shut them down. That never stopped him from having them though.

One of the instances that has always stuck with me happened at Terry Melcher's old house on Cielo Drive. Terry and his girlfriend, Candace Bergen, had moved out of the house near the end of 1968. Strangely, Sharon Tate, the actress that I met on my first date with Vicki, and her husband, movie director Roman Polanski, had moved in.

I was familiar with Polanski from *Rosemary's Baby*, his film about a woman who was unwittingly pregnant with the spawn of Satan. It was a pretty freaky flick that upon its release, stirred up lots of attention and controversy. A few of us had taken a trip down to L.A. to check it out. It reminded me too much of my bad acid trip, so I wasn't a fan. A lot of people really liked it and although Polanski had already directed several previous films, this one put him on the map in the States.

The odd thing is that neither Polanski or Tate were at the party that was going on at their own house. They were both out of the country on separate movie projects and had left their home to the care of two houseguests. They were the ones that had thrown the party and from what I gathered, it was a common occurrence. While I had been invited to the party as Vicki's guest via Jay, several other members of the commune attended as well, although I don't think many of them stayed very long.

Charlie was there briefly, but left very early on. Sadie and Squeaky put in an appearance and I seem to recall Ruth Ann weaving in and out of the crowd. I didn't see Tex, but he could have been there.

It was a who's who of the Hollywood elite. Warren Beatty, Jane and Peter Fonda, Joan Collins, Steve McQueen, the list went on and on. I didn't recognize everybody, but Vicki pointed out everyone she knew and introduced me to a number of them. When Jim Morrison and Jonie Mitchell stopped to say a quick hello, I returned the favor of introducing her to them. It was surreal to see Mia Farrow, the actress from *Rosemary's Baby*, stroll by.

In addition to all the A-list celebrities, there was a large contingent of people who looked a lot like the kids at the ranch. In contrast to the hundred-dollar suits and dresses, there were a lot of bare feet and bell bottoms walking around. Amidst a bunch of rich celebrities were a bunch of young hippies. Some, very young. There were multiple girls there that couldn't have been more than twelve or thirteen years old. I wondered if their parents knew where they were....or if they cared. The drugs and alcohol flowed freely and no one questioned anything. Welcome to Hollywood.

Vicki and I found a corner of the pool deck, sat down with our drinks, and watched the people walk around us. Jay wandered over and welcomed us before he blended back into the scenery. Vicki pointed out a man and woman who looked to be in their early 30s. The woman was an attractive brunette but was dressed conservatively. The man resembled John Lennon of the Beatles.

"That's Gibbie and Voytek," she informed me. "They're watching the house while Sharon and Roman are away." Judging by the steady stream of people going in and out of the house, it didn't look like they were watching it very closely, but it wasn't my house.

The woman had a wine glass in one hand and a joint in the other. She smiled and nodded to a few people but struck me as being polite more than actually hosting. The man was a totally different story. He was drinking heavily, laughing, and going from person to person. Every stop he made, he either gave or took a different drug. After watching him do this for most of the evening, I wasn't sure how he could still be standing, but there he was, still going strong.

"Voytek is a friend of Roman's from Poland," Vicki explained. "According to Jay, Sharon doesn't much care for him, but lets him stay because she doesn't want to upset Roman."

It was hard to put the party animal I saw in front of me and the soft-spoken Sharon Tate I had met previously under the same roof. From all indications, Roman was pretty wild. Stories of his womanizing were widespread. I had heard enough about Jay's history to know that he could be out there too. I guess that was Sharon's type. I later overheard Steve McQueen, another of Sharon's former boyfriends, confirm this by complaining that "I never had a chance. I was too tall and too blond." Opposites do attract I suppose.

"What about the girl?" I asked.

"That's Gibbie, Abigail Folger. Her family owns the Folger's Coffee Company."

"Wow. Maybe I should try to hook up with her," I teased.

"Too bad. She's with Voytek and you're already hooked up with me."

"Hmmm. Do I want to have nice nails or do I want to live like a king and drink great coffee? That's a tough choice."

I would have continued this banter for a while longer, but a commotion broke out near the gate and we, along with most of the other guests, rushed over to see what was going on.

Jay and Voytek were squared off against three guys in their late 20s. They must have arrived with Mama Cass, as she was pleading with them to "come on" and let's just leave." The three guys were having none of it. We squeezed through the crowd to get a little closer and I recognized the group. I had met them all at another party Cass had thrown a few weeks prior.

Pic Dawson was a little shorter than me. He had long, dark hair and a bushy mustache. He was yelling about Jay and Voytek owing him for the blow and mescaline they were giving away at the party. He had his chest poked out but seemed to be more talk than action.

Tom Harrigan was about my size with dirty, limp brown hair hanging in his eyes. He looked stoned and not involved in the confrontation, even though he was right in the middle of it.

The real instigator appeared to be a guy named Billy Doyle. When I had met him at Mama Cass', all he wanted to do was brag about what a big drug smuggling operation he had going on. He claimed that he and Harrigan flew drugs in from Canada that supplied half the west coast. I pegged him as a little guy, he was maybe 5'7" or so, who wanted to come across as important. It looked like tonight he may have sampled too much of his own product because he was tripping out of his mind.

Family Man

"Billy! Come on, we can deal with this later, let's go!" Mama Cass pleaded.

"I'm dealing with it right now!" he screamed, pulling a revolver out of his waistband and waving it around carelessly.

People scattered in all directions. I grabbed Vicki and pulled her away. Looking back over my shoulder, I saw Jay Sebring execute some kind of karate move to disarm him. The gun tumbled to the grass where an almost as out of control Voytek recovered it and pointed it at Doyle. Doyle continued to hiss, spit, curse, and kick like a wild, rabid animal, but was finally dragged away by Dawson and Harrigan.

"I'll kill you, you pollock fuck!" he screamed as they drug him away.

"Fuck you!! I didn't step on your fucking shoes! Fuck you!!!" he yelled the whole time his friends were hauling him through the gate.

Cass was shaking and crying. She also was apologizing profusely to everyone she came in contact with as she backed her considerably large hind quarters through the gate. She was one of the people I knew best at the party, and for all her shortcomings, she was a very kind hearted, sweet person. I was fond of Cass and didn't want to leave her alone with these jackasses. We followed her through the gate and asked if we could give her a lift home. She looked from us to the guys struggling with their still flailing cohort, and gratefully accepted.

Doyle was experiencing a major freak out. Harrigan and Dawson wrestled him to the ground and proceeded to tie him up with a piece of chain before picking him up and dumping him into the trunk of their car. As they were loading him in, I observed that he had pissed himself.

CHAPTER 54

I climbed in the back to allow Cass to have the front seat beside Vicki.

"I'm so sorry! I can never show my face there again!" she wailed.

"It's not your fault," Vicki comforted her.

"But I brought them. I knew Billy was tripping on mescaline, but I didn't know he was going to freak out like that!"

"There is no way you could have known," I assured her.

"I'm so glad that Sharon and Roman weren't there. I am so ashamed," she continued.

"I'm pretty sure that wasn't the first time that someone has freaked out on drugs at that house," Vicki stated.

"They came with me. I didn't know he had a gun. What if someone had gotten shot or even killed?!" Cass rambled on.

"But they didn't," I reminded her. "Don't blame yourself. It's all on Billy."

It felt strange calling someone else Billy. After tonight's scene however, I'm glad that everyone knew me only as Shep.

We arrived at Mama Cass's to find that her "friends" had arrived first. Pic approached the car as we came to a stop.

Family Man

"That son-of-a-bitch has lost his mind," Dawson said. "He tried to fucking bite us when we got him out of the car. We had to chain his ass to a tree."

We followed his eyes to a tall palm tree in the front yard. Cass's property was lined with trees and set back from the road a ways. Hopefully passers-by wouldn't spot the half-naked man who was chained to the tree and howling like a maniac.

"Is he going to be okay?" Vicki asked.

Dawson didn't appear to be concerned. Just another day of chaining a friend to a tree for him, I supposed.

"He'll be fine once he comes down. He's been on a three-day mescaline trip. He needs to get it out of his system."

"Where's his pants?" Cass asked.

"Pissed himself. Didn't want to leave him in them."

"Everybody needs a friend like you," I commented. The sarcasm was lost on him.

"He would do it for me," Dawson reasoned. "Call us when he comes down and I'll come back and cut him loose," he said to Cass.

Dawson and Harrigan loaded up and drove off, leaving Cass to deal with the mad dog chained up in her yard all alone.

"Do you want to come home with me?" Vicki offered.

"Thanks, but no, I'll be alright. I need to be here when he comes back around."

I felt conflicted about leaving Cass like this, but she insisted. I figured she had more experience dealing with bad drug trips than I did, so after several more assurances from her, we left. The last time I saw her, she was watching Doyle hugging the tree like the Earth was falling away and that tree would be the only thing left.

It was well past midnight and the evenings adventures had left us a little shell shocked. We drove silently until suddenly Vicki slowed and looked back in her mirror at the only two cars that had passed us since leaving Cass'.

"That looked like Jay's car," she said with both curiosity and certainty.

I turned to look, but all I saw were tail lights fading into the night. Even if it had been a black Porsche, it wouldn't have been uncommon. It was Beverly Hills, after all.

"Should we go back?" I asked.

She slowed to a crawl and looked thoughtful for a moment, then accelerated and continued on our way home.

I later heard rumors that Jay and Voytek, along with a few other guests from the party, had driven to Mama Cass' that night. When they found a pantless Billy Doyle, unconscious and still chained to the tree, Voytek anally raped him while the rest of the group cheered him on. I don't know if that's true. Doyle himself stated that he couldn't remember enough to honestly say whether it happened or not. That sounded like an admission to me. Thankfully, Vicki and I were long gone by then.

CHAPTER 55

The summer of 1969 was blistering. Having grown up in South Carolina, I thought I was used to the heat. This would be the third summer I had spent in California, but for some reason, whether physically or emotionally, this one felt hotter than any I had ever experienced. Little did I know that the real heat was just beginning.

It was in late June or early July, as I recall. according to sources that came after the fact, it was July 1st, which sounds about right. I know it was the middle of the week because I had borrowed Vicki's car while she was working. She rarely worked on weekends unless it was an extremely special situation.

I had made what was becoming a fairly common trip down to San Francisco to visit the Haight-Ashbury Free Medical Clinic on Clayton Street. While I had personally taken advantage of the clinic one or two times myself, many of the family had been constant visitors. Lately, Charlie had begun sending me on the trip to pick up his medicine. All that was required of me was to check in at the front and tell them I was there to pick up for Charles Manson. I would instantly become Doctor Smith's next patient. He would make a little small talk, asking how specific members of the group were doing by name, and then hand me a sealed paper bag to take to Charlie.

After making a few of these runs for Charlie, I noticed that we always had big LSD parties on the same night that I returned. I never looked in the bag. It was sealed when I got it and sealed when I gave it to Charlie. In retrospect, it seemed to be more than a coincidence.

I had just made such a medical run and then picked Vicki up at work. She dropped me off at the ranch a little after midnight. I was walking toward the boardwalk when Tex came bursting by me and ran inside. I entered just as the phone was ringing. I looked around but didn't see Tex anywhere. Charlie picked up the phone as I was handing him the bag so I was close enough to hear a hysterical, crying woman on the other end.

"Charles?!" the voice cried.

"Yeah, this is Charles," said Manson.

An angry black man's voice replaced the woman on the other end of the line. "Give me back my money muthafucker or I'm going to kill this bitch first and then me and my boys are going to come down to that ranch of yours, rape all yo bitches and kill every last one of you muthafuckers before we burn the place to the ground!" the man yelled.

"Whoa, whoa, whoa! Hold up just a minute brother, now let's talk this out," Charlie said calmly.

"I ain't talkin' shit, muthafucker! I want my money or I want my dope! That's all I got to say!"

"We can work this out. Tell me where I need to come, and I'll come see you. Ain't no need for nobody to get hurt," Charlie reasoned.

I was impressed by how calm Charlie stayed through all this. He had told me about the deals he had to make to survive in prison. Now I was seeing one of those deals in action.

"We at the same bitch's house you left me waiting for you outside. You the one's been fuckin' her, you know where it is."

"I think you got the wrong Charles, Jack. But that's all right, I'll come down and talk to you. It's cool."

Family Man

"You got an hour, bitch!" The phone went dead.

"Dammit, Tex! What have you got me into this time?" Charlie spun around. I didn't see Tex anywhere.

"You going to take care of this, or you going to hide under that bed like a little bitch?" Charlie scolded.

Tex crept out and looked around cautiously.

"What the hell am I getting into?" Charlie pressed.

Tex went on to explain that he had set Rosina up to make a drug deal. He said he wanted to buy $100 worth of grass, which was about one kilo, but that his vending machine connection (Geno), would only sell him 25 at a time. He asked Rosina if he could borrow the $2500 from her, but she said she didn't have it. She told him she would make a few calls. Within minutes, Rosina had lined up a buyer for the whole 25 kilos.

Tex told Rosina that he knew a way to sweeten the deal. They would get the $2500 from her buyer, some guy named Bernard Crowe. I felt sick - the dumb sack of shit had ripped off Lotsapoppa. After he got the money from Crowe, she would stay behind while he went to make the buy for the grass. they would then sell Crowe 22 kilos at a markup of 25 bucks each and he would keep 3 kilos to share with the family.

To make it worth Rosina's time, he would pass a cool $200 to her just for setting up the deal. Once Tex got the money, he decided he would burn both Crowe and Rosina and keep both the grass and the money for himself.

The plan backfired once Crowe realized what had happened. Instead of just being pissed off, he held Rosina hostage and she told him about the ranch.

"Well, go over there and make this shit right," Charlie told him.

"He won't listen to me Charlie! There's three more of them. they'll kill me as soon as I walk in the door. Probably Rosina too! Then they'll come here and burn down the ranch. Maybe you can talk some sense into him!" Tex whined.

"You stupid asshole," Charlie fumed. "Come on, Shep, TJ. Let's go fix this shit."

I wasn't crazy about accompanying Charlie on a suicide mission, but I had seen Charlie talk people into, and out of, things that I wouldn't have thought possible. I also knew Lotsapoppa and thought maybe I could help settle him down.

Charlie picked up the .22 Buntline revolver and stuck it into the waistband of his pants and we hopped in Johnny's Ford. I had been to Rosina's apartment before so I offered to drive. Charlie rode shotgun and TJ jumped in the backseat.

Charlie was jumpy and fidgety all the way over. He was muttering under his breath and I couldn't make out whether he was going over what he was going to say or if he was still cursing Tex. Probably a little of both.

Being that it was in the early morning hours of the middle of the week, parking was not an issue this time. There were a few cars at the curb, but not many. Standing out conspicuously was the long black Cadillac that belonged to Bernard Crowe.

"Drive by it and come back around," Charlie instructed. "I want to make sure he don't have his boys outside to ambush us."

I did as he said and circled the block. there was no sign of movement or anyone in or near the car.

"That's good," he said. "Park in front of it and let's go in."

When we were all out of the car, Charlie repositioned the pistol at the back of his pants.

"Let me do all the talking," he said. "Both of y'all stand behind me. I don't want them to see the gun. I'm going to try to explain things to him, but if that don't work, on my signal, TJ, pull the gun out and shoot the bastard."

Both TJ and I nodded.

"Alright. Let's go."

Charlie made his way up the stairs to the apartment that I had told him belong to Rosina. My palms were sweating, but I noticed TJ was dripping wet, and I could see his hands shaking. At that point, I knew that TJ would be useless in the event of trouble. I'm sure Charlie knew it too. Charlie didn't knock. When he got to the apartment, he turned the knob, pushed the door open, and walked in with his hands up.

Crowe was beside a chair with a frightened Rosina sitting in it. Two mean looking guys that I didn't recognize were standing on each side of the door with their arms folded. It was a good thing Charlie had us standing behind him to block their view of the gun or things could have gotten ugly before they did. A big guy that I remembered as Bryn, was at the table on the other side of Rosina. I saw both recognition and confusion cross his face when he saw me.

"Let the girl go. Let's talk about this like men," Charlie began.

"I done told you this bitch ain't going nowhere unless you got my money or my dope," Lotsapoppa responded. Then, seeing me for the first time, his brow wrinkled.

"Shep, what the hell you doin' hanging with a jive ass bunch of bitches like this?

"Come on Poppa. You don't need to do this. Charlie will make it right," my voice portrayed more calmness than I felt.

"Now it's like this," Charlie started. "I ain't got it right now but I will get it to you, if you will just let me do it a little at a time."

"I need it now," Poppa replied.

"I ain't got it now, but if you give me some time, I can get it," Charlie reasoned.

"This ain't about me. I got other people to take care of. No bargaining. My money or my weed. I done told you, you ain't got that, I'm coming to burn that fucking ranch to tha ground," Poppa insisted.

"Does it take a life to settle this?" Charlie asked.

"Yeah. If you ain't got my money, it takes a life," Crowe answered.

Charlie reached behind him and pulled out the gun. He held it by the barrel and offered it to Lotsapoppa.

"Then here. I stand in my brother's place. If it takes a life, take mine. Just leave my people alone."

"Fuck that," Crowe stood up. He reached his right hand towards the gun. Charlie spun the pistol around and pulled the trigger.

Click.

Click.

A smile spread across Lotsapoppa's face and he began to laugh.

"Jive ass fucker wanna come after me with an unloaded gun," he said to his friends.

He took a step towards us and grabbed Charlie by the throat. As he did, Charlie fired again. This time the sound of the explosion from the gun coincided with the red explosion that appeared on Lotsapoppa's white shirt. his eyes grew large and he fell first to his knees, and then face down on the carpet. The other three guys stopped mid stride as Charlie swung the gun around wildly pointing at each of them. They held up their hands slowly and backed away. Charlie waved them all behind the table and waived Rosina out the door. All of them followed his directions. I went over to Lotsapoppa and kneeled beside him during the commotion. His eyes were open wide, and his breathing was ragged and shallow. I heard him breathe my name. I bent closer to him.

"Shep, get that crazy fucker outta here. Tell him I'm dead," he rasped.

"Charlie, come on," I said. "Let's get the hell out of here!"

Charlie stood still for another minute, his gaze shifting from one henchman to another. TJ was still frozen in the same spot he was when the gun went off. Charlie started backing towards the door but motioned for us to go out first. He took a step back inside and told Bryn that he liked his shirt and that he would really like to have a shirt like that.

"Go ahead, Brynn, give him the shirt. Just do it," said the other guy.

"Shit, Del, what the fuck?" said Bryn, disgusted, but he took off the shirt and tossed it to Charlie. Charlie struggled to put on the shirt and handed me the gun to keep them covered. It was a pullover buckskin looking thing that was probably drenched with sweat from the confrontation. TJ helped Charlie pull it over his head and rolled the sleeves up. The shirt was huge on him and hung all the way to his knees. He didn't take the shirt because he liked it, he took it because he could see the fear in their eyes and knew he could. I saluted them with the gun, and we all ran down the stairs and sped back to Spahn.

CHAPTER 56

The next day at the ranch was crazy. As much as Tex tried to avoid Charlie, their paths still crossed. Every time they did, Charlie would scream and berate him, telling him how stupid he was and because of him, he had been forced to kill a man. The biggest problem with this was the fact that he didn't bother taking Tex on a walk and talk, but screamed it out in front of whoever happened to be there. By mid-morning, everyone on the ranch knew about it. I pulled Charlie aside at one point to ask him why he was screaming about this when he had told me and TJ to keep it on the down low.

"That's for people out there, like your little girlfriend. People in here already knew about it. They're in the soul, so they already knew. It's in the thought. I ain't telling them something that they didn't already know," He explained.

I nodded and said, "Ah." If Charlie hadn't berated Tex so publicly, I doubted that "the soul" would have had a clue.

Everything went completely crazy after the news was announced that the body of a Black Panther had been found that morning. One of the girls had heard it on the news while she was in George's trailer. The unidentified man had died from a single gunshot wound and the body had been dumped in Canoga Park.

Charlie instantly went from pissed to paranoid. He let Tex have it even more. Not only had the dumb bastard made him kill somebody to clean up his mess, now he had brought the Black Panthers down on the ranch! Tex just stood there with his lip stuck out. He stared at the ground and his face turned red but he knew better than to speak at that time. He had fucked up and he knew it.

When a police car came cruising down the main drag, everybody scattered. Tex and Charlie took off to hide. I was one of the few that couldn't think of where to run, so I just stood there. I pictured going to jail as an accessory to murder. Crowe wasn't dead though. Nor did I think that he was a Black Panther. I was standing in the middle of the road, so they stopped beside me. Two cops got out of the car and walked to where I stood. The driver was tall and skinny while his partner was short and fat. I instantly named them Laurel and Hardy.

"What's your name, son?" the first Officer Laurel asked me.

"Uh, John. John McCartney," I answered, pulling the name from the two most famous Beatles. Everyone else at the ranch had an alias for just such an occurrence. Why shouldn't I?

"I hear you and your friends have been running an illegal nightclub here, Mr. McCartney. Is that true?"

I felt a flood of relief wash over me. For the past month or so, we had been operating a nightclub out of the saloon building. It had a stage and a dance floor so we figured we would make the most of it. Charlie, Clem, and I, along with Bobby when he was around, would play guitars and sing and the girls would play records in between our sets. The girls had decorated the place with black light posters and painted the ceiling black. They had added stars to make it resemble the night sky.

Word had gotten around, and people from town would show up. It was a bring your own booze place, but we charged 2 dollars at the door to get in. We had asked for George's permission to open the club and after some

207

reservation, he had agreed. We gave George half the money we made so I'm sure that influenced his decision. The door of the club was painted and decorated with poetry and words, including the name of the club - Helter Skelter. Dumbass Pat, however, had mistakenly spelled the first word with an added "a." Instead of "Helter Skelter," the door said, "Healter Skelter." While that was not such a big deal at the time, it would become a major point for the prosecution later.

"Uh, yeah," I answered. "It's just for kicks, though. We don't serve drinks or anything."

"Well...the problem, John, other than the fact that you don't have a license to operate a club, is that you don't check IDs either, looks like," said Officer Hardy.

He went on to explain that the previous night, two teenage boys had come to the club and had gone home wasted. They had ratted us out and their parents had called the cops and reported that we were running an illegal club.

"We're going to need to talk to Mr. Spahn," Laurel informed me.

I reluctantly took them over to George's trailer and turned them over to Squeaky.

"Can I go?" I asked.

"Did you have anything to do with giving those underage boys dope?" Hardy asked.

"No sir! I wasn't even here last night, I was over in Hollywood Heights!" Great. Not only had I blown my alibi, I had actually put myself at the location of the Crowe shooting.

"Then you're free to go, John."

I breathed a sigh of relief and went to find Charlie to tell him that we were in the clear.

George was beyond upset that we had brought the police to his door yet again. He promised them that he would make us shut down the club and apologized to the officers for their troubles. That must have been all they wanted because they drove away none the wiser about our involvement in the Crowe affair. That was the end of the Helter Skelter club though.

CHAPTER 57

In addition to the album that Charlie recorded for Terry Melcher, they had also decided that a great way to help create a buzz for that album would be to film a documentary of life at the ranch. Gregg Jakobson suggested this after spending so much time around the group. In light of the mobile recording failure, Terry had enthusiastically agreed.

Camera crews had spent days at the ranch over the past several weeks following everyone around and telling them to act natural, all the while giving them instructions on what to do. My shyness made me do my best to avoid being on camera. I preferred to watch what the crews were doing and learn how things worked behind the scenes anyway. I was extremely grateful in the coming months and years that I had never allowed myself to be filmed.

There was a camera man named Mike who saw the fun everyone was having and decided that he would like to participate in one of the LSD parties. Much like my own first experience with the drug, it did not go well for Mike. He started freaking out, saying that he was dying, and begging Charlie not to kill him. Charlie struggled to free himself from Mike's vice like grip on his feet, and tried to explain to him that no one was trying to kill him. Clem and I tried to take Mike out to the woods to get him away from everyone else and try to get him some peaceful scenery to bring him down. He insisted that only Charlie could save him. When Charlie came to try to comfort him,

Family Man

Mike went right back to screaming that Charlie was trying to kill him. I guess that's the wonders of LSD for you.

Once Mike finally came down from his high and went home, he took the film with him. We never saw Mike or the film again. Terry, after hearing Mike's tale and catching wind of the Lotsapoppa shooting, sent word back by Gregg that he was backing out of both projects. He was negotiating a network deal but he said that once the record company and TV producers heard that Charlie had shot someone, they wouldn't touch either one of them.

Charlie was irate. He said that Terry had gone back on his word, so he was dead to him. He gave his "your word is your bond and your bond is your life" speech. He raved and fumed, but within a few hours, he was laughing, singing and playing his guitar again like nothing had ever happened. I don't think Charlie wanted the trappings of stardom. I just think he wanted to play his music and that would be enough. He had never brought up the talk of fame and a record deal. That was pushed on him by first Dennis Wilson, then later, Terry Melcher, along with encouragement from people like Frank Zappa and Neil Young. Their thought had made its way into his thought. Now he was free of that and content just to play and sing. It was a long time before Terry or Gregg came back to visit us. A few of us did drop in on Terry at his new Malibu beach house from time to time. On one occasion, Dean Martin's daughter Deana was there playing the piano. She sang and played as beautifully as she looked. Terry did eventually come back to hang out with the family and partake of the offerings, just not until after we had moved the entire commune to Barker Ranch.

CHAPTER 58

The paranoia seemed to grow day by day. Charlie was still convinced that Lotsapoppa had been a Black Panther and that because he had killed him, his Panther brothers would be coming for us. He refused to believe me when I told him Poppa wasn't dead. He said that they would inflict all the carnage that Lotsapoppa had threatened. He ended up doing probably the worst thing he could have done under the circumstances.

He asked Danny DeCarlo if he could bring his motorcycle gang friends to the ranch to offer us protection. Charlie promised that the bikers could have sex with the girls any time they wanted and that we would share our grass and LSD with them. Obviously, Danny didn't have to make this offer twice. In a matter of days, both Danny's gang, the Straight Satans, and an affiliate Club, the Satan's Slaves, roared into the ranch.

Along with the "protection" the bikers brought, they brought even more with weapons, bad behavior, and hard drugs. While grass, LSD, and mushrooms had always been welcome, Charlie had tried to forbid drugs like cocaine and MDA. With the bikers' arrival, these became commonplace.

The bikers were really rough on the girls, too. Now don't get me wrong, I had seen Charlie slap a girl or two, but nothing like what the motorcycle gangs did. There had been plenty of orgies and girls asked to do "favors" before, but those were done willingly. The girls could opt out if they wanted. Now, I heard plenty of girls say "no," but were forced to comply anyway. I addressed this with Charlie, but he just said, "So long as they keep their mouth shut and do what they're supposed to do, they'll be fine."

Lookout posts were established at each end of the ranch. Guys were stationed at these posts night and day, armed with long range shotguns and rifles. Charlie insisted on this because he was so paranoid that the Black Panthers had us on their radar.

It got to the point that I would walk down to Corriganville Ranch, a couple miles away, if I were meeting up with Vicki. I didn't feel safe having her come to the ranch anymore. I didn't tell her about the Crowe shooting, I just told her that a bunch of bikers had moved in and that I didn't trust them. I think she knew that she wasn't getting the whole story, but to her credit, she never questioned me.

CHAPTER 59

I spent a lot of time away from the ranch over the next couple of weeks. I was very conflicted. On the one hand, the people that I had come to think of as my family were still there. On the other hand, a bunch of people that didn't belong and weren't part of our family were there, too. The whole vibe was different, just like a couple of years earlier in the Height, peace and love had turned to violence and fear, almost overnight.

I spent several nights a week at Vicki's. We even attended another party at Cielo. Again, Sharon and Roman were absent and Gibbie and Voytek were the hosts. My impressions of them were reinforced as they behaved virtually the same as the first time I had come in contact with them. There was the steady stream of many of the same celebrities with a few new faces thrown in and there was no shortage of whatever your drug of preference might be. This time the only strange occurrence happened as we were leaving. We ran into Pat Krenwinkel. She was with a couple of her friends that I had never met before and they were leaving from the guest house. They had spent the night there with an old friend of hers, a girl who she introduced as Debbie, and her boyfriend, Darrel, who Pat said was an old friend of the current caretaker. It was another one of those things that seemed insignificant at the time, but would play an important part in the events that were about to unfold.

When Vicki had to go out of town, I stayed a night or two at Gary Hinman's. Even the vibe at Gary's Place felt all wrong though. It always did without Bobby there, so when I went back by the ranch and saw that Bobby had returned, this time with a pregnant girlfriend named Kitty Lutesinger, I decided to go back.

Bobby and Charlie were as close as Charlie and I were. Bobby's easygoing attitude and smile had a way of disarming situations and Bobby always seemed to be able to figure things out. I pulled Bobby aside and apprised him of the recent events and told him how much the bikers had upset the balance of everything we stood for. He listened carefully and then said he would talk to Charlie and see if we could figure something else out.

I felt better after talking to him. I thought that if anybody could settle things down and help put things right around the ranch again it would be Bobby.

Boy, was I wrong.

CHAPTER 60

We took the bread truck down to Los Angeles. I believe the original purpose was to dumpster dive and pick up some supplies. Charlie, Squeaky, Sandy, and I were walking down the sidewalk when we came upon a Black Muslim.

The Black Muslims were religious and racial separatists. They preached the superiority of the black race. They mocked Christianity by saying the Christian God must be weak if he would allow men to nail him to a cross. They claimed Allah would have never done that. He went on to say that the overthrow of whites was contained in the Muslim holy book and that soon the "white devils" would be wiped off the face of the Earth.

If that wasn't enough to freak us out, around the next corner was a group of Black Panthers, wearing their black berets, with their fists in the air, yelling things like "the revolution has come" and "death to pigs!"

I looked at Charlie and he was deathly pale. We all turned and made a hasty retreat back to the bread truck and the safety of the ranch. We could get supplies another time.

That night at the ranch, Charlie held court. We were all sitting around the fire, many of us lost in thought after what had happened in town. Charlie was especially in a state of high awareness.

"War is not murder," he began. "What you do for a brother is not a sin or a crime."

Family Man

While I think he was trying to reinforce the fact that we should all stay alert and watch out for each other, I think he was also trying to justify in his own mind that he had shot Lotsapoppa to get his brother, Tex, out of a bind. That way it was not a sin or crime as long as it was in that thought. After all, if something is done in the name of love, how can it be wrong?

"I'm kind to kindness, I'm love to love, and a fool to a fool," he continued. "I love myself and now that's all of you. I can reflect bad and death and fear as well as I can reflect good and gentleness. Most people are raised to do right but don't know right from wrong because it's all programming. Right and wrong for who or what? On what level do you learn honor, grace or survival? Is Mama Lion wrong when she kills a deer to feed her baby? Good and evil is related to the balance for survival."

They were thought-provoking words for sure, some of the thought may have been applied a bit too literally by some who heard it. Maybe I didn't apply it literally enough.

CHAPTER 61

There was a group of over forty black people that showed up at the ranch that weekend. We rarely had any blacks at the ranch. Maybe a couple here and there, but never a party this big. We barely had enough horses for them to ride, a few even had to double up on one horse.

Charlie sent Clem and Bruce into the hills to watch them, but neither reported them doing anything that appeared suspicious at all. Charlie was concerned that they were a scouting party for the Black Panthers, but in retrospect, it was likely just a bizarre coincidence.

The same weekend, the long-gone Shorty Shea reappeared to introduce his new wife around the ranch. He said that she was a Las Vegas showgirl. What Shorty didn't tell anyone until his blushing bride came out of one of the trailers was that she was black. While normally that wouldn't have been a big deal, in light of recent events, it put more space and animosity between Charlie and Shorty. Charlie wasn't even sure that the lady Shorty introduced as Magdalena was even his wife. He was suspicious of her and thought that Shorty had brought Magdalena to the ranch to spy on us for the Panthers. The union between Shorty and his new bride was a rocky one and she left him after only a few weeks to return to her showgirl gig in Vegas. Nevertheless, the gap between Charlie and Shorty had widened to the point that it could never be bridged.

Magdalena and Kitty Lutesinger were not the only new faces to arrive in July. Gypsy had picked up a girl hitchhiking and brought her to live with us. She was a short, plain, but not totally unattractive girl named Linda Kasabian. Linda had a two-year-old little girl named Tanya and had just separated from her second husband, though she was only nineteen.

Linda reminded me of a more militant version of Sadie. She often talked of revolution and came already equipped with her own folding buck knife that she carried with her at all times. She was the first white person that I ever heard refer to the police as "pigs." We called them "the man" or "cops" and Gypsy referred to them as the "Blue Meanies," in reference to characters in The Beatles "Yellow Submarine" cartoon. While none of us had a fondness for the police, Linda snarlingly called them pigs and had a particular disdain for them. She was far from the "peace-loving hippie girl" that Vincent Bugliosi described her as at trial. She had been hardened by life already and seemed to have a chip on her shoulder all the time. Is it any wonder that she and Tex hooked up almost immediately?

CHAPTER 62

In the quest to acquire as many dune buggies as possible, Tex was the leader of the pack when it came to coming up with money. He had used the $2,500 he had bilked Lotsapoppa for to purchase a couple of dune buggies and bought some parts to convert a few more.

A couple of days after Linda had shown up, she and Tex had come up with a plan to steal $5,000 from her estranged husband, Robert Kasabian. Supposedly, her ex-husband and a partner had saved up the money to go to South America. Linda knew where he kept the money, so she and Tex went to her old house and stole it. Not long after they returned, an understandably angry Robert turned up with his friend at the ranch and demanded for "that thieving little bitch" to give him his money back. Once again, Tex was nowhere to be found and Linda hid behind Charlie, terrified. Charlie came to her defense saying that he didn't know anything about his money and that Robert should leave.

"Not without my money!" Robert yelled.

"I don't have your money so I guess you'll just have to kill me," Charlie said, producing the Buntline and offering it to Robert. I had seen this scenario play out before and I didn't want to see it end the same way. Clem and I eased our way up beside the two strangers.

"It'd be best if you just went back where you came from, friend," I told Robert. "There are things that are worth way more than money."

Family Man

The two men looked around to see that they were outnumbered and outgunned. They backed away.

"I'll be back, you crazy bastard, you'll see," Robert threatened.

"That would be a bad idea," Clem said, fingering the blade of his knife.

Fortunately, Robert took our advice. He must have gotten the hint that his life was more valuable than his money. I personally didn't want to see Charlie shoot someone else to clean up another one of Tex's messes. The $5000 never made its way to the group coffers. Tex and Linda had other plans for it. It became the seed money for what would become one of the most infamous crimes of the century.

In the neverending dash for cash, Bobby became the next player. Charlie always spoke of the evils of money and how people could lose their souls in the pursuit of the almighty dollar. In spite of his words, the quest to get to the desert as soon as possible and some very bad decision making, led us down that rabbit hole at breakneck speed.

Danny DeCarlo had mentioned to no one in particular that the Straight Satans were having a big anniversary party on Friday night, July 25th. He went on to say that the club had given him $1,000 to spend on some mescaline if anyone had a hookup. Bobby piped up and said that he had a connection that he could get the drug from before Friday if Danny was cool with $100 of the investment being used by the family.

"As long as my brothers and sisters have a good time, I don't care what you keep," Danny responded.

Bobby gave $100 to Charlie to buy dune buggy parts and took the other $900 to our old friend Gary Hinman up in Topanga Canyon. Gary told him he would have the mescaline to him by Friday afternoon. Bobby drove up to

Gary's on Friday and Gary produced the drugs. They returned to the ranch with big smiles on their faces.

"Your man hooked me up," Danny beamed, straddling his bike.

"Glad to hear it," Charlie replied. "Bobby's alright."

"Yes, he is," Danny grinned, roaring off to the Satans celebration.

In less than 24 hours, alright would go all wrong.

CHAPTER 63

Danny DeCarlo and a few of his biker friends roared up into Spahn the next day. It was late afternoon when Danny and a couple of his brothers came tearing into the saloon and went straight to Bobby and jacked him up against the wall. Bobby had been sitting at a table, playing strip poker with a couple of girls. Danny banged into the table, knocking drinks and cards flying in his haste to jerk Bobby up out of his chair.

"What the hell, man?!" Bobby exclaimed.

"Where the fuck did you get that dope?!" Danny growled.

For a biker, Danny was usually pretty laid-back, no one had ever seen him behave like this.

"What do you mean, man?" Bobby stammered.

"That shit was bad, man. Tell me who your dealer is. We're gonna go kill that son of a bitch," a huge dirty biker with a beard, who hadn't bothered to take off his sunglasses said. All three bikers were between me and Bobby and I was more concerned that they didn't go after one of the girls than I was with trying to save Bobby's hide.

"No dude, he wouldn't do that," Bobby protested.

Bobby's resistance got him nothing but his head banged back against the wall and a couple of hard backhanded slaps across the face.

"I'm telling you," Danny continued, "that shit was bad! Half of us have been puking our guts out all morning and one of our old ladies miscarried from that shit."

223

Charlie walked up to Danny. I wasn't sure how long he had been in the room or exactly what he had heard, but the sight of him made Danny relax his grip on Bobby. "Wait a minute, man," Charlie started, "Bobby wouldn't burn you, man. Let us work this thing out. If he got a bad batch, that's on the supplier. That ain't on Bobby here."

"That's who we want. Whoever he got his shit from," Beard and Sunglasses interjected.

"Well, you see it don't work like that. He's a friend too and I ain't sending a bunch of pissed-off dudes to go after a friend. Give us what's left and we'll take it back to him. If it's bad, he'll make it good," Charlie said.

They said that they had used it all and didn't have any to give back. Charlie told them that plenty of people in our group had used that same drug and none of them had gotten sick. They wouldn't hear of anything but getting their money back.

"Bobby," Charlie relented, "take a ride up the hill and tell Gary we gotta a little problem here and we need to get these cats their money back."

"Sorry about your old lady," Charlie said to the bikers. "Mistakes happen. You can't hold us accountable for something that was in the will of God."

The bikers looked at each other for a minute, then Danny let go of Bobby. "C'mon," Danny said to his companions. "Charlie's good for this, I'll stand for him." They turned and left the saloon, Danny turning back at the door. "Charlie," he began, "I can't hold them off forever."

"You do what you got to do, Danny. In other words, you live with your judgments and I'll live with mine, ya dig?"

Danny pushed through the saloon door and the motorcycles roared to life, slowly blending into the hum of a box fan sitting near the door. The room was silent until Charlie finally spoke up.

Family Man

"Shep. Take Bobby over to Gary's and let him straighten this out. If Gary don't give him no shit, drop him off and we can go get him later. Bobby, It's in your hands. Handle it however you have to, but get these bikers off our backs."

Bobby had gathered himself up by now. I went to locate a car and left Charlie and Bobby talking. I passed Bruce Davis going in as I was coming out.

An old Chevy that had appeared in the past few days was sitting outside and the keys were in it, so I pulled it around to the saloon. Bobby and Bruce exited together and both got in the car. I had barely started rolling when Susan and Mother Mary, who had not seen the confrontation in the saloon, came up to the car.

"Where are you going?" Susan inquired.

"To see Gary," Bobby answered without elaborating.

"Can we come?" Mary asked.

They didn't wait for an answer before hopping in the back seat. I liked having the girls along, even Sadie. Their presence helped ease the tension and almost made me forget that this was a business trip. We came to a stop outside Gary's Topanga Canyon home. Susan and Mary bounded out of the car and up the stairs to Gary's front door. Bobby remained behind in the car for a moment.

"Don't forget what you're here for," Bruce cautioned him.

"I won't," Bobby responded, unconsciously touching his jaw.

Bobby took a couple steps away from the car when Bruce called him back. Bruce produced a small caliber revolver and handed it to him.

"If he doesn't want to cooperate, show him this to prove that you're serious."

"I don't think I'll need that," Bobby protested.

"Just in case," Bruce said.

"Just in case," Bobby echoed, taking the gun from Bruce and tucking it under his shirt.

We sat and watched as Gary opened the door and welcomed Bobby and the girls in. He waved to me and Bruce and we waved back. Gary followed them in and shut the door behind them. I looked at Bruce.

"The last time we brought a gun along 'just in case,' Charlie ended up shooting Lotsapoppa," I reminded him.

"This'll be different," Bruce assured me.

I've wished a thousand times that I had stayed at Gary's, but I didn't. I shifted the car into drive and went back to the ranch.

CHAPTER 64

Around 1 a.m., the phone rang at the ranch. Assuming it was Bobby calling for me to come get them, I answered. It was Bobby, but he wasn't calling for a ride. He asked to speak to Charlie. I handed the phone over to him. After a few minutes of heated conversation, Manson hung up the phone.

Charlie and Bruce had been horsing around with the Satans' sword and a small tree branch that Bruce had fashioned into a sword of his own.

"Bruce, Shep. Let's go," Charlie was all business with this and the mood became somber immediately.

We walked over to the old Chevy to go back to Gary's. As we all got in the car, Bruce tossed his "sword" aside. Charlie did not. During the 20 minute or so ride over to Gary's, Charlie filled us in on what Bobby told him had happened in the hours since I had dropped them off.

Everything had gone cordially until Bobby had brought up the subject of giving back the $1,000. Gary denied that the drugs were bad and refused to give the money back. When Bobby pressed him on it, he insisted that he couldn't give it back if he wanted to because he had already spent it booking a religious pilgrimage to Japan to pursue his interest in Buddhism.

They discussed a few other things and then Bobby told Gary that the Satans were demanding their money back and that he seriously needed it. At this point, he followed Gary into the kitchen and pulled the gun out, out of sight of the girls, to prove his point. Gary grabbed the gun, trying to wrestle it away from Bobby and it went off. Jerking it away, Bobby then turned it around and hit Gary in the head with the butt of the revolver several times. Bleeding badly from the back and side of his head, Gary staggered back into the living room and sat down on a chair, holding his head. Bobby gave the gun to Sadie to hold on Gary while he went back into the kitchen to call Charlie and ask him what he should do next.

The conversation was interrupted when Bobby heard a struggle in the next room where Gary knocked the gun away from Sadie. Sadie then got on the phone to say that Bobby had reclaimed the pistol and was holding it on Hinman until we could get there. Relaying the story had taken up most of the drive so I didn't get to ask Charlie why we were there until we were going up the stairs.

"To teach Bobby how to be a man," he answered.

CHAPTER 65

Gary screamed for help when Mary opened the door for us. He must have thought we were there to rescue him. Ironically, I thought that's why we were there too. It seemed that way at first. When we went in, the others all went into the kitchen, leaving Charlie, Bruce, and me in the darkened living room with Gary.

"Please, Charlie! Bobby's gone crazy. Just please take him with you. I don't want any more trouble," Gary pleaded.

Gary looked at, and spoke to, only Charlie. He didn't even acknowledge that Bruce and I were in the room. Maybe he was in shock, maybe he didn't recognize us in the darkness, I'm not sure. The cuts on Gary's head looked bad, it was possible that he had a concussion.

"Well you see Gary, we got a little problem here," Charlie began. "You see, we got some pissed off motorcycle riders back at the ranch saying you sold 'em some bad mescaline."

"I didn't, I didn't know," Gary protested. Charlie cut him off.

"I'm telling you what's gonna happen, Gary. You're gonna give me that $1,000 back and we're gonna walk out of here."

"No, Charlie I don't..."

"I ain't asking you, I'm telling you! I been doing what you told me to do for twenty years. Now it's time for you to do what I say!"

"But Charlie..."

229

Gary then did something that after all these years, I still can't figure out why he did it. He reached for the sword. When he did, Charlie smacked him sideways across the left side of the face with it. Gary let out a wail that I'll never forget and fell to his knees grabbing his face. Charlie cursed and ran off to the kitchen, sucking the fresh cut to the index finger on his right hand and switching the sword to his left.

I immediately rushed to Gary's side. He was sobbing and howling like a wounded animal. "Gary! Why the hell did you go for the sword?" I cried. I only received wails and pieces of chants, which I assumed were Buddhist prayers, in response.

I finally pried Gary's hands away from his cheek to assess the damage. He reluctantly let me lower them. He was still on his knees, rocking slowly back and forth. I took off the shirt that I was wearing and used it to try to dab away the blood on Gary's face. As soon as I could staunch away some blood, a new stream took its place. I eventually ascertained that Gary had around a 5-inch gash extending from his lower jaw upwards. His left ear had been split in half, the lower part dangling sickeningly sideways.

Mary and Sadie came in from the kitchen with some towels. They coaxed Gary over onto his side, Mary resting his head in her lap while Sadie alternated between wet and dry towels, attempting to clean his wounds. After an hour or so, Gary quieted. While it had become quieter, a heaviness descended on all of us. Between the tension and the humidity, it felt like being covered with a wet blanket.

Charlie went over to Gary and squatted down next to him. He told him that if he didn't have the money to return to the Satans, we had to have something. Gary offered to sign over the pink slips of his Fiat and his Volkswagen van if we would just leave him alone. Bruce retrieved the titles from the drawer where Gary kept them and brought them over for him to sign.

"There," Gary said after signing the papers. "Now please just leave me alone."

Charlie took the papers and began his walk to the door. "No calling the cops Gary," Charlie told him. "This was a deal among friends and it's settled, right?"

"Yes. It's settled, just go. I won't call the cops, I promise," Gary assured him.

"Let's go," Charlie directed to me and Bruce.

"Charlie, he needs to go to a hospital," I suggested.

"Hospitals ask questions. Sadie, can you fix him up?" he called back.

"I saw some dental floss in the bathroom," she offered.

"He'll be alright. Y'all take care of Gary and come on back to the ranch when he's feeling better. If he'll come with you that would be good."

We left the house, none of us speaking. Charlie took the keys to the Fiat and he and Bruce drove back in it. I returned in the Chevy that we drove up in. I sat in the car a long time once I got back to the ranch. The first hints of a sunrise were appearing behind the Santa Susana Mountains before I drug myself from behind the wheel. I trudged up to one of the outlaw shacks to spend the rest of the night alone. I could still hear Gary's screams of pain. The good news was that the problem had been solved. We could sell the cars to pay off the Satans and Mary and Sadie would nurse Gary back to health. At least those thoughts helped me go to sleep that night.

231

CHAPTER 66

Sunday evening, I saw Bobby at the ranch. I had spent a good part of the last three years around him, but this was no longer the Bobby I knew. His eyes were glazed over and he was moving around as if he were in a trance.

I made several attempts to talk to him. I hoped to find out what was going on with him and whether I could help. I had witnessed Bobby stoned on multiple occasions. This was different. He would walk right by me without even acknowledging my presence. He wasn't just avoiding me either, he was avoiding everyone. I kept thinking of an old zombie movie that I had watched once, *Night of the Living Dead*. Bobby was the living dead. Since I couldn't get to Bobby, I tried to track down the girls. Mary was nowhere to be found. No one had seen her all day. Someone said she might be back with the children. Eventually I found Susan and cornered her.

"What's wrong with Bobby?" I asked.

"He's just going through some changes," she responded. She was avoiding the question. I grabbed her by both arms and pinned her back against the wall. The smirk on her face made me want to hit her, but I didn't. I had been taught that you didn't hit women. Sadie had a way of making that difficult sometimes.

"What kind of changes?!" I demanded. "What the hell is wrong with him?!"

"He's adjusting to the fact that Gary is floating in the cosmos," she said.

Family Man

I let go of her. Susan lied all the time. She must be lying now. If she wasn't lying, she was saying that Bobby had killed Gary. I couldn't accept that fact. I knew Bobby, and I knew that he did not have that in him.

"You're lying," I told her. "Why do you always say such stupid shit?"

"What's the big deal, Shep?" she spat back. "There's no such thing as death!"

She pushed by me. I stood there unbelieving. This couldn't have happened. I knew Gary was in bad shape when we left, but there was no way he should have died from those wounds. Maybe he had set up an infection. If that was the case, surely they would have taken him to the hospital. If he died from an infection that wasn't Bobby's fault. That had to be it. Bobby was feeling guilty for hurting Gary and was blaming himself for Gary's death. I had to find Bobby and talk to him. It was an accident; it must have been. I had to help him realize that. I had completely convinced myself that I had figured out what happened. When I did get to talk to Bobby, I found out that I was completely wrong.

I came upon Bobby over by the horse stables. He was sitting behind the wheel of Gary Hinman's Fiat. The car wasn't running. Bobby was just sitting there, looking straight ahead with a thousand-yard stare. I Spoke to him several times before he responded.

"Bobby."

No response.

"Bobby!"

Nothing.

"Bobby, can I get in? C'mon man, let's talk."

He remained in his zombie-like state. A small murmur escaped from his lips. I wasn't sure if it was a yes, but I took it as such. I opened the door of the Fiat and sat down.

"Bobby, you gotta talk to me, man."

"I fucked up, Shep."

"Tell me what went down, man, let me see if I can help."

"It's all on me man. Gary was gonna tell on us. There was no way out.

"What did you do?" I knew the answer but I needed to hear Bobby say it.

"I killed Gary, man. I held a pillow over his head. Now he's gone. He was my friend. He didn't do anything to deserve this."

Bobby went on to tell me that they had stayed at Gary's all of Friday night and Saturday. He and the girls had tried to take care of him. They tried to talk him into coming and living at the ranch. Barring that, they tried to ensure that he would not call the cops or tell anybody about what had happened.

Gary initially agreed to this, but as he began to recover his strength, he became defiant again. He told them that he was calling the cops and that we were all going to go to jail.

Bobby called the ranch again late Saturday night and spoke to Charlie. He asked what he should do.

"Be a man," Charlie told him. "You don't need me to tell you what to do. Follow your love. Do what it tells you to do."

The next morning, Gary was feeling even better and confronted Bobby in the hallway.

"I stabbed him, man. I stabbed him right in the heart. I didn't know what else to do. I drug him into the living room. He refused to die, so I held a pillow over his face to make him stop breathing."

Bobby then told the girls, who had stayed in the kitchen while all this was happening, to wipe the place down and try to erase all signs of them being there.

Family Man

They wiped down the house and bagged up all the evidence they could think of, including their bloody clothing. Bobby stuck his palm in Gary's blood and fashioned a paw print on the wall. He then took a hand towel from Gary's kitchen and wrote the words "Political Piggy" in Hinman's blood. The intention was to make it look like the Black Panthers committed the crime. As they were leaving, they heard the loud, raspy sounds of Gary breathing.

"I can't go in there again," Bobby had told the girls.

Sadie and Mary then took turns holding the pillow over Gary's face until he was dead. Sadie returned to the kitchen and informed him, "It's all over." Bobby then called the ranch asking if someone could come give them a ride back.

"You're on your own, Jack," Charlie told him. "I ain't coming to get you and I ain't getting nobody else into this. You did what you did and that's your cross to carry."

Charlie had taken the keys to both of Gary's cars when he left, forcing Bobby to hot-wire Gary's VW van to get it started. After spending the $20 bill they had taken from Gary's wallet for food, they returned to the ranch.

"I knew I'd end up going to prison," Bobby said. "Gary would tell on me for sure. He would tell on Charlie and everyone else. It was at that point I realized I had no way out."

I sat in stunned silence. I'm not sure how long I joined Bobby in his zombie stare through the bug-stained windshield of the Fiat. I eventually got out and left Bobby sitting there. I didn't say a word to him. What was there to say?

CHAPTER 67

Gary's death affected all of us in different ways. Word had spread fast and by late Sunday night, almost everyone knew about it. Things had changed so fast. There was a darkness of mood that had overtaken us all. Charlie must have spoken with Bobby either shortly before or after I had. We had become so close that our thoughts almost intertwined.

"I've got to get away, Shep," Charlie said. "I'm going up north for a while. I can get some stuff up there to give the bikers. That should get them off our backs. Man, I gotta clear my head. I'll be gone a few days."

"I was thinking the same thing," I agreed. "I just can't be here right now. I need a day or two to process all this."

"Bobby left," he informed me.

"Did he say where he was going?"

"No. I didn't want to know. I don't think he knows."

"I get that," I responded.

Charlie straightened and gave me a weak smile.

"He needs to just keep going, don't look back," he said.

"Yeah, he does," I concurred.

"Shep, old friend, I'll see you soon."

"Yeah. I'll be back," I promised.

"I know you will."

Charlie climbed aboard the bread truck and headed north. I called Vicki and asked her if she could pick me up. I told her I just needed to get away for a few days. She said of course she would. I told her I would start walking in her direction and she could pick me up off the side of the road. I was relieved that she didn't ask why. I felt that I could not stand being on the ranch for one more minute right then. We hung up and I hit the road.

The toot of a horn and a lady's voice brought me back to earth. Vicki slowed the Corvair and I got in. We rode silently the rest of the way to her apartment. I'm sure she sensed that I needed time to think, and she gave it to me. After a couple of hours, I started a trend that I would continue for the next several months – lying to my girlfriend.

"What's wrong Shep?" she finally asked. "Even the most patient people can only wait so long."

"My friend Gary is dead," I told her.

"Oh no! What happened?"

"I'm not really sure. He was found dead at his house. I think somebody killed him."

"My God! That's terrible, do they know who did it?"

At this point, it would be another 24 hours before the body was discovered. I didn't even think about that. I had to tell her, she knew I was hurting. Behind every lie is a little bit of truth, right? I gave her as vague a story as I could, telling her truthfully that a mutual friend had told me about it.

"I just need to be away from the ranch for a while," I explained. "Everybody is so bummed out there about Gary's death that I needed a happier place."

"I'll do anything I can," she consoled me. "I am so sorry about your friend. I can only imagine what you're going through."

In a little over a week, she wouldn't have to imagine how it felt to lose a friend. She would know the experience first-hand.

CHAPTER 68

I stayed with Vicki the rest of the week. Other than the time she spent at work, we were inseparable. For the first time in almost two years, I began to give serious thought to leaving the ranch.

Everything had changed. It seemed like just days ago that everything was fun and games and there was hardly a care in the world. Now, Charlie had shot Lotsapoppa and Bobby had killed Gary. Even though I doubted that we were on the Black Panthers' radar, as Charlie believed, the Straight Satans were a whole different story. I had no idea what they might do if we couldn't come up with their money, but I knew that it wouldn't be good.

As the days passed, my mood began to lighten. As Sunday turned to Monday and Monday turned to Tuesday, I began to rationalize what had happened at Gary's.

Just like at Poppa's, I was there but I hadn't harmed anyone. I had no clue that things would get violent at either place and there was no blood on my hands. I couldn't bring Gary back. I could only hope that Bobby and the girls had done a good enough job covering their tracks and that they would get away with it. I had already lost one friend forever; I didn't want to lose another. I would rather never see or hear from Bobby again than to see him go to the gas chamber, or spend the rest of his life in prison. Tuesday night I was almost feeling like myself again, then Wednesday rolled around.

On the evening news, it was announced that Bobby Beausoleil had been arrested in connection with the Gary

Hinman slaying. Gary's car had been spotted, stopped on the side of the road, on Route 101 between San Luis Obispo and Atascadero. The car had broken down and Bobby had climbed in the back seat to go to sleep. He was still asleep in the broken-down Fiat when the cops found him. Some of Gary's friends had found the body late Monday and reported the cars stolen. The knife Bobby had used to stab Gary was hidden in the spare tire well in the trunk of the car. It still had Gary's blood on it.

CHAPTER 69

Vicki was appalled at what she had just heard. I had to do my best to perpetuate the myth that I was hearing this news for the first time. She never met Bobby but she had heard me talk about him on a regular basis. I couldn't pretend that I didn't know him.

"I don't believe it!" I explained. "There's no way Bobby could have done this. We were all friends!"

I felt like a complete shit putting on this performance for her, but I couldn't just tell her that I already knew about it. I thought back to Charlie telling me to never lie. Now it registered even more why he said that. Once you told a lie, you had to keep telling more just to cover your ass from the first one.

"Oh, Shep," Vicki cried. "I am so sorry. What in the world could have happened?"

"I don't know. I don't believe it." And I wouldn't have, if I hadn't heard it from Bobby's own mouth. "They have to have the wrong guy." And the hole got deeper.

Vicki took me in her arms and we held each other. I relished the opportunity to not have to look her in the eyes. Maybe burying my head in the softness of her hair would help me keep my big, fat, lying mouth shut. The rest of the night was spent in quiet, my eyes downcast. Vicki thought that I was dealing with the shock and grief of one of my friends killing another one. I found it preferable for her to think that than to know that I was actually just wallowing in the self-pity and guilt that I felt for betraying her.

Family Man

I lay awake in bed that night listening to the soft sounds of Vicki's breathing. The thoughts were running through my head like a hamster on a wheel. Should I turn myself in? But to what point? I promised Charlie that I wouldn't lie and I wouldn't snitch. We had made that bond in brotherhood. I couldn't betray him, too. Would Bobby spill his guts and implicate Mary and Susan? What about Charlie? Would he even include me and Bruce even though we didn't actually participate? Bobby was our brother. We could trust him to keep quiet, couldn't we?

What if I just left the ranch? Would that make things better, or worse? And what about Vicki? Should I come clean and tell her the truth about everything? Would she understand, or would she hate me forever? I heard the clock alarm at 6:30 am. I had still not been asleep.

I got to sleep a little while after Vicki left for work. The guilt lifted some without having her lying there beside me. The phone woke me up a little after noon.

"Hey!" Vicki's voice came from the other end of the line. "Did you get some sleep? I noticed you were restless all night so I let you sleep in."

Great. More guilt.

"Yeah, I'm sorry. I hope I didn't keep you awake too much."

"Here and there, but not too bad," she responded. It wasn't like her to call during her work day.

"That's good," I said. "What's up?"

"Well, Jay has bought some kind of fancy new video machine where you can watch movies at your house. Isn't that crazy? He asked if we would like to come over and break it in with him tonight. I thought that might help you get your mind off things."

I thought it sounded crazy too, but that was when Charlie had shown up with one at the ranch. Another thing I decided not to tell her. In this case, I didn't really think it mattered. Charlie told me about it and what it was, but I hadn't watched it with him. I didn't even know if he had.

"Sure. Sounds fun," I replied. "I could use a stress-free evening."

"Great, I'll tell him that we're in."

A stress-free evening. There was no such thing for me anymore and I should have known better. Vicki and I arrived at Jay's house just before seven. Amos, the butler, opened the door for us and directed us to the living room.

Sharon Tate was sitting on the sofa. She turned around and gave a little wave and smile. Jay welcomed us and introduced me to his other two guests, Abigail Folger and Voytek Frykowski. I had seen Abigail and Voytek at several of the parties at Cielo, but had never formally met them.

Abigail gave us a friendly smile. She was polite, but seemed a little distant. Voytek was off in his own world. Jay introduced us, snapped his fingers in front of his face and waved his hand in front of him, but Voytek never even blinked. Abigail, or Gibbie, as everyone else called her, was a little put off and embarrassed by his behavior. Jay explained that Voytek was doing a 10-day MDA experiment and was currently on day six.

"What's the experiment?" I asked. "To see how many brain cells you can destroy and still function?"

Sharon laughed softly and Vicki turned red. Apparently, no one else got the joke.

"We never really had an end goal in mind," Jay mused. "I'm on day 3 myself. I guess we just wanted to see what it would be like to be high for an extended period of time without coming down."

Jay, strangely, was showing little effects of their experiment. I expected Gibbie would have to be wiping the drool from Voytek's chin within the next few days, if not the next few minutes. Maybe that explained her distance.

I enjoyed seeing Sharon Tate again. Her big brown eyes and bright smile could really light up a room. I didn't realize how long it had been since I had last seen her until I noticed that she was probably eight months into her pregnancy.

Amos rang a bell in the dining room and we went to have our seats at the dinner table. It took Gibbie several minutes, and more than a few tugs on Voytek's sleeve, to snap him awake enough to join us. It was as if he were listening to music that only he could hear.

We were having steak and it was nothing short of fantastic. When Vicki and I went out we ate well, but nothing like this. Tender filet mignon with twice baked potatoes and fresh garden salads followed by a key lime pie were the evening's courses. I can only imagine how much this meal must have cost.

On the ranch, we ate mostly vegetarian. Meat was rarely thrown into dumpsters and when it was, it was usually spoiled. Occasionally, we would get lucky and find some hamburger or pork chops still on ice and have a nice treat. Charlie practiced a mostly vegetarian lifestyle due to his love of animals, but he was also strictly against wasting food. If meat was found, he was okay with eating it.

After the meal, Jay told Amos that once it was cleaned up, he could go for the night. I would estimate that he left a little before 8:30 p.m. Jay ushered all his guests into his master bedroom. There, he proudly showed us his brand-new RCA video cassette player. Dennis Wilson had given Charlie a very similar one a few months back. Sharon commented that Jay's was even nicer than the one her husband, Roman, had at their house. While most people were unaware that video cassette players even existed in the late 60s, now I knew three people who had one.

243

Chuck W. Chapman

Jay said that he had paid $5,000 for the machine, so he thought it deserved a party for its christening. He broke open a bottle of champagne and proposed a toast to the second-best form of entertainment that you could have in the bedroom. We clinked glasses to celebrate the occasion and settled into our places to watch the movie.

"What are we watching?" Sharon asked.

"You'll see," Jay replied mischievously and went to load the tape. He had just closed the lid when there was a loud pop and the lights flared really bright for a moment before dimming to very dim and staying there.

"What in the hell?!" Jay exclaimed.

The tape machine light had gone out and the television screen had gone to static.

"Just a minute," Jay said. He looked thoughtful for a moment and then walked toward the door. "I'm going out to see what's going on."

Vicki and I got up and followed him out. The street lights were still bright, and we could see neighbors houses through the trees. It was only Jay's house that had gone dark. In the quiet of the evening, we could hear a rustling in the ivy behind Jay's house, near the road. It sounded like a couple of large animals running through the vegetation. We rushed around to the side of the house and looked in that direction. Jay had brought a golf club and brandished it over his head, ready for whatever wild beasts we might encounter. Nobody saw anything. However, I could have sworn that I heard a man's voice say my name.

"Hello," I called. "Is anyone there?"

We waited a few minutes, but there was no reply so we went back into the house. Jay phoned an electrician that said he would be right over to check things out.

Paul Greenwell, Jay's electrician, arrived a little after 9:30 p.m. He looked around and said that there were some large nicks in the wires leading inside. Once we told him

244

what we had heard, he said it could have been a wild animal but that it looked like someone had tried to cut the power to Jay's house. He could fix it tonight, but it would take a few hours. Movie night was off.

Sharon and Gibbie discussed going to The Daisy, a popular nightclub in L.A., for a while. They asked if we wanted to accompany them but we declined. As far as I know, Voytek and the girls went there while Jay stayed home for the electrician to fix his power. Vicki and I went back to her place.

Once we were in the car, I asked Vicki again, "While we were outside, during the rustling, you didn't hear someone say 'Shep!' like they were trying to be quiet?"

"No babe," she answered. "I heard the rustling but I didn't hear anyone say anything. I think it was probably a mountain lion. They wander down out of the hills sometimes looking for food. You were imagining things. You've had a rough week."

That was a major understatement. What neither of us knew yet was that the bad week had just gotten started.

CHAPTER 70

Vicki got a call early Saturday morning from her mother. Her father had suffered a heart attack and was in the ICU in Sacramento. Vicki said that she would drive down immediately and asked what I wanted to do. I told her to drop me back off at the ranch. I had, after all, committed to working for George Spahn and had done nothing of the sort all week long. Even though I was having second thoughts about whether I would continue to live there, I did miss my friends and wanted to check up on them. I had a place to go if I wanted out. Many of them did not.

I started throwing some bales of hay around immediately upon my arrival, before I even spoke to anyone. I had just begun this task when I saw Charlie drive up in the bread truck. He disembarked, followed by a girl who looked a few years younger than me.

"You came back," he stated.

"I told you I would," I reminded him.

"How long you been here?" he asked.

"Ten, fifteen minutes," I answered.

He introduced his new "young love" as Stephanie. He had picked her up near Santa Barbara and said she would be staying with us for a while. Our conversation was interrupted as a swarm of the girls descended on Charlie. They had basically ignored my arrival but came out of the woodwork when Charlie pulled up.

All of them were talking at once. Sadie, Linda, Mary, Leslie, and Squeaky informed Charlie of Bobby's arrest. I pretended this was the first I had heard of it. My acting skills were improving on a daily basis. Linda went on to repeat the phone conversation she had with Bobby from jail. As of now, she said, he was only being held as a suspect and had not been formally charged with Gary's murder. The girls told us that they had thought about something. What if other crime scenes looked the same as Gary's? Then wouldn't the police have to release Bobby? Wouldn't that prove that he couldn't have killed Gary after all?

"That's crazy talk," Charlie said. "What we need is some more money to get Bobby a good lawyer."

Even though we still hadn't come up with the money for the straight Satans or to make our move to the desert, I still had to agree with Charlie. "The cops will never fall for something like that," I argued.

"It would work!" Sadie protested. "What if they wrote words like 'Political Piggy' on the wall again? Then the cops would think that the Black Panthers did it, just like you said!"

"You fucking people are gonna get me sent right back to prison," Charlie countered. "I'm loading up my shit and getting the fuck out of here. I ain't going back to prison cause a bunch of kids can't handle their own problems."

"You can't go. Love is one," Squeaky spoke up. "We are one soul, one love."

Charlie and I looked at each other. I could see in his eyes what I felt in my heart. The sinking feeling that we were all going to go down together.

"Shep, help me grab my shit out of the truck, will you?" Charlie sighed.

I didn't answer. I just did as he asked. I noticed that someone else had remained silent through all this. Tex Watson was standing there the whole time, but never uttered a word. Charlie and I walked by him carrying Charlie's bags.

"Hey man, how are you?" Charlie spoke.

Tex's head lolled around for a minute before his eyes focused on us. A stupid smile spread slowly across his face.

"Hey! Charlie, you're back!"

Charlie and I traded a quick glance. Tex had been standing right there the whole time.

"Guess you heard about Bobby, right?" Tex drawled.

Pause. Another glance.

"Yeah, I heard about Bobby. Tough way to see a brother go down," Charlie replied.

"Did you see the girls? Have you talked to them yet?" Tex asked, oblivious to the conversation that had just taken place 6 feet in front of him.

"Yeah, I talked to them. What they do, they do on their own. I ain't going back to jail again," Charlie answered.

"How's your head, Tex?" I interjected. "You okay, man?"

"Sure man," Tex said. "I'm on my feet and talkin' ain't I?" He stared at me, his mouth hanging half open for a minute before continuing. "Well, I got a plan. You see, these fuckers stuck me and Linda on a drug deal a couple nights ago and I'm…."

"Don't tell me about it. Either be a man and do what you got to do, or shut the hell up," Charlie interrupted.

"Well, I was going to give you…."

"Listen," Charlie cut him off again, "you remember that little deal I did for you? Bobby is my brother. You owe me, you pay it back to Bobby."

Charlie and I headed to the boardwalk. Mary and Sandy were outside laughing at Clem doing imitations of the ranch hands.

Family Man

"Everybody's bummed about Bobby," Charlie said. "Why don't you go into town and see if you can talk to him? Get a couple of credit cards from Squeaky and buy some zuzu's and trinkets to cheer everybody up."

The girls went to do what he had asked. Zuzu's were what Charlie and the girls called candy. I never asked why; it never mattered. Charlie went back to show Stephanie around the ranch and I went back to finish my chores.

I worked until almost dark. I had just gotten cleaned up and walked inside when the phone rang. It would have been somewhere around 10 p.m. It was Sandy. She and Mary had gotten arrested for using the stolen credit cards. Charlie was livid. He stormed out and was kicking and stomping around outside yelling at no one in particular. I thought I would give him some time to cool off before trying to talk to him. Maybe half an hour or so later, Pat came in and made a phone call. I overheard her talking to a guy named Bill. I missed the first part of the conversation, but caught the end of it.

"Look out the window and see if her car is there," Pat told him.

"Okay. We're coming over there later. Make sure you stay inside," Pat instructed.

At the time I heard this, I thought Pat was telling Bill not to leave because she was coming to visit him. I soon discovered that wasn't what she was saying at all.

CHAPTER 71

After half an hour or so, I went out to look for Charlie. It took me a while to find him. He had been in one of the trailers with Stephanie and was coming down the steps when he saw me.

"I was just about to come looking for you," he offered.

"Yeah? I was looking for you. I wanted to give you time to cool off," I answered.

"I need you to do me a favor," he said.

"Sure, what do you need?" I asked.

"I need you to go check on Tex and the girls."

"Where are they?"

"They went up to Terry's old place. Tex and Linda were pissed about some people up there ripping them off and said they were going there to collect from them."

A lump formed in my throat. Terry's old house. That was where Sharon Tate lived now. It didn't register at first. Sharon was eight months pregnant; she wouldn't be involved with any drug deals. Then it hit me. Voytek and Abigail were staying there with Sharon while her husband was away. Jay would more than likely be there, too. Jay had mentioned in passing last night that he and Voytek were working on a big deal with Joel Rosteau. That had to be it. Linda and Tex had gotten burned by Jay and/or Voytek. My thoughts went back to what the electrician had said last night at Jay's, "It looks like someone tried to cut the lines."

"How did they go?" I asked.

Family Man

"They took Johnny's old Ford," Charlie answered. "Sadie and Katie went with them."

Shit. Tex, Sadie and Katie. The three speed freaks. Great. It took me a few minutes to locate another operational vehicle, but when I did, I stopped back by Charlie.

"You coming with me?" I asked.

"I don't want to be a part of whatever they got in mind. Just try to get there and make sure Tex doesn't do something crazy."

I hit the accelerator and sped off towards Cielo Drive. It was quiet when I cut the engine and coasted into place in front of Johnny Swartz's old Ford. It was near the end of the street facing away from the gate. I listened for a moment then got out and started walking towards the gate. I noticed two cables hanging loosely from a power pole on my left. I was just about to push the button to open the gate when Linda came scrambling down the embankment on the right and grabbed me.

"Holy shit, you scared the hell out of me!" I gasped.

"Shep, you gotta help," she pleaded.

"Whoa, what's happened?" I asked.

"It was going good. We opened the door and walked right in. Voytek was in the living room and Tex told him we needed the money back. The other guy and two girls came in and it was cool, but now they're fighting. I'm afraid they're going to hurt Tex! Come on. Quick!" she said, turning and running back towards the house.

I hurried up the embankment after her automatically instead of using the gate like I had planned. As I descended the other side, I could hear Tex and Jay arguing on the front porch. When I regained my feet, I saw that they were not just arguing. They were fighting. The hedges on either side of the front door kept them confined to a small area. Then all hell broke loose. Even in memory, it seems that everything happened at once. I heard a scream and saw Sharon Tate at the door, with Sadie trying to hold her back. Sadie had her black-tape-handled knife held on Sharon. In the struggle, Sadie had slashed Sharon's cheek before they quickly disappeared back inside the house.

Almost immediately, the space was filled with Voytek running through the doorway, slamming into Tex and Jay, knocking them both into the hedge beside the door. A gunshot rang out and Jay fell to the porch. Tex stood up and started kicking Jay brutally in the face. The force of the impact caused Voytek to lose his balance, stagger and fall face-first onto the grass. Abigail came running from the pool area, blood pouring down the front of her white nightgown. Pat was chasing her with an upraised knife. By the time I looked back, Tex had abandoned Jay and was on top of Voytek, stabbing him over and over.

"Please make it stop!" Linda screamed.

The last minute or two seemed to have played out in silence and slow motion. Linda's scream brought me back to the moment. I started to run towards Tex when, immediately to my left, I heard tires squeal. I saw the white flash of a Nash Rambler smash backwards into the white picket fence then head straight for me. Before I could get out of the way, the car shot forward then slammed on brakes, but not before knocking me to the ground.

"Please! I won't tell anyone!" I heard the driver plead. I then heard a scream of pain that was quickly silenced by four gunshots in rapid succession. The motor came to an abrupt halt.

I brought myself to my hands and knees, struggling to get back to my feet as the chaos continued around me. My head pounded and I felt as if I were going to be sick. The next thing I remember is seeing Tex's cowboy boots inches from my face. I looked up.

Family Man

"What the fuck are you doing here, Shep?" he growled down at me.

"Charlie told me to come check on you," I replied weakly.

"Well, I don't need no babysitter," he spat.

Pat came rushing from the direction of the guest house.

"It was empty. Nobody was home," she said.

"What about those fucking dogs?" Tex asked. I heard the muffled barking of two or three dogs coming from that direction for the first time. "Who's taking care of them?" Tex turned and took a step in that direction before Pat stopped him.

"That's him in the car," she said. "Come on, let's go." I felt a couple of hands tugging on my arms. Sadie and Linda pulled me upright.

"Come on Shep, we got to go," I heard Sadie say through the fog in my head.

"Sharon?" I asked looking around.

"Everybody's dead," she said calmly. "Let's go."

I don't remember getting in the car or driving back to the ranch. The only thing I remember, before finding myself back at Spahn, was at some point I heard Linda say, "Fuck, I lost my knife."

CHAPTER 72

I must have been in shock. I sat in the car until I heard the four doors of Johnny's old Ford slamming behind me. Charlie must have heard them too, because I saw him coming out from the saloon. I numbly opened my door and got out.

Sadie was the first one out of their car and approached Charlie with vigor. She proceeded to tell him all about the events of the night and how they had "offed five pigs," concluding with, "Oh Charlie, we did it! I took my life for you."

"You fucking cunt," Charlie explained, looking at her incredulously. "All you've done for me is sent me back to prison."

Sadie poked her lip out and disappeared into the saloon. Linda and Pat looked exhausted from the evening's activities.

"I just want to go to bed," Pat resigned.

Linda silently stared at the ground.

"Go on," Charlie told them and they walked away. Sadie came back out a few minutes later with a bucket and sponge and started washing down the car.

"What about you?" Charlie asked Tex.

"It was crazy, Charlie," Tex smiled. "It sure was Helter Skelter."

"Did you cover your tracks?" Charlie questioned.

"Linda threw our clothes and knives out the window over a cliff," Tex answered.

"I mean at the house. Did you wipe the place down before you left?"

"Huh?" Tex gazed at him dumbfounded.

"Did you get rid of any fingerprints, confuse the scene, leave something witchy?" Charlie demanded.

"Oh. I didn't think about that," Tex admitted.

"You stupid fucking hillbilly! You're gonna get us all sent to the gas chamber. Get in the fucking car! Shep, come on."

"I'm not going back up there," I protested.

"I'm not taking this stupid bastard without some help. You're my brother, Shep. I need you."

I gave in and reluctantly got back in the car. On the drive over Charlie asked if they had at least gotten what they came for. Tex admitted that they had not.

"We got a couple hundred dollars and a few grams of weed," he explained. "But they said the whole shipment of MDA hadn't arrived. Then Sebring made a move on me and things got all crazy. I didn't have a chance to look for any more."

Tex went on to say that after leaving Cielo, they had attempted to go by Jay's house to see if the stash was hidden there. They had accidentally gone up the wrong street. When they attempted to cut through a neighbor's yard to go in the back way a man came out and asked what they were doing. Tex spotted a garden hose in front of the house. Thinking quickly, he told the man that they were walking and had just stopped in his yard to get a drink of water. Seeing the car sitting at the curb a short distance away, the man didn't believe him. He followed them back to the car and tried to take the keys. Tex sped away and gave up on the idea of breaking into Jay's house.

Johnny Swartz's Ford rolled up to the gate at Cielo for the second time that night. Charlie cut the engine and waited, listening for anything that sounded out of the ordinary. The place was eerily quiet. After a couple minutes he nodded and we got out, closing the doors softly. Charlie reached to push the gate button, but I warned him of the bell that sounded when the gate opened. Tex claimed that he had pushed the button when they left and didn't hear a bell. Charlie said we weren't taking any chances so we scaled the bank again.

I froze when I saw the bodies of Abigail Folger and Voytek Frykowski lying on the grass. I had just spent time with these people last night. Now they were gone at the hands of people I considered to be my family. I noticed for the first time that the bright Christmas lights that had lined the property since Terry Melcher had lived there were still on, mocking the bodies on the lawn.

Charlie took a slow look around, noticing the lights on in the guest house. "Did you go in there?" he asked.

"No," Tex replied. "Katie checked it. It's all locked up. That's the caretaker in that car." He pointed to the Rambler. At that time, we had no reason to doubt his assessment.

"Let's go," Charlie replied in acknowledgement and we headed for the house.

"I need to wait out here," I begged. "I can't go in that house."

"I need you inside," Charlie insisted.

I continued to walk. As we approached the porch, I saw Jay lying almost in a fetal position. He was surrounded by a large pool of blood. There was a spray of blood on the opposite side where Susan had slashed Sharon's face during their scuffle. Charlie and Tex stepped around his body, carefully avoiding stepping in the pools of blood. I followed their lead, except I turned my head away so that I wouldn't have to look at him. When I stepped through the door and into the living room, my stomach lurched. I staggered back and reached out to the wall to steady myself.

Sharon Tate lay on her side in front of the couch. She was clad only in a bra and bikini panties. Her right arm was extended above her and across her forehead as if she had swooned. Her left hand was clutched near her heart. She was covered in blood and lying in a pool of it even bigger than the one on the porch under Jay. A rope was looped around her neck and thrown over an open beam in the ceiling. The bile rose in my throat and I had to force myself to swallow it down. I charged Tex.

"You son of a fucking bitch!" I screamed, launching myself at him. Tex stumbled back, tripping over a corner of the sofa. Charlie grabbed me and kept me upright. Tex grasped for the rope to catch himself, causing Sharon's body to rise sickeningly. Charlie stepped in to keep us apart as we screamed back and forth at each other. He finally calmed me enough to be convinced that I wouldn't kill Tex on the spot. Tears stung my face and my hands were shaking.

"We gotta do what we came here to do. We ain't got time for this right now," Charlie reasoned.

"Why are we here?" I demanded. "This is bullshit!"

"We're here to keep another brother from getting caught," he reminded me.

"I don't care if he fucking gets caught!" I railed. "Sharon didn't burn you on no fucking drugs!"

Tex, still breathing heavily, stared at me with that same stupid slack jawed look.

"Then you're doing it for Bobby. And for me," Charlie said. "Help me move that guy out front inside."

"Make him do it," I insisted, glaring at Tex.

"Come on, Tex," Charlie told him.

Tex opened his mouth, but didn't say anything. He gave me an "eat shit" look but followed Charlie out to the porch. I looked down and saw two pieces of the broken grip from the Buntline lying on the floor. I didn't bother picking them up.

I heard them grunting as they lifted Jay's body and maneuvered him into the house. Rigor mortis had already set in. His body was so stiff that it remained in the same position it was in on the porch. I stared at the ceiling as they lay him on the floor a few feet away from, but facing, Sharon.

"Put that rope around his neck. Isn't that what he was into." Charlie said. It was a statement, not a question. I wondered how he knew.

They must not have noticed they had placed Jay on top of the rope. I gently lifted Jay's head up and loosely wrapped the rope around his neck. "I am so sorry, man," I whispered to him.

Charlie had brought a few things with him to throw the cops off and confuse the scene. He had an old pair of eyeglasses that a tourist had left at the ranch and a couple of candles and some other things. He dropped these around the room while Tex was pushing a couple of steamer trunks out of the hallway and stacking them on end. Charlie told me to go get a couple of towels from the bathroom.

"How many rooms were you in?" he asked Tex.

"Just this one," Tex answered. He didn't bother to cover for any of the girls who may have gone into the other rooms. Pat left a bloody fingerprint in one of the bedrooms as she was chasing Gibbie through the house. He didn't even tell us to look there. I brought a couple of hand towels into the room.

"Give me one of those," Charlie instructed. "You take the other one and wipe everything down in here the best you can."

Family Man

I did a half ass job at best. I really didn't care if we got caught at that point. While I wiped the walls and tables, Tex and Charlie rearranged the room and tossed a few things on the floor, in hopes of making it look more like a robbery that had gone wrong. They set some silverware and glasses on the table, pouring them half full and taking care to wipe everything down.

"Done," I said. "Let's get out of here."

The plan had been to make it look like the Black Panthers had been involved and to duplicate the Hinman scene. That had almost gotten lost in the chaos. Charlie took his towel and dipped it in the pool of blood on the carpet. He proceeded to write the word "PIG" on the front door in Sharon Tate's blood.

"Do something witchy," he told me.

I took my towel and layed it over Jay's head, covering his face. Charlie stared at me for a moment, then nodded and followed Tex out the door. I started after them, pausing briefly by the chair in the living room where I saw Linda's prized knife sticking up at the back of the cushion.

"Fuck it," I said to myself, and left the way we had come, careful to avoid the puddles on the porch.

Tex made it a point to kick Voytek as we passed his body on the lawn. I went after him again. I'm sure this was the "sound of men arguing" that some neighbors claimed to hear around 4 a.m. Tex pressed the button to open the gate as we left and Charlie didn't stop him. We got in the car and drove back to the ranch in silence.

CHAPTER 73

I don't know if it was shock or exhaustion. Somehow, I went straight to sleep when we got back. It was well into the afternoon when I woke up. I dressed and made my way outside. I was still in a fog. It felt like I was recovering from a hangover. I almost succeeded in convincing myself that I had been drugged and dreamed or imagined the events of the previous night. The news on the radio soon erased those thoughts.

Sadie, Pat, and Linda appeared to be proud of what they had done. They were all smiling and whispering back and forth. Charlie and Tex were nowhere to be found. I overheard Linda bragging about stealing a set of silverware and hiding it along the road. She planned to go back for it later after the heat had died down. I couldn't believe what I was hearing. How could they feel anything other than the shock and horror that I was experiencing?

My horror soon turned to complete revulsion as the details of last night's murders were painted in chilling detail on the evening news. The carnage was even worse than I remembered. Jay Sebring had been shot once and stabbed seven times in addition to multiple kicks in the face from Tex's cowboy boots. Sharon Tate had been stabbed 16 times, not including the cut on her cheek. Abigail Folger had been stabbed a total of 28 times. Voytek Frykowski, obviously the target of Tex's rage, suffered a staggering 51 stab wounds and was hit over the head at least 13 times with the Buntline revolver.

Family Man

The driver of the Rambler was an 18-year-old kid named Steven Parent. He was slashed once with a knife and shot four times. He was also not, as Pat had claimed, the caretaker. The real caretaker, another 18-year-old named William Garretson, was hiding inside the guesthouse all along. Garretson was being held as a suspect in the murders. When this was announced, Pat and I locked eyes for a moment. Now I thought I knew who Bill was. I also learned why he told her that Sharon wasn't home. Sharon had recently wrecked her car and while it was being repaired, she was driving a rental. Bill had no way of knowing that. Why Pat chose to protect him, I never found out.

I returned to one of the trailers and went back to sleep. It was the only way I could escape the thoughts running through my head. By the time I awoke, it was late evening. It had begun to get dark out. I had made up my mind. I was leaving. I located my old duffle bag and was stuffing it with my belongings when Charlie came in.

"I need you to come with us tonight, Shep."

"I'm leaving, Charlie. I can't do this. I can't kill people."

"Whoa, whoa, whoa, now. Back up a minute. Who said anything about killing people? I'm not into killing nobody. They did that shit on their own. I wasn't no part of that scene," he protested.

"I knew those people, Charlie. I don't care how bad Tex got fucked on his drug deal. They didn't deserve that."

"You don't know what they deserved! If you saw what kind of movies they was making up there you might change your mind!"

My resolve wavered. "Nothing will ever change my mind about that." I continued to pack my bag.

"Don't be so sure about that. The thing you don't agree with today, you might tomorrow." I ignored him and zipped the bag. His mood switched again. "I need you tonight. This is my life on the line," he stressed.

He proceeded to tell me about visiting Dennis Wilson again. He had asked Dennis for some more money to pay off the Satans and to try to get Bobby out of jail. He figured Dennis still owed him for using *Cease to Exist* and another one of his songs on their record.

"But Dennis says he'd like to help but he ain't got no money. Their manager keeps all their money and makes those decisions. So I go see this manager, guy named Nick Grillo, and he says 'Fuck you, Charlie. You want any more money, you'll have to sue us.' Now he knows I ain't got no money to sue nobody, so I jack him up and say, 'You give me my money or else!' and he shakes me off and tells me to get the hell out of his office or he'll call New York and he starts dialing the phone. Now, he's threatening me with a mafia hit you see? So I tell him I got friends in New York too, and I cut outta there. On my way out though, I stop and chat up his pretty little secretary and I ask her 'Who'd your boss just call for me?' and she gives me the number. But it ain't a New York number, it's a number out in Los Feliz. So I need to pay this guy a visit and get things straightened out before he comes down on me, ya dig?"

I let out a big sigh. "There can't be any weapons, Charlie. No guns, no knives, no anything."

"We don't need no weapons. I'm going to have a little chat with him and get that book that's got those names in it. We'll try to get some money out of him to pay the Satans if we can. I ain't killing nobody. If I can get that book, he won't be coming for me or anybody else in there. That's why I need you and Tex to come along. I need some backup in case he wants to make a move on me."

"Why in the hell would you bring Tex?" I asked, incredulous.

"Cause you and him are the biggest cats around here. All these dudes understand is intimidation."

I stared at the wall for I don't know how long. I couldn't let Charlie face a guy that could be a mafia hitman alone. I didn't trust Tex to do his part without me, so I gave in.

"After this, I'm out of here," I told him.

"If that's what you need to do, brother, then do it," he stated. He turned and I followed him out the door.

CHAPTER 74

We left a little after 10 p.m. For such an important mission, Charlie seemed to be in no hurry to arrive. He drove around seemingly aimlessly, occasionally breaking into song with the girls joining in happily. Again, I began to wonder if I had been secretly dosed with LSD and was experiencing another bad trip. The whole scene seemed so surreal.

The rear seat had been removed from Johnny's old Ford. Sometimes this was done to make space for groceries on the garbage runs. In this instance, it was to accommodate more passengers. Charlie, Linda and I occupied the front bench seat while Tex, Sadie, Pat, Leslie, and Clem sat in the open back floor space. We appeared to be taking a scenic tour of Los Angeles. I was beginning to believe that Charlie was lost. The singing and merriment continued until all of a sudden Charlie stopped and got serious. We had pulled into the parking lot of a church.

"What are we doing here?" Linda asked.

"I'm gonna go kill the priest," he deadpanned. "Come on, Shep." The celebration in the car instantly stopped. I got out and quickly followed Charlie around to the back of the building, rushing to catch up with him. When we got behind the building Charlie looked around and began to unzip his fly.

"What the hell, man?" I asked.

Family Man

"I had to take a piss," he stated, matter of factly, starting to water the lawn. I didn't know whether to laugh or to be angry about this.

"Why did you tell them you were going to kill the priest?" I questioned.

"Had to tell them something. It was a stupid question. What the hell did she think I was stopping for?" He laughed and zipped up, walking casually back to the car.

"What happened?" Linda asked immediately as Charlie climbed behind the wheel.

"Eh, nobody answered the door," he answered. This little joke would come back to bite Charlie in the ass when Linda portrayed it as a serious occurrence on the witness stand. After that, Charlie appeared to have a definite direction in mind. He made a straight path to a house on Waverly Drive. He pulled into the driveway of the house where Harold True used to live.

"Is this where we're going Charlie?" Sadie piped up from the back. "This is Harold's house."

"No, we're going next door," he answered.

I looked at him skeptically.

"Are you sure this is it?" I asked.

"I confirmed it with Joe this morning," he said. "This is the place."

The only Joe I could think of was a biker named Joe Dorgan that hung around at the ranch with the Satans sometimes. I didn't know what Joe could have known about a guy that supposedly had underworld connections so I assumed that Charlie was talking about someone else. When it came to light that Joe Dorgan was the boyfriend of Suzan Struthers, the daughter of one of the inhabitants, it gave that assumption a little more validity.

Charlie got out and turned back to the car. "Shep, Linda, Tex, come with me. The rest of you, wait here." As we walked up the driveway, Charlie turned around and spoke directly to Tex. "I'm going to show you how to do this. You don't have to panic anybody and you don't have to kill anybody. We get what we came for and we leave." He then cut through the yard and moved quietly up to the house at 3301 Waverly. He peered through a couple of windows, then motioned us over to join him. "Our guy is asleep on the sofa. I don't see anybody else, but there's supposed to be a woman inside too. Be quiet and calm and this will go smoothly."

He walked to a side door and tried the knob. It was unlocked. He eased the door open into a kitchen area. Three dogs competed for space to get to the door and see what was going on. Charlie kneeled down and shushed the dogs and started petting them. They instantly calmed down and never made another sound. He stood up and stealthily approached the sleeping man. He produced a gun from under his shirt and nudged the man in the shoulder. The man jolted awake.

"Wh…? Who are you? What do you want?" the guy exclaimed. He appeared to be in his mid to late 40s with a balding head and a large belly. I supposed he looked Italian, but he didn't fit my idea of what a mafia hit man would look like.

"Calm down, brother," Charlie started. "I'm not here to hurt you. I'm here to get a book from you and to get some money. Be cool and nobody will get hurt."

The man relaxed a little, but how relaxed could he be with four strangers in his house and a gun in his back?

"Is anybody else in the house?" Charlie asked him.

"My wife's in the bedroom, but leave her out of this. I'll give you whatever you want."

"Where's the black book?"

"I don't know what you're talking about," the man answered.

"Listen now," Charlie raised his voice. "The sooner you give me what I came for the sooner I will get out of here."

"The side table, the man relented, pointing to a roll-up style desk against the far wall. "It's in there. There's some money in there too."

"Tie him up," Charlie instructed Tex. Linda pulled a couple of 3-or-4-foot-long leather thongs from her pocket and gave them to Tex. He pulled the man's hands down, securing them tightly behind him.

Charlie rifled through the desk drawer. He stuffed a small black book in his jeans along with a couple of twenties. "Is this all there is?" he asked.

"Leno? Is everything all right?" An attractive dark-haired woman in her late 30s appeared in the bedroom doorway. Her hands immediately flew to her mouth.

"It's okay, Rosemary," Leno assured her. "They just need some money. Give them what they want and they will leave."

"My purse is in the bedroom," Rosemary said, turning to go back into the room.

"Whoa, wait a minute," Charlie stopped her. "Linda, go with her."

Linda came out a few minutes later holding the woman's wallet. "There's less than fifty dollars and some credit cards in here," she reported.

"That's not going to work. We need more than that. Is this all you have?" Charlie repeated.

"There's more down at the store," Rosemary volunteered.

"Okay. Come with us," Charlie told her. "Tex, you stay here and keep an eye on him. As long as he's cool you be cool."

Tex nodded. The woman called Rosemary asked if she could change clothes.

"Just put something on over what you're wearing," Charlie told her.

Linda followed Rosemary to the bedroom. She returned a short time later wearing a black and white striped house dress over her nightgown. Rosemary accompanied us outside. Passing through the door, Charlie warned her against making a sound. She stayed quiet.

Upon reaching the car, Charlie told Pat and Leslie to go in and keep Tex and Linda company. He directed Rosemary into the front seat between us while Clem and Sadie remained in the back. The lady directed us through the 15-minute drive from her home on Waverly to a place called the Boutique Carriage on North Figueroa Street. Charlie accompanied her inside, where she removed $2,000 in cash from her safe. We then made the drive back. So far, so good. When we arrived back at Waverly, we led Rosemary up to her house.

"No cops," Charlie cautioned. "We're done here, but if you call the cops, we'll be back."

She readily agreed and we walked her back into the house. Tex and the girls were in the kitchen eating watermelon and drinking chocolate milk when we arrived. Leno was still tied up on the sofa. I noted that a pillowcase was placed over his head and secured with a lamp cord.

"All right, we got what we came for, let's go," Charlie told them. Linda started towards the door and I turned to leave.

"I'm going to stay a little while," Tex declared.

"We're done here," Charlie reiterated. "Let's go."

"You go. I'm staying," Tex insisted.

"I'm staying too," Pat said.

"Me too," Leslie concurred.

"Well, we're leaving and we're not coming back. Find your own damn ride."

Family Man

Charlie stalked towards the door. Linda and I looked at each other confused, each one trying to will the other to say something.

"What the hell, Tex?" I asked. "Let's go!"

"Fuck off, Shep. You can be Charlie's lap dog if you want. I do what I want to do."

I looked from Pat to Leslie. They both made it a point not to make eye contact with me. I turned and went after Charlie. I was unsure if Linda was coming or staying but after a moment of indecision, I heard her at my heels.

"What the fuck, Charlie?" I demanded. "We can't leave them here. You know what that fucker's gonna do!"

"I can't control what Tex does. Whatever he does is on him. I got what I came for." He made his way back to the car. I looked at him across the roof refusing to get in.

"Give me the gun," I fumed. "I'll stop his ass."

"The gun's not even loaded," Charlie smiled, and got in the car.

I stood there for a minute. Linda pushed by me and got in. If I had any chance of stopping what I knew was going to happen, I was on my own. I heard the first screams and realized I was already too late. I slammed my fists down on the top of the car and after a quick look back at the house, I climbed inside.

CHAPTER 75

Once in the car, Charlie headed to Venice. The Straight Satans headquarters were there and now we had enough money to pay them back for the bad mescaline they claimed they had gotten from Bobby. Charlie was in good spirits, happy to finally get the Satans off our backs.

Linda still clutched the brown wallet she had taken from the woman's purse. She also had a gold bracelet and a watch that I assumed she had lifted from the bedroom as well.

We stopped in Sylmar at a Denny's. Charlie offered to buy everyone's milkshakes. I passed. The thoughts of food right now did not appeal to me. There was a Standard gas station next door.

"Anything left in there?" Charlie asked, referring to the wallet.

"Some change, credit cards, and a driver's license," she responded.

"Take the money out and throw the rest of that shit away," he instructed.

I looked over Linda's shoulder as she was going through the wallet. Rosemary LaBianca was the name on the license. For the first time, I knew the last name of the people my friends had killed and that I had unwittingly facilitated.

Charlie went to the Denny's to get the milkshakes and Linda went over to the ladies' restroom at the Standard station. instead of throwing away Mrs. LaBianca's purse and jewelry as Charlie had instructed her, for some reason she hid them in the back of the toilet tank. My only guess is that she planned to come back later to retrieve them, just like she had planned to do with the silverware from the previous night.

The story she told on the stand that Charlie told her to hide them there to frame a black person doesn't hold up. Sylmar was a predominantly white neighborhood. Charlie knew California like the back of his hand. There is absolutely no chance that he mistook that for being a black area. If that had been his purpose, he could have fulfilled it just a few blocks away.

As we approached Venice, Linda mentioned that she knew an actor there that she could probably get some more money from. Instead of giving directions, Charlie pulled over and let her drive. She drove directly to a five-story apartment building on Ocean Front Walk. Linda, Sadie, and Clem got out and went to the building. None of them had weapons that I was aware of although they all usually carried knives in their sheaths just like the rest of us. Charlie slid back into the driver seat and after a brief visit to the Satans' headquarters to pay off our debt, he drove us straight back to the ranch.

CHAPTER 76

I went straight to the trailer that had been my quarters recently. When I got there, Leslie was already inside. I turned to leave but she stopped me.

"Shep, I need to talk and I know I can trust you. Can I stay a while?"

She had a pleading look in her eyes and that one time not so long ago, I had been particularly fond of her. I let out a long sigh, then relented.

"Okay."

She wanted to talk about what had happened after we left the LaBiancas house. I didn't want to hear it, but at the same time I had to hear it, and she had to tell it.

She claimed that she and Pat...well, *she* at least...first thought they were going to get more money or valuables from the people. She really wanted to help Bobby get out of jail and she thought if they were friendly and explain their plight, maybe the LaBiancas would be willing to help and less likely to call the police on us.

When Mrs. LaBianca returned to the house, they had complimented her dress. She was nervous, but accommodating and told them to look in her closet. If they wanted any clothes in there, they could have them.

Everything seemed to be going smoothly. She and Pat followed Rosemary into the bedroom. She opened her closet doors and started going through dresses when they heard Mr. LaBianca's screams coming from the living room. Tex had started stabbing him with a kitchen knife from the couple's own drawer. Hearing this, Mrs.

Family Man

LaBianca instinctively turned and ran to help her husband. Pat jumped on her back and wrestled her to the ground while yelling for Tex. Tex then attacked Mrs. LaBianca with the same knife he had used to stab her husband. Somewhere in the confusion, another kitchen knife appeared and Pat joined in the stabbing. Leslie had shrunk back into the corner in horror.

Once Mrs. LaBianca became still, Tex stood up, handed his knife to Leslie, and told her she had to participate. "You're not gonna stand there and watch without getting your hands dirty," he said. Leslie shied away but Tex forced the knife into her hand.

"Do it!" he ordered.

She knelt down behind Rosemary, who was now face-down and unmoving beside the bed. She raised the knife and plunged it into her back and legs she guessed about 16 times. She said that she thought Mrs. LaBianca was dead before she stabbed her, at least she hoped so.

"But why 16 times, Leslie?" I asked her.

"I don't know," she replied. "Once I started, I just couldn't stop."

Once the deed was done, they pulled a pillowcase over Rosemary's head and tied it with a lamp cord to match her husband. They returned to the living room, where Pat stabbed Leno multiple times with a two-pronged fork that she left sticking in his abdomen. Leslie wasn't sure whether it was Tex or Pat who carved the word "WAR" into his stomach, but she knew it was Tex who then stuck one of the knives into the man's throat and left it protruding.

Pat took a page from the newspaper that Mr. LaBianca had been reading. Using it as a makeshift paintbrush, she printed the words "Death to Pigs" and "Rise" on the walls and "Healter Skelter" (accidentally misspelling "Helter") on the refrigerator. The three then used the LaBianca's shower to clean up and hitchhiked back to the ranch.

She seemed calmer after getting the story off her chest. She lay down beside me and I held her until she went to sleep. Then I got up and went to the outlaw shack, where I spent the rest of the night alone.

The gruesome details were all over the news the next day. Over the next few months, more facts were learned about the LaBiancas. Leno LaBianca had managed a chain of supermarkets. He was being investigated for embezzling over $200,000 from them. He was also a steady gambler, placing bets on horse races of up to $500 per day. He owned several thoroughbred race horses that very few people knew about until after his death and was deeply in debt. If Mr. LaBianca had anything to do with the mob, my guess would be that he was on the wrong side of it. He had been stabbed 12 times and punctured seven times with the fork in addition to the word "WAR" carved into his belly.

Rosemary LaBianca had been a waitress before she married Leno. She had in the past several years amassed a large amount of wealth, in the neighborhood of half a million dollars. It was questionable whether all that came from her dress boutique. Tex, at least, believed that she was a drug supplier. Much like the night before with Voytek Frykowski, he had inflicted his rage upon her when she couldn't deliver the drugs he demanded. Mrs. LaBianca had 41 stab wounds. There was a smear of blood approximately two feet under her body, suggesting that somehow she had briefly survived the vicious attack and casting doubt on Leslie's assertion that she was already dead when she stabbed her.

CHAPTER 77

The next several days were chaotic. The paranoia that had pervaded the place since the shooting of Lotsapoppa had now reached a fever pitch. Everybody's concentration was on moving to the desert. Although the bikers were now off our backs, it was only a matter of time until the blacks or the police came calling.

Another call I had been dreading came on Tuesday. Vicki had returned from Sacramento to the horrors of her employer and his friends' murders. She called the ranch, and Lynette came looking for me. Jay Sebring's funeral was to take place the next day and she wanted me to attend it with her. Knowing what I knew, there was no way I could go to that funeral. While I hated to leave Vicki on her own, I felt it would be sacrilege for me to attend.

I put on my weakest voice and told her that I had been really sick and just wasn't up to it. I explained that there was a bug going around the ranch and that it was highly contagious. I didn't want her coming by and getting sick, nor did I feel like being around anyone else and exposing them to it. She was disappointed but understood. I didn't tell her that it was a murder bug and while I didn't have it, I had been exposed to it. I highly doubted that it was contagious.

I didn't know what I was going to do at that time. Even though I had not participated, I was now complicit in seven murders. I felt trapped. I wanted to leave but I also felt a strong sense of there being honor among thieves. As long as we all stuck together, maybe we could do as Charlie planned. If we disappeared into the desert to the Barker Ranch, we could start fresh and everything could go back to the way it used to be. On the other hand, maybe I should turn myself in, throw myself on the mercy of the court and tell everything I knew.

"Your word is your bond and your bond is your life." These words constantly echoed in my head. *"You don't lie and you don't snitch."* I realized I had no choice but to follow the plan and hope for the best.

The plans for the desert were progressing. Several trips were made to carry supplies and gasoline. It seemed more frantic by the day. Charlie wanted the ranch guarded 24 hours a day. He created outposts and stationed armed guards with shotguns. Field telephone lines were laid so that the sentries could alert the main house if an invasion was underway by the Panthers or by the cops. Despite this, early in the morning of August 16th, the Los Angeles sheriff's department conducted a raid, arresting 26 of us. As I stood in a row with my hands cuffed behind my back, I felt both alarm and relief that it was over.

Like most everyone else, to make things as difficult as possible, I gave an alias. Once again, I became John McCartney. Charlie asked what we were being arrested for. When they told him suspicion of auto theft, several people actually laughed. Twenty-four hours later, we were all released. We spent the night in holding cells, but most of us were not even fingerprinted. The official reason for the release was that the warrant had been misdated. More likely, it was simply that so many people were there, they couldn't prove who did what. Regardless, I escaped with my true identity still concealed.

A week later, Charlie and I were driving into town to get some of the final supplies we needed to move to Barker Ranch. We were only a few minutes away from Spahn when Charlie told me to pull over behind a car parked on the side of the road. As we came to a stop, I recognized the car as belonging to Shorty Shea.

Charlie got out and started down a steep embankment beside a culvert. I followed, curious. Looking over the side, I witnessed a battered and bleeding Shorty being held by Bruce and Larry Bailey. Clem and Bill Vance were there as well. Tex was standing in front of him with a bayonet.

"Why Charlie, why?" I heard Shorty moan.

"Because this is what happens to snitches," Charlie told him, and punched him in the stomach.

Charlie turned and trudged back up the hill as Tex delivered the final blow. It barely fazed me when he climbed back in the car and said, "Let's go."

The details were filled in later, Charlie, and several of the others, were convinced that Shorty was responsible for bringing the cops down on us a week earlier. They had gotten into a heated argument earlier that day. Inexplicably, just a few hours later, Shorty apparently agreed to drive Tex, Bruce, and Clem into town to pick up some auto parts.

Just after leaving the ranch, Clem, who was in the backseat with Bruce, hit an unsuspecting Shorty over the head with a lead pipe. Tex, seated beside Shorty in the front seat, grabbed the wheel, forcing the car off the road. They dragged a bleeding Shorty, who probably had a concussion, down the hill to finish him off. I'm not sure if Larry Bailey and Bill Vance were waiting for them or were in another car up ahead. When we stopped, they were already there. This is the one murder that feasibly Charlie could have "ordered." There's no doubt he knew about it beforehand and had no qualms letting Shorty know what had led to his demise.

CHAPTER 78

A couple days later, we made the move to the desert and our new home at Barker Ranch. I called Vicki to inform her that I would be away for a while. At that point, I wasn't sure how long. I gave her the address of the store in Ballarat and arranged for them to hold any mail for me. I apologized for stringing her along but explained that I had some issues that I needed to work through. At the time, it seemed like the best solution. I was hopeful that escaping to the desert would help me escape from my bad memories. The only problem was most of those memories moved there with me.

Three weeks or so into our time at Barker, we had established ourselves comfortably. For the first time since the move, late one evening, Charlie asked me to join him for a walk and talk.

"I think it's time for you to go, Shep," he told me.

"What?!" I was totally taken aback.

"You're too good for this," he stated.

"But you're my family, Charlie," I protested.

"No. You'll always be my brother, Shep, but you're not a part of this. Shit's about to go down and when it does you need to be far away from here."

"I was there, Charlie. I'm in this as deep as you are."

"Listen, boy!" he said, getting angry. He grabbed my wrist and held my hands out. "There ain't no blood on these hands. You keep it that way! You take that little girl of yours and you run as far away from this place as you can get. Don't look back. You don't belong here and you don't belong in jail. In the morning, I want you to get away from this place and don't ever come back. I ain't asking you, I'm telling you!"

He turned and walked back to the ranch. Charlie had a way of knowing things. He wasn't a wizard and he wasn't Jesus. Nor did he claim to be, at least not yet, but he was in tune with things. If he said I should go, then it was time for me to go. Several of the girls in the group - Barbara Hoyt, Stephanie Schram, Kitty Lutesinger - had already taken off. Even Little Paul Watkins and Brooks Poston had abandoned the ship. It was only a matter of time before someone started talking. Charlie would always be my brother, and just like a big brother should, he was protecting me.

The next day, I climbed into Charlie's dune buggy with the few belongings I still had left. Although the sheriff's office had released us, they had retained almost all of our belongings. Once again, even my beloved guitar was gone. The bouncy ride through the desert went by quickly. Charlie dropped me off at the store in Ballarat. He didn't get out of the buggy. We didn't hug, we didn't shake hands. He smiled at me and gave a small wave before shifting gears and driving away in a cloud of dust. I watched until he disappeared over the horizon. I never saw him face-to-face again.

Upon entering the store, I asked if there was any mail for me. There were two letters, both from Vicki. The first told me that her dad was back in the hospital and asked me to call when I read this. The second was a little over a week ago. He had passed away and I had left her alone at another funeral.

Placing the phone call, I wasn't sure that she would even answer. She did. I did my best to apologize for being so absent. I then swallowed my pride and told her where I was and that I would like to see her if she would be willing to come get me. She made a three-and-a-half-hour trip in just under three hours.

We spent most of the trip with me listening to her talk about her father. Her mother wasn't doing well either. She was afraid that she would be losing her soon too.

When we arrived at her place, I sat her down and told her my whole lurid story, sparing no detail. Tears rolled down her cheeks but she never interrupted me.

"What now, Shep?" she asked once I had finished.

"I don't know," I answered truthfully. "Charlie says I should get as far away from here as I can and never come back."

"Is that what you're going to do?" she asked.

"I guess so. It makes as much sense as anything."

"No sense makes sense." Another of Charlie's phrases popped into my head.

"You could turn yourself in. You could tell them everything you just told me," she suggested.

"I've seen what happens to snitches," I reminded her. "No thanks. I'm doing what Charlie said. I'm going away. I would like for you to come with me."

"It's all too much, Shep," she replied. "You have to give me time to process this."

"Take your time, Vick, but I can't wait too long or my choice may be made for me."

She took me to a small motel down the street, checking me in under her father's name. I spent a sleepless night wondering if I had done the right thing. If Vicki decided to call the cops on me, then it was on her. I hadn't snitched.

The next morning, she knocked on my door. I opened it to see the redness around her eyes showed that she didn't sleep much either. She had made her decision though.

Family Man

"Let's go, Shep. Let's go as far away from here as we can. I've already lost most of the people I care about. I don't want to lose you too."

I took her in my arms and we both broke down in tears. I promised her that I would never leave her again. We rented a truck, packed up her small apartment, and drove far, far away. The only time we returned to California was a year later for her mother's funeral.

This time, I was right by her side.

CHAPTER 79

Charlie was right, again. Only a few weeks after he had told me to leave because "The shit's about to come down," it did. It came down in buckets.

First, on October 10th, and then again on October 12th, a joint task force consisting of the Inyo County Sheriff's Department, the California Highway Patrol, and the National Park Service Rangers, raided the Barker and Myers ranches. The first day, Charlie wasn't there. The second day, he was. He was found hiding under the sink at the Barker Ranch. He somehow folded himself into an area less than nine square feet. If not for a lock of his hair hanging over the cabinet door, he possibly would have evaded capture again.

The ironic part of the capture was that once again, it had nothing to do with the murders. The Park Service had left a large earthmover blocking one of the entrances to the ranch. In his anger, Charlie and a few of the others doused the machine in gasoline and set it on fire. The arrest was for destruction of public property.

The murders came to light only after a jailhouse confession by Susan Atkins. Just days after Sadie was booked and charged in connection with the Hinman slaying, she was visited by two-high profile and high-priced lawyers: Richard Caballero and Paul Caruso. Though she was destitute, she somehow retained their services. With their cooperation, noted author and screenwriter Lawrence Schiller released Susan's story of the murders, and with the help of the District Attorney's office, created the myth of Helter Skelter. Schiller also somehow managed to be present for the "confessions" of Lee Harvey Oswald and Jack Ruby. The story ran in the Sunday, December 14th edition of the *Los Angeles Times*. It was quickly released as a pulp paperback entitled *The Killing of Sharon Tate*. It was an almost word for word retelling of her grand jury testimony. Shortly after the story's release, Susan recanted her testimony and voided her deal with the D.A.

Charlie, Sadie, Tex, Pat, and Linda were indicted for the murders of Sharon Tate, Jay Sebring, Voytek Frykowski, and Abigail Folger as well as Leno and Rosemary LaBianca. Leslie, having not been present the first night, was indicted for the murders of Leno and Rosemary LaBianca only. Charlie, Susan and Leslie were already in jail on other charges. Tex, Pat, and Linda, had gone back to their home states and were not in custody. Pat and Linda, upon hearing of the warrants for their arrest, returned to L.A. and turned themselves in. Tex turned himself in to the sheriff in his hometown who was coincidentally his cousin. He fought extradition for nine months. Because of this, he was tried separately. Linda Kasabian was offered immunity in exchange for her testimony for the prosecution escaping any charges. Charlie, Susan, Pat, and Leslie were tried together.

Just before the trial, I made a call to prosecutor Vincent Bugliosi's office. I used a pay phone in a neighboring state and identified myself as John McCartney. After a brief conversation, Mr. Bugliosi asked me if I would be willing to corroborate the story of Charlie being a cult leader and wanting to start a race war by killing "pigs."

"No," I replied. "It wasn't like that at all."

"Thanks for calling, John," he responded, "but I don't think I can use you. I'm looking for people who knew Charlie a little better than that."

Like most of America, and a large part of the world, I watched the drama of the trial unfold in the morning paper and on the evening news.

After Crowe, and more specifically after Hinman, Charlie changed. The paranoia begun to increase until it had boiled over by the time of Shorty Shea's murder. Sometime between my departure and the start of the trial, I think Charlie had a psychotic break. He carved an "X" in his forehead to proclaim that "I have X'ed myself from your world." He shaved his head, he claimed, "Because I am the devil, and the devil always has a bald head."

The fact that so many of the "family" members followed his lead, I can only attribute to their own confusion. My feeling is that they were doing it to protest the injustices being heaped upon the defendants in general, but Charlie in particular. The result was that they only reinforced the prosecution's narrative.

The trial began on July 15, 1970. The prosecution started presenting their case on July 24th and rested almost 4 months later on November 16th.

Charlie had asked to present his own defense. It was denied. He asked to testify. He was once again denied on the basis that he could "hypnotize the jury." Immediately upon the prosecution resting their case, the court-appointed attorneys for the defense rested theirs, without calling a single witness. They were never allowed to put on a defense.

On March 27, 1971 all four defendants were sentenced to death. Tex Watson would receive the same sentence in a separate trial seven months later. in 1972, the state of California abolished the death penalty and all were commuted to life sentences with the possibility of parole.

CHAPTER 80

It's been said that the "Manson Murders," a misnomer if there ever was one, were the end of the sixties and the end of the hippie movement. In a sense, that is true. Everyone from President Richard Nixon, to California Governor Ronald Reagan, to Attorney General Evelle Younger were opposed to the counterculture movement and the opposition of the war in Vietnam. With Charles Manson and his band of "drug addled hippie followers," they had found the perfect scapegoats. District Attorney Vincent Buyliosi was given unprecedented latitude in his prosecution. Judge Charles Older was very lenient in his rulings in favor of the prosecution and ignored or overruled multiple opportunities to declare a mistrial.

On November 5th, LA County police were called to a home at 28 Clubhouse Avenue. The home belonged to Mark Ross. Mark was always open to letting us stay with him. I and other family members had crashed at Mark's house numerous times. In the bedroom was the body of Christopher "Zero" Haught. Zero died from a single gunshot wound to his right temple. Present at the home were Cathy "Cappy" Gillies, Bruce Davis, "Country Sue" Bartell, and Madeline "Little Patty" Cottage.

According to Little Patty, she and Zero were in bed together when he saw a .22 revolver lying on the bedside table. He picked up the gun and stuck it to his head with the intent of playing "Russian Roulette." The odds were against Zero. The gun was fully loaded. Although Bruce admitted picking up the gun afterwards, neither his nor

Zero's fingerprints were found on it. The death was officially ruled a suicide.

In December of 1971, Steve "Clem" Grogan was convicted of the murder of Shorty Shea. He was sentenced to death but the judge commuted the sentence to life on the basis that he was "too stupid and hopped up on drugs to have decided anything on his own." The judge didn't know Clem very well. "Stupid" was one thing Clem was definitely not. He made a deal with the court and after agreeing to reveal where Shorty Shea was buried, he was paroled in 1985.

In 1972, Bruce Davis was convicted and sentenced to life in prison for two counts of murder in the killings of Gary Hinman and Shorty Shea.

On August 21, 1971, Dennis Rice, Kenneth Como, "Mother Mary" Brunner, Catherine "Gypsy" Share, Larry Bailey, and Charles Lovett were involved in an event known as the Hawthorne Shootout. The group drove a van to the Western Surplus gun shop on Hawthorne Boulevard with the supposed intention of stealing all the weaponry. The spoils were to be used to break Charlie out of prison. An employee tripped the silent alarm. By the time they had cleaned out the gun store and made it back to the van, they were surrounded by police. They engaged in a seven-minute gun battle. Gypsy, Mary, and Larry were injured in the ensuing shootout.

In June 1972, Charles Lovett was sentenced ten-years-to-life. Dennis Rice was convicted in 1973 and sentenced to six-months-to-twenty-years. He was released two years later. A few months later, Catherine Share was sentenced to ten-years-to-life. Kenneth Como, fifteen-years-to-life; Mary Brunner and Larry Bailey both received twenty-years-to-life. All members of the Hawthorne Shootout have since been released.

Family Man

On September 5, 1975 Lynette "Squeaky" Fromme pointed a loaded gun at President Gerald Ford in Sacramento's Capitol Park. Squeaky, clad in a red robe, was quickly apprehended by the Secret Service. She was convicted and sentenced to life in prison. She escaped on December 23, 1987, but was recaptured two days later. She was released from the Federal Medical Center in Carswell California on August 14, 2009.

CHAPTER 81

I never spoke to Charlie after we parted in Ballarat in 1969. I did occasionally write him letters over the years, always without a return address and postmarked from a neighboring state. He could, obviously, never reply. He did, however, let me know he had received them and sent me his love through hand signals in some of his televised interviews. I never betrayed Charlie and, true to his word, he never betrayed me.

Charles Manson died in prison on November 19, 2017. He often dropped hints, but he never revealed the true motives for the Tate-LaBianca murders. Till the day he died, he maintained that he never killed, nor ordered anyone to kill. He also held fast to the fact that he was never given his constitutional right to present a defense.

Susan "Sadie" Atkins died in prison from brain cancer on September 24, 2019.

Charles "Tex" Watson is serving a life sentence. He has been denied parole 17 times.

Patricia "Katie" Krenwinkel is the longest serving female in California prison history. She has been denied parole 14 times.

Bobby "Cupid" Beausoleil serving a life sentence for the murder of Gary Hinman. Although Bobby has been recommended for parole, the same mechanisms that turned Charles Manson into an icon of evil, have kept Bobby incarcerated. His parole was overturned by the Governor of California.

Family Man

Bruce Davis has been recommended for parole 5 times. California Governors have reversed each recommendation.

Leslie "Lulu" Van Houten was denied parole 19 times. At her three most recent hearings, she was granted release, only to also have those reversed by the Governor.

Fifty years later, the political piggies are still pushing their own agendas and pursuing greater personal political power.

Prosecutor Vincent Bugliosi died of cancer on June 6, 2015.

EPIL⦿GUE

Vicki and I have been living under assumed names on the East Coast since October of 1969. She opened her own nail salon and I ran a second-hand music store. I ended up giving away more than I sold. We both retired last year. We live frugally, but comfortably. We never had children due to the fear of my former life being exposed. I also never returned to my parents' home for the same reason, though I did call now and then. The promise that Charlie and I made to each other, Vicki has maintained. She never snitched and she never lied. For my part, at Charlie's recommendation, Billy "Shep" Shepard has "ceased to exist."

Until now.

ACKNOWLEDGEMENTS

I could not have completed this book without the cooperation and support of the following people. To them, I owe a huge amount of gratitude.

To my wife, Brigitte, who's learned more about Charles Manson than she ever cared to know; who read and reread my longhand scribbles and assisted in converting them into a typewritten manuscript.

To my publisher, Nicholas Grabowsky, and Black Bed Sheet Books, thank you for taking a chance on a new author and a controversial subject. Thanks to you – the truth is out there.

To the following people who were willing to share their expertise and opinions: Jon Aes-Nihil, Edwin Colin, Brian Davis, John Michael Jones, Marlin M. Marynick, Matthew Roberts, Nikolas Schreck, Deb Silva, and Stoner Van Houten.

Extra special thanks to Billy "Shep" Shepherd for accompanying me through this entire process and baring your soul.

Recommended Reading and References:
Chaos by Tom O'Neill
Charles Manson by David J. Krajicek
Child of Satan, Child of God by Susan Atkins
Goodbye Helter Skelter by George Stimson
Helter Skelter by Vincent Bugliosi with Curt Gentry
Manson by Jeff Guinn
Manson in His Own Words by Nuel Emmons
Member of the Family by Diane Lake

Chuck W. Chapman

The Myth of Helter Skelter by Susan Atkins-Whitehouse

Reflexion by Lynette Fromme

Restless Souls by Alisa Statman with Brie Tate

Will You Die for Me? By Charles Watson

With thanks for their personal help with this book, I highly recommend the following:

Charles Manson Now by Marlin M. Marynick

The Killing of Shorty Shea by Edwin Colin and Deb Silva

The Manson File: Myth and Reality of An Outlaw Shaman by Nikolas Schreck

The following websites contain a wealth of information:

www.CieloDrive.com

www.Mansonblog.com

The following YouTube channels and podcasts are highly recommended:

The Tate-LaBianca Radio Program hosted by Brian Davis

Spahn Ranch Worker hosted by Stoner Van Houten

Other research sources:

Newspaper and magazine articles, court and parole hearing transcripts, radio, television, and telephone interviews, police and coroner reports.

About the author

Singer, songwriter, actor, director, and author, Chuck W. Chapman is from Greenville, SC. He has toured the US in various rock bands and recently wrote, directed, and starred in the Rondo Award-nominated indie horror film, *"He Drives at Night,"* with Butch Patrick of "Eddie Munster" fame. Chuck has been a featured actor on nationally syndicated television and a background actor in major motion pictures.

Look for us wherever books are sold.

If you thought *this book* was cool, check out these other titles from the #1 source for the best in independent horror fiction,

BLACK BED SHEET

www.blackbedsheetbooks.com

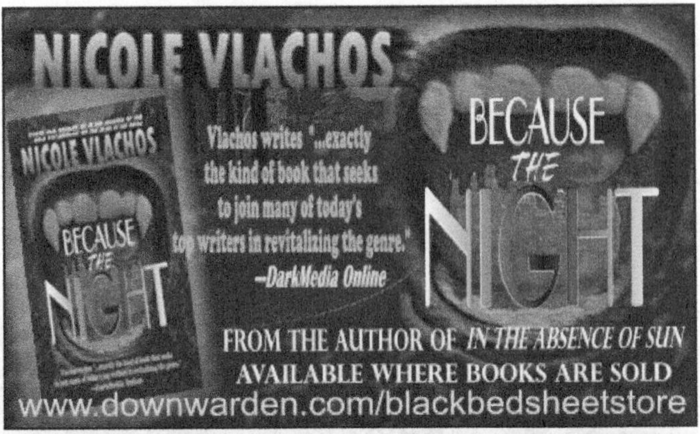

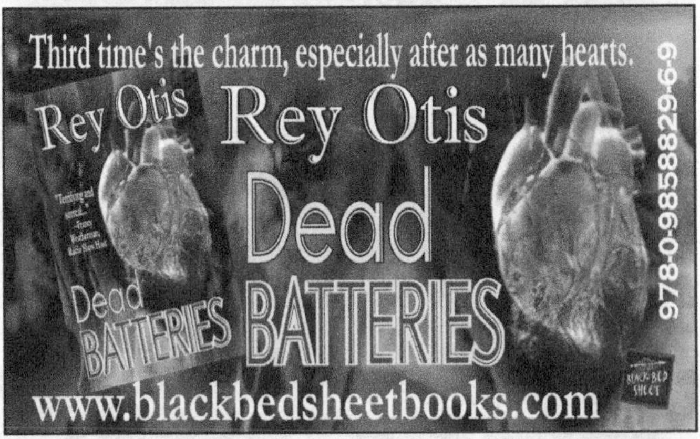

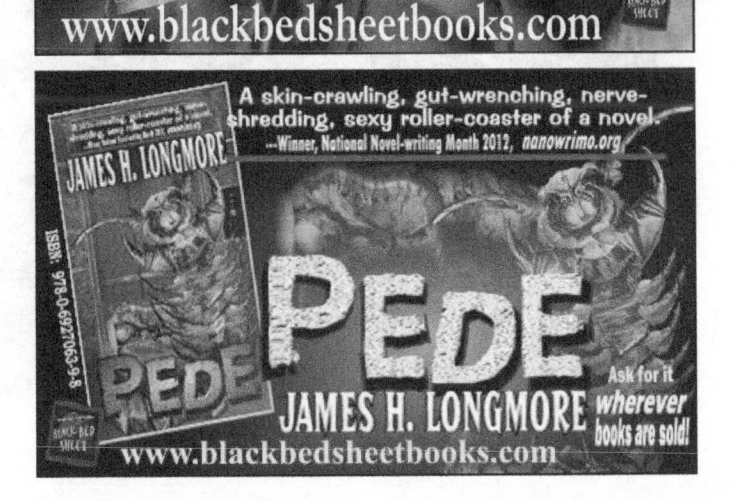

Made in the USA
Monee, IL
12 February 2024